In Between Men

By Mary Castillo

IN BETWEEN MEN
HOT TAMARA

MARY CASTILLO

In Between Men

AVON
TRADE

An Imprint of HarperCollins*Publishers*

HarperCollins books may be purchased for educational, business, or sales promotional use. For information please write: Special Markets Department, HarperCollins Publishers Inc., 10 East 53rd Street, New York, NY 10022.

FIRST EDITION

Interior text designed by Diahann Sturge

Castillo, Mary, 1974–
   In between men / by Mary Castillo.—1st ed.
      p. cm.
ISBN-13: 978-0-06-076682-5
ISBN-10: 0-06-076682-4 (acid-free paper)
1. Women teachers—Fiction. 2. Divorced mothers—Fiction. 3. Mothers and sons—Fiction. 4. Los Angeles (Calif.)—Fiction. 5. Soccer coaches—Fiction. I. Title.

PS3603.A876I5 2006
813'.6—dc22   2005016563

06 07 08 09 10 WBC/RRD 10 9 8 7 6 5 4 3 2 1

This book is dedicated to four special women in my life:
Ilona, who is a woman of strength
and lives with grace and dignity.
Betty and Pam,
who are my mom's friends,
come rain or shine,
through thick and thin.
And finally, my Grandma Margie,
who planted the seed
that grew into a career of telling stories.

1

ISA AVELLAN'S HOROSCOPE FOR SEPTEMBER 7

What's happening here? Appreciate this
as a transformative experience and remember that
someday soon you'll even be able to laugh about it.

Isa demanded a recount.

Rereading the poorly photocopied "Sex Savvy Senior Survey," she felt something break off inside her and land with a thump.

The last thing she expected to learn that Tuesday afternoon at the emergency staff meeting was that the student body of Isa's alma mater and current employer had voted her the unsexiest teacher alive.

Actually the survey was a little more specific: the most *un*fuckable teacher alive in big bold letters next to her admittedly unfuckable staff photo.

Intellectually she knew better than to care about a high

school prank. And Isa damn well knew if she put her mind to it, she'd be a helluva good lay.

She conceded that four years was a long time between men. Well, maybe it was longer than that, but *this* was ridiculous. She was a modern twenty-nine-year-old woman whose ESL students had the highest GPA in the entire district.

No, this wasn't just ridiculous. This was insulting. Especially considering the competition she had in the category: Myrtle the ancient librarian, Celeste the bearded lunch lady, and Bill Weisshaar, the twitchy biology teacher the kids called Bildo.

Damn right she deserved a recount. This was a matter of principle.

"I wanted everyone to know about this little survey our students circulated," Principal Quilley said as the shock settled among the crowded lounge. "We confiscated it when Carrie Barcus and Addison Pinchly were smoking behind the bleachers."

Isa turned when she heard a woman's voice catch. Myrtle, who happened to be a delightful and intelligent woman, held a shivering hand to her candy-pink lips.

"I . . . I never thought . . ." Myrtle sobbed. "This is . . . oh this is just . . ."

"Nice to know some of us are so highly regarded," Stan Fields boasted.

Outrage boiled up Isa's throat, tasting nasty and metallically sweet. She could barely breathe while the others—mainly the athletics department—chortled. With his one-size-too-small shorts and carefully styled white-boy do, Stan had been voted the sexiest in the male category.

Of course that *pinche reina* enjoyed this. Isa's hand itched to deliver an Alexis Carrington–style slap across his smug face. Stan might be a former all-star athlete and head of the PE department, but that mama's boy made Steven Cojocaru look straighter than Trent Lott.

"Quite." Principal Quilley clipped off the laughter in his Shakespearean voice. "I spoke with their parents and they will be composing a letter of apology to the staff here at the school."

"That's it?" Isa's question killed what was left of everyone's amusement. "I'm sure Carrie and Addison didn't have the only copy," she added. Did she really have to say the obvious? "Do we want our students circulating this around about us?"

"They will also be suspended from school for one week," he answered, his eyes dark with compassion. "Anyone who is caught with a copy will be given a week of detention."

Isa glanced at Myrtle, who now cried quietly into her hankie, and at Bildo—*Mr. Weisshaar*—who stared wide-eyed at the table. The three of them would have to face the students every day for the rest of the year, knowing how they looked at them, judged them. At least Celeste had the power to spit in their food.

No punishment would be good enough. Isa's inner Alexis Carrington insisted she speak the hell up. Like the episode when she wrested Denver Carrington from Blake and threatened the board of directors with dismissal if they crossed her. And girlfriend did it in a fabulously massive shoulder-padded suit. If Isa had a little less Krystle Carrington and more Alexis in her, she'd get her recount.

Stacking her hands on top of the other and pulling her unpadded shoulders back, Isa did her best.

"I think this is indicative of the general lack of respect we have from the students," she heard herself saying out loud. "I think we should use a class period to have an open discussion of respect not only for men, but women as well."

A tide of outrage and complaints drowned Isa's voice.

We don't have time to discuss this on class time with the state exams next month.

We shouldn't be perpetuating this behavior by addressing it in the classroom; let their punishment speak for itself.

"Ms. Avellan, remember you have students who also rely on you," Principal Quilley said gravely when the clamor ebbed away. He had been her favorite teacher when she was in this high school, he encouraged her to take a full AP load, and then helped her find scholarships for college. He knew her better than her own father did and in spite of all her personal failures, Dr. Quilley's respect never faltered.

"Frankly, I feel any further discussion will only make it worse," he continued. Why, she asked silently, why would he not take her side? "Better to let this little incident die down and focus on education.

"Don't you think?" he asked, looking up at Isa like a patient father ministering to his complaining teenager.

"No," she spat, shoving her chair back. "I really don't."

"Girl, I thought you were going to castrate him with your eyes, I swear you were," June declared. The school secretary's stiletto boots clattered to keep up with Isa's red Keds.

Isa could almost hear the creaking hinges as she forced her lips into a grin. She was almost angry enough to say something against Dr. Quilley. But not quite. "You made out well."

The approving glow in June's eyes dimmed. "I'm a married gal," she countered. "Ted will really appreciate that high school guys jerk off to thoughts of me."

Maybe they wouldn't if June started dressing like an adult. Then again, part of Isa envied June for just letting it all hang out there in clothes that inspired cattiness.

The whisperings that went on behind June's back speculated that she got her secretary job because of her bra size rather than her typing speed. It didn't help that June wasn't shy about sharing her opinions, which further alienated every other woman in the school, except for Isa. Now she likened the friendship to being adopted by a cat.

June planted a hand on a sassily cocked hip when they stopped at Isa's mobile classroom, on what the kids called Trailer Trash Row. As budgets tightened and the student population swelled, mobile buildings crept up like mushrooms after the rain. "Now will you go out with my brother-in-law?" June pleaded.

"No."

June's sly grin collapsed. "Why not? He's a good guy, he has a great job and trust me, what happened back in that room is already makin' the rounds. You need damage control, girl."

Why her, Isa pleaded. Why? June had only been living in Sweetwater, an L.A. suburb wedged between Montebello and Norwalk, for a few months and she knew full well how fast word got around. And around here no one needed the Internet, cell phones, or TV. All you needed was to tell Susan Contreras. Isa loved her best friend's mother, who had taken her and her son in when they had nowhere to go. But no secret was sacred when it landed in Susan's ear.

"I'm not dating Alex so people will think I'm—" she looked over her shoulder and whispered, "fuckable."

"Oh, but honey, I've lived in his house long enough to know that he is," June remarked and then saw Isa's look of *eww*. "I'm just being honest."

June's brother-in-law was the first guy in a long time who made Isa nearly forget her hard-won lessons about men. Guys like Alex were too charismatic, too . . . too much for a girl like Isa. In some ways, he reminded her of her ex husband when she had first fallen senselessly in love at fifteen. Now she was almost thirty and she'd learned never to make that mistake again.

"Alex is Andrew's soccer coach," Isa informed June.

"More reason for you to get in there and snatch him up before them other soccer moms do." Inspired, her drawl sharpened. "This is what we'll do: new hair, a little makeup to bring out your eyes and shorter, tighter outfits . . . we'll make you a MILF!"

"A what?"

"MILF. Mother I'd like to—" June looked over her shoulder and finished clearly. "Fuck."

Isa shook her head. Just because they were in a high school didn't mean they had to talk like they were students. "I promised Andrew I wouldn't be late for his practice," she said with as much dignity as she could muster on a day like this. "See you at lunch tomorrow?"

"Soccer practice? You'll be there tonight?"

"Well I thought so since my son is on the team an—" Isa realized the direction where June's thoughts were headed. "Oh no. If you try to set me up with Alex I'll never speak to you again."

"Just an introduction?"

"No. I already met him."

"And?"

"He shook my hand and gave me the schedule."

"That's it?"

"I have work to do."

"You're telling me," June said before wiggling back to the main building. June reminded Isa eerily of her mother, Dara. The same Dara from whom Isa hadn't heard in four months. Aside from her blue eyes and boobs, Dara hadn't ever given Isa much.

But where Dara had been the MILF of all MILFs, her daughter drew her sweater closed and resigned herself to being the dependable mom she'd always been.

2

"That was quite a turn," Alex called out when Isa slammed the car door shut, dropping her backpack while hugging a store-bought potato salad she'd artfully arranged in a ceramic bowl to look like homemade.

Backpack forgotten, she looked up and saw *him*—Alex—hefting a net of soccer balls over his shoulder. "Ready for the new season?" he asked.

Remembering that the air-conditioning died in her classroom, Isa clamped her free arm to her side. And she wondered why she beat out Myrtle, Celeste, and Bildo for the title?

"Hardly." She sniffed the coconut oil in his sunscreen as he bent down to pick up her backpack. "How about you?"

He shrugged her backpack up on his shoulder and Isa bit back a sigh. "Can't back out now."

Isa wondered what that meant, noticing his brown poet's eyes were underlined with dark half-moons and that melt-in-your-mouth smile was nowhere to be seen.

"Have you heard from your brother?" she asked, remembering that Ted Lujon had originally been the head coach but had been called to active duty.

"Uh, no," he answered as if he'd already forgotten they were walking together. "Not in a while."

See, Isa would've told June. This is why she would not go through the humiliation of a makeover for a man who couldn't remember her presence while he carried *her* backpack.

"I've been waiting fifteen minutes for you to get here," Susan Contreras shouted at Isa from the gazebo. "And honey, how many times do I have to tell you to get rid of that ratty old backpack?"

Isa had known Susan since she was six years old and interpreted this greeting: "Hi. How are you?" in Mexican Mama speak. But she'd really wished Alex wasn't holding the offending backpack right this very second.

"I was so worried and you never answer your cell phone," Susan complained, wrapping Isa into a hug and the Carolina Herrera she sprayed on religiously every morning. She looked like a tropical cocktail garnish in her straw hat and lime Capri set. "And everyone's talking about the, you know, that *thing* that happened at your school."

"Here you go," Alex offered, holding out her backpack from its duct-taped strap.

"Thanks," Isa murmured.

"Go take your balls to the field," Susan ordered him. For the first time Alex grinned at Isa, and even though she felt so inelegant, his brief attention felt like the sun warming her bare skin.

"And *m'ijo*, make sure you take some bottled water," Susan continued as if time hadn't stopped and Alex wasn't looking at her. "It's very hot out there."

"I will." He turned and every female eye watched him bend down over the ice chest, except for Susan, who started lecturing Isa about her backpack. Isa took in the other moms in their colorful, cute clothes and shoes.

You know better, a voice spoke unheeded. Isa heaved in a breath when Susan swatted her arm. "I was wondering when you'd notice."

Isa immediately cleared all thoughts in case Susan really could read minds. Ever since her best friend Tamara brought her home that day after kindergarten, Susan had treated her like a second daughter. She set her potato salad on the table, which was already crowded with homemade brownies, cookies, salsa, salads, and beans.

Susan narrowed her eyes behind her sunglasses. "Why aren't you wearing makeup or at the very least lipstick?"

"Well I—"

"And I hope you're drinking more water and wearing that sunscreen I gave you. It's not too greasy, is it?"

"Uh, no, not at all." Not that she'd know, as it had been tossed in her drawer with all the other stuff Susan bought for her.

"Good because trust me, now that you're about to hit thirty"—Isa turned twenty-nine two months ago—"it's all over. So if you want another husband, get started now."

Strategically changing the subject, Isa scanned the field. "Where's Andrew?"

Isa found him pumping his legs as fast as he could to keep up with the other kids. With a power she'd never seen before, his foot slammed the ball and Alex ducked out of the way before it hit him in the face.

Mother and son cringed, but Alex yelled out, "Good kick. Next time aim the other way."

* * *

Alex knew the second he jogged off the field that he'd been had.

Eleven weeks wasn't that long, he told himself as he eyed Susan Contreras standing as the ringleader in a circle of single and married soccer moms who watched their sons' soccer practice. Why did he let Ted talk him into this? Why did Ted have to be called up for active duty *now*? Alex had other things to do, but as always, what he wanted would have to come second.

"Alex, could you help me with the ice chest?" Susan asked.

Pulling the corners of his lips into a smile, he set his clipboard on a picnic table. "Sure. Where do you want me to move it to?"

"Oh, over there somewhere," she cooed, waving her hand around. "How's *tú papa*?"

"Fine."

"And your sister Christine?" she asked and he paused to answer.

"I got an email from her today," Alex said, tension coiling in his neck. Christine's next tuition payment would be due at the end of the month.

Alex hoped he would walk out of tomorrow's meeting with his boss with a nice healthy raise. Hopefully, a raise that would allow him to keep paying Christine's tuition with some left over for him to go back to college, part time, of course. It would be a start. "She's already studying for mid-terms."

"Hmm. So have you been keeping busy?"

"Yeah. Not too busy, though." Unease chilled his skin, warning that this wasn't a casual conversation. But the

shade was such a relief after getting beaten on by the swel-
tering September sun. His eyes already burned from the
sunscreen sweating down his face and he wanted nothing
more than to dunk his head in ice water.

"That's nice. So will you be at Josie's barbeque on Saturday?" Susan asked.

Here it comes. Some unlucky lady was about to get
shoved in his path. "Maybe."

"Well, I was thinking if you're seeing someone and you
want to bring her to these things, I'd welcome her completely. Just as *tú mama* would."

He flinched, not expecting that one. "Ohh-kay. But I'm
not seeing anyone—"

"Oh!" A delighted smile popped on her face. "I see."

"You want to set me up, don't you?"

That rattled the smile off her face. "How do yo—I mean,
what would give you that idea?"

"I've known you since I coached Memo's team."

"If you want me to introduce you to some nice girls, I'd be
happy to—"

"That's okay." He thanked God that Susan's daughter
was with that fireman guy in L.A. "I can look on my own."

"Do you have anyone in mind? I mean, I was saying to
Isa the other day that you two should—"

So that's what they were talking about on the sidelines.
He'd seen them standing arm in arm, watching and talking.

Isa was . . . *Isa*. Don't get him wrong, she was cute, if a little too quiet for his taste. He glanced past Susan's shoulder
and looked for Isa. One of the moms caught him looking and
bent forward to show off her cleavage. Alex blinked and
turned back to Susan.

"Uh. I don't think so," he stammered, searching for an escape.

Her hand curled into a fist. "¿Con permiso? There's nothing wrong with her."

"I just don't see it happening right now."

"Why not now?"

Isa wanted a soda but her feet ground to a halt when Susan all but demanded to know why Alex Lujon did not want to date her.

Before she could tell her feet to run, Alex said, "I don't think that would work." He laughed. "I'm sure she's really sweet but—"

"But you'd go as friends," Susan insisted, as if they were haggling over a rug.

"I'll think about it."

"I'm sure Isa is available Saturday night."

"I'll have to double check an—" He stepped back, bumping into her, and Isa lost her chance to escape and pretend she never heard any of this.

"Isa?" he asked as if he couldn't believe she was standing there.

Susan gasped but quickly recovered. "I was just telling Alex that I . . ."

Her voice drifted away and Isa's mind grasped at something smart to say. It had to be cool and unruffled. But what came to mind was the memory of Tamara telling her ex-boyfriend who had just proposed that she had to go to the bathroom in front of God, family, and a horrified Susan.

That would not work. But what would Alexis say? *You will all be fired*—

No. Not that either.

"I need to go do something that I've been meaning to do," Susan said. "Talk soon!"

Staring out at the field, Alex took a deep breath before asking, "You heard all that, didn't you?"

"Don't worry about . . . any of it," Isa managed as she dipped down and yanked something that felt like a bottle out of the cooler. Water dripped down her hand. "I mean that's Susan for you, right?"

"Still, I don't want you to think . . ."

Isa clutched her bottle to her thumping chest with both hands. "It would be weird."

"No, of—"

"You should get back to practice."

He shifted his weight on his other foot and the sun burned her eyes. Birds darted about the rafters of the gazebo, blithely unaware of Isa and Alex shuffling their feet and hoping no one else was paying attention.

"Isa, I'm really sorry for all of this," he started. "I think you're—"

BONK! Her bottle went airborne. Alex's mouth dropped open and he rushed forward. Somewhere behind her she heard Andrew yell sorry. As her vision went to static, Isa had this vague sense of falling and her last thought before kissing the dirty pavement was, *damn it*.

3

ALEX LUJON'S HOROSCOPE FOR SEPTEMBER 7

With Mercury out of retrograde you are now free to open your eyes to see more of the world around you. However, this expansive feeling does not include romance. In fact, starting a romantic relationship is highly inadvisable until late next week.

Isa's eyes snapped open when Susan shouted in her face, "Isa, say something! Anything!"

"Anything?" Isa managed.

"*¡Gracias a Díos!* You're alive."

"Don't move her," Alex commanded.

"Is she okay?" Andrew whined somewhere behind her. "I didn't mean to."

Isa pulled her eyes open and saw three heads staring down at her. The pain in her head forced them shut, but Susan dug her nails into the soft of her palm.

"Ow," she moaned. "Stop hurting me. I'll wear the damn sunscreen."

Her hand fell onto the concrete. "But you said you were wearing it!"

"I'm taking her to the hospital," Alex decided, and Isa opened her eyes. There was Susan looking indignant about the sunscreen, and Alex. But then there was also Joan Collins. Isa shut her eyes. She had a head injury. She really didn't see what she just saw.

"Isa," Alex said. "Open your eyes."

"He seems so masterful, darling."

Isa opened her eyes and saw Joan Collins standing next to Alex, her eyes admiring his broad shoulders.

Frowning, she asked Joan, "What are you doing here?"

"Oh my God! Does she have anemia?" Susan gasped, clutching her hand tighter.

"Amnesia, which I don't have," Isa corrected. Her eyes fluttered shut and when she reopened them, Joan was gone. "What happened?"

"A ball hit you in the back of the head," Alex explained.

A head injury, she told herself. Joan was a mild hallucination brought on by a soccer ball, not insanity.

"Ice! Someone get some ice!" Susan demanded. "Honey, you'll be just fine."

"Am I bleeding?"

Two gasps and Susan fell back into the arms of two mothers standing behind her. They practically fell out of their tops trying to catch her.

Alex bent closer and Isa pressed her head into the ungiving concrete, thinking he was going to kiss her. But she felt his strong fingers in her hair, feeling her scalp. When he touched the tender lump she couldn't help but hiss back the pain.

"Sorry," he murmured. His eyes met hers and a jolt lit through her. "You're not bleeding but I'm taking you to the hospital."

"Where's Andrew?" she asked.

"He's fine. But Susan—" He glanced over and then rolled his eyes. Isa snorted and when he looked down amused, she curled her toes tightly.

"I should've been paying closer attention," he apologized and she started making sounds that it wasn't his fault. "Not just the ball, but what I said."

Oh, that's right. How could she have forgotten? As far as she was concerned, that particular incident now made all of this Alex's fault.

"*Darling, make him pay for this,*" Joan said from out of nowhere.

Isa shifted her eyes to the right and saw only Susan's knees, which were now dirty from kneeling beside her. Joan was right even if, well, she wasn't real.

"Can you sit up?" Alex asked.

"You owe me," came out of Isa's mouth.

"What?"

"Nothing."

"She's right," Susan insisted beside her, having made a miraculous recovery. "You were facing the field and you should have done something. Now you need to make this up to her."

Isa shut her eyes and prayed for unconsciousness to take her away.

"I can take her to the hospital," he offered.

Wow, what a hero, Isa thought sourly. She sighed and sat up, the world shifting treacherously in front of her eyes. Alex's arm shot around her shoulders, "Whoa, take it easy there."

"I'm not a horse." She braced herself up on her free hand in case she plopped down again.

"Alex, I think you owe Isa dinner." Susan cast an unmerciful eye his way.

"I don't think—" Isa started, when Alex surprised the hell out of her by saying, "Sure."

Carefully she turned her head to face him. "You don't have to."

But Alex did and now he felt even shittier remembering how his first thought when Susan started singing Isa's praises was that Isa had put her up to it. His conscience couldn't bear the claws of guilt that he'd embarrassed her and then watched her take a ball to the head.

"I'd really like to make this up to you," he kindly insisted.

Her lips pressed into a thin line like he'd just called her a skanky crack 'ho.

"Well thanks, Alex. But I can feed myself. Can someone help me stand up here?"

He took her arm and she glared at him with eyes so blue that they hit him like a punch to the gut. As she gathered her backpack and Andrew while waving off Susan's help, he wondered why he hadn't noticed her eyes before.

Two hours later, Alex staggered through the front door and smelled cigarette smoke drifting into the house from the back patio. His dad wasn't supposed to be smoking, which would be a double death wish with his lung condition and living with Ted's wife. Hoping to call Isa to try to apologize again, Alex put that in the back of his mind as he pocketed his keys.

"We're gonna have words you and I!"

Before he appeared on the steps leading to the back patio, Alex took a moment as he prepared himself to deal with *her*.

Her, being Ted's wife, whose face was slathered in green stuff, making her eyes look huge with vengeance. Unable to afford the apartment she had shared with Ted in Irvine, June forced her way into the house where Alex and his four siblings had grown up.

"How much longer do we have until you can't move your mouth anymore?" Alex asked.

"Hey son, you're home early," his dad said cheerfully, appearing from the patio off the kitchen. "How was practice?"

"Great."

"It's a nice evening, care to bring out a couple of beers?"

June made sure no one forgot she stood there by drumming her nails on the counter.

His dad assessed the situation. He leaned on the counter, eager to see what his daughter-in-law was so mad about now.

Alex really wanted that beer and the only way he'd get it was to get this over with. "Okay, what?" he asked her.

"You insulted my friend and then hit her with a soccer ball!"

"Look I never meant to hurt Isa's feelings. It was Susan who—"

"What's so wrong with her that you won't at the very least get to know her?"

Alex realized she had no way of knowing, unless . . . "How do you even know about this?"

Her eyes narrowed. "That's not the point."

"Well since Isa has now been voted team mom, looks like I'll have plenty of time to get to know her now, won't I?"

"Who are we talking about?" his dad asked innocently.

"No one," June and Alex barked.

"Oh that girl! Isa is her name, *sí*?"

June nodded, a long crack in her green mask forming across her brow.

"You know, *m'ijo*, from what I've heard she sounds like a really nice girl. Did you really hit her in the head?"

Alex pressed the jumping muscle under his right eye to make it stop. Wishing all of this would just stop. "Can I have my beer please?"

"Call her an' apowogize," June mumbled, little cracks forming around the corners of her mouth, which just weirded him out. "And then take her out."

"She doesn't want a pity date," he said. "And even though it's none of your business, I was planning to call and make sure she's okay."

"What's a pity date?" his dad asked.

June stiffened, practically shaking from wanting to tell him off but her mask had probably solidified so she couldn't.

"Do you have any opinions you want to share?" Alex turned to his dad on his way to the refrigerator.

Stifling a laugh, his dad ran the back of his hand across his mouth. "Like I always say, never say never. When you call this girl one thing might lead to another and . . ."

The muscle twitch nearly shut his eye. Alex was going to have to take this one looking like a major jerk. Simple fact: Alex didn't mess with single moms, no matter how beautiful their blue eyes were.

Number one, they didn't just want a guy around; they

also wanted a father for their kid. Number two, they had ex husbands or boyfriends. Number three, as the oldest, Alex had spent his life taking care of his siblings and then after mom died, his father, so he really wasn't looking for any more responsibilities.

And finally, from the way Isa got all prickly on him, she didn't exactly jump at the chance to go out with him.

The refrigerator door slammed with a clink of bottles.

"This does not leave this kitchen," he started.

June and his dad leaned in ever so slightly.

"She's not my type, okay? I didn't want to come out and say it because Isa seems like a nice woman. But it ain't gonna happen."

"Ash-ho," June mumbled, pivoting on the heel of her poofy heeled slipper and marching down the hall. The wall clock bounced and settled crookedly when she slammed the bathroom door.

Taking a deep breath and raising his salt-and-pepper eyebrows, Alex's dad murmured as he walked back outside. "I hope you know she'll be in there all night. That's not good for a man my age and my kind of problems. This is your fault."

"Wha—why—I didn't marry her," Alex sputtered.

"Yeah, but you let your brother talk us into taking her in," his dad muttered. With one cutting look, he then slammed the screen door shut. Alex looked down and realized his dad took his beer.

4

By seven that night, Isa realized that her plans to move somewhere far, far away, like Ohio, would have to be postponed. At least until after the soccer season ended. God forgive her, she would pray every night they didn't make it into the finals because Andrew could talk about nothing except soccer.

But as a mother, her son's happiness was much more important than her pride.

Great. Not only was her head killing her, she now had the guilt of wanting to move Andrew far from all this on top of dragging him away from the picnic with his friends.

"Did I say I was sorry enough? Because I really am," Andrew said, looking up from his fries.

"I know you are, honey."

"Does it hurt?"

"Not anymore." She hoped she had something for the pain.

"Do you think Alex is mad at me?"

"Why?"

"He told me to watch where I kick the ball."

She paused, holding her burger just so from her mouth. "Did he yell at you?"

So help Isa but if he so much as looked at her son the wrong way she'd—

"No. But I felt bad for hitting you. And he told me to make sure I took good care of you tonight."

This was one of those moments when as his mother, she needed to say something wise, except she didn't know what that could be. However, she did know that the idea of Alex lecturing her son did not sit well with her.

"Is that why you've been so quiet?"

Andrew nodded his head and a pang hit her right in the center of her chest.

"Well, don't feel bad. It was an accident. But you've got one thing going."

She waited for him to peek up. "What?" he asked.

"You have a heck of a kick."

His grin started at the corner of his mouth and then spread. "Alex said I might get to play goalie or center forward. He wants me to try both."

Isa curled the corner of her mouth. At least Alex wanted to play with one of them.

"He said he wanted me to show up early for practice so we could see." Andrew munched happily on his fries, having cleared his conscience with his mother. "Do you think Tía Susan can take me on the days you have to stay late?"

"Maybe. What about asking your dad?"

"Alex might be able to pick me up."

She looked down and realized she'd eaten nearly all of her fries. She could almost hear the fat stampede to the backs of her thighs. No amount of butt clenches she would do while grading papers could stop the infestation of cellulite.

"We'll see," she grumbled.

"Okay." His socked feet bounced off the legs of the chair. "Are you going to tell Dad about my games?"

"I think you should."

Andrew shrugged, keeping his eyes glued to his plate.

Her maternal antenna picked up on something.

"Is there something you want to talk about?"

"No." He stabbed a fry into his ketchup.

She pushed her plate away. "Is the weekend bothering you?" Andrew's last visit with his father hadn't gone well.

"I wish you had stayed together. I want to be in one place."

As a kid, she thought her father had the handle on guilt, but in truth, no one could send you on a guilt trip like your own kid. "I wish you could, too. Do you know what you guys are doing this weekend?"

"Nothing. I'll probably stay at Grandma and Grandpa's like I always do."

"Well, maybe your dad will get his own place soon." As soon as Isa made the dig, she regretted it. She didn't want to be one of those mothers.

"I'd rather stay here this weekend so I can go to Josh's house."

"Maybe your dad will take you."

"I asked and he said I had to stay with the family cuz it's the only time he gets."

Even though it was the last thing she wanted, she asked anyway. "Do you want me to talk to your dad?"

"No."

"Maybe I can see if he wants more time with you."

Andrew gripped his fork in one hand but shrugged his shoulders. "It would've helped if you stayed together."

"Andrew—" She caught herself before she said something he didn't deserve to hear. Anger flared hot and fresh inside her, darkening her cheeks and tightening her grip on her fork.

She was trying; boy, was she trying to forgive Carlos for not being man enough to keep his family together. He never even made an effort. He just did whatever he wanted without caring that it cost them their savings and their home. Isa's blood still simmered when she remembered the afternoon she came home and found him and a nineteen-year-old in their bed when he was supposed to have been at work.

And how many times had Isa slept in those sheets before she caught them?

Don't. Don't go there. She loosened her hold on the fork and forced herself to breathe.

"I want to stay with you." With sorrow in his eyes, Andrew blinked and then looked down at his plate.

She grinned, barely keeping from bursting into a million pieces. "Me too."

"I'm so sorry I'm late," Susan cried, sailing through Josie's new French doors into the new sunroom. Why Josie's husband and not Susan's husband built one for his wife irritated her, especially since her friend—God bless her soul—decorated with fake flowers.

Bending down to give her comadres, Josie and then Patty, pecks on the cheek, she took her chair facing the roses that Josie's husband planted around a stone birdbath he installed for Josie's fiftieth birthday.

"I have something very important to tell you," Susan started.

"I was just telling Patty that Mireya was arrested for check fraud," Josie bragged excitedly. "She made copies of her own checks and then cashed them at one of those check and go places."

"And I was telling Josie that Yolanda cancelled her weekly mani-pedi just the other day," Patty added, not to be outdone. "Yolanda hasn't been seen ever since."

This was good dirt, Susan realized. But hers was more important. "I need to get Isa and Alex Lujon together."

Patty winced like she bit into a lemon. "That old *viejito*?"

"No not that one!" Even though she didn't need it, she slid a cookie off the plate. "His son, Alex Lujon."

"Ohhh," they both chimed knowingly.

"*Pero* what about Tamara and Will?" Josie asked.

"They're getting married," Susan said confidently, sneaking another cookie off the plate. "I know it's happening this year. I can feel it."

Josie and Patty exchanged dubious glances that Susan chose to ignore. "Has Tamara said anything?" Josie ventured diplomatically.

"Not yet. But they've been together long enough."

"Young people don't do it like we did, Susan," Patty said through the cookie in her mouth. "They could be like that . . . that Susan Sarandon or Oprah."

Susan slowly lowered the rest of the cookie from her mouth. Her daughter wouldn't dare do that to her. And Will, she had made sure he understood that the only reason why she allowed Tamara to move in with him was on the condition of marriage. Now Tamara had her degree and they had a home. Any day now, she reminded herself as the menopausal heat flushed her cheeks.

But she was here to talk about Isa and Alex. "We'll worry about Tamara later."

"Pish. Don't get your hopes up," Patty muttered while Susan dotted the crumbs off her lips with a napkin.

"They have the spark," Susan insisted. "I saw it with my own two eyes."

Josie started, "Susan, we shouldn't—"

"Spark? What spark?" Patty demanded. "There's no such thing as no spark."

"They're attracted to each other and they're perfect." She didn't refer to Alex's less than enthusiastic response to her suggestion that he ask her out. "Alex will make the perfect Daddy for Andrew and he'll take care of Isa."

"But he ain't going to want another man's child," Patty blurted and then wilted under the scathing looks from both Josie and Susan. "*Es cierto.*" She crunched on another cookie.

"Maybe you should let nature take its course," Josie suggested. "Remember what happened when you made Ruben propose to Tamara at Mireya's party?"

"I didn't *tell* him to propose," Susan argued. "I just suggested that because he and Tamara were arguing that he might want to think—"

Patty swatted Josie in the shoulder. "Please. This is us you're talking to. Remember when you nosed into Memo's business with that girl he brought home? That *pobrecita's* never been seen since."

"You know I forgot all about that," Josie mused. "Susan, let the kids figure it out on their own. They get so embarrassed when you—"

"But wait," Patty cried, reaching around for her ten-pound purse. She muttered as she shoved around the accumulated flotsam until she pulled out a bite-sized camera. "We could try this."

"Try what?" Susan asked skeptically.

"It's the Magic Eye camera." Patty widened her eyes and held her hands up. "It takes pictures of your aura."

"Oh, Patty," Josie sighed.

"We could take their photos and see if their auras match up," Patty continued, ignoring Josie who attacked a cookie in exasperation. "If they match, we'll set them up."

"Let me see that," Susan insisted, holding out her hand. "What does it do?"

"It takes a photo of the person and their aura energy around them." Patty wound her hand in the air. "It's like reading their mind."

Susan turned it over. It was made in China but she liked the part about reading someone's mind.

5

HEADLINE FROM THE *SWEETWATER STAR NEWS*:
CHEERLEADERS SUE DISTRICT
FOR WRONGFUL SUSPENSION
PARENTS ALLEGE A PRANK TAKEN OUT OF HAND.
SCHOOL OFFICIALS WILL NOT COMMENT ON SUIT.

"Are you done yet? My arm's tired."

Isa tore her eyes from the headline to Andrew who held up the soggy edition of the *Star News*. She ripped it out of his hands and read the story. The edges of the paper gave under the pressure of her fists as she took in quotes about how suspensions on the students' records could compromise future college careers. A livid flush burned her skin when she got to the thinly veiled attacks on the eleventh-grade ESL teacher the girls claimed had been persecuting them since last year.

"Shit!"

"You said a—"

She handed him the keys. "Get in the car. And I know what I said but do not repeat it."

The reporter mentioned nothing about Myrtle, who broke down in the library when students started laughing behind her back or the snickering that followed Isa every time she walked through the halls. Now her humiliation was complete.

"Am I going to school today?" Andrew asked.

"Yes."

She threw the paper back where it belonged, down in the gutter filled with a shallow puddle of sprinkler water.

"What was it about?"

"Three bi—" she cleared her throat. "Girls who go to my school."

"Oh. You're not mad at me, are you?"

"Of course not." Do not take this out on him, she warned herself as she got into the car. With a deep breath she started it and sat there, dreading to go to work while the engine warmed to life.

"Who's taking me to practice after school?" Andrew asked.

"We've already been through this, Andrew. Your Tía Susan will pick you up."

"Are you sure you can't come?"

Isa sucked in breath to keep from exploding at her son who had done nothing to deserve it. "I'm sorry, but I have open house tonight. It's the only practice I'll ever miss."

"I hope Dad will be there this time."

Tears bit the back of her throat but she managed to put the car in gear. "I'm sure he'll try."

"I doubt it," he muttered as they pulled away from the curb.

Thank God Andrew said nothing more about this afternoon's practice or else she might not have made the drive without losing hold of her tears. When he hugged her good-bye, she almost didn't let him go.

The second she stepped on school grounds she was hav-ing a few words with Dr. Quilley. She would be professional and matter of fact, but something had to be done about this. She worked too damn hard for her reputation to be de-stroyed again. She wouldn't be the subject of anyone's pity, derision, or contempt.

When Isa arrived at her class, she'd worked herself into a quivering froth. Breathing fire from her nostrils, she nearly marched past Mr. Weisshaar and some of her first-period students outside her classroom. But when he ran over, his eyes filled with tears, she immediately knew something was wrong.

"I swear I didn't bring it to school," Mr. Weisshaar sobbed. "I'd never in my life . . . I don't want to lose my job. I swear, I'd never even seen one—"

"What?" she demanded in front of several curious students.

"Th-th-this—the—"

A chorus of excited students rose up all around her while Mr. Weisshaar babbled about the cops and parents.

She took his arm, steering him to his class across from her mobile unit. "Show me."

And when she stepped into his class, Isa didn't see what was wrong. "I don't know why this is happening," Bildo said. *Mr. Weisshaar*, she reminded herself. "All I want to do is teach. It's all I ever wanted to do and look how they—"

Isa couldn't handle the man falling apart on her. Not with heckling high schoolers smelling blood and fear through the thin wall of the mobile class unit. She turned to buck him up and then her eyes snagged on the blonde blow-up doll seated behind Mr. Weisshaar's desk.

"What the fuck?" she exploded.

"Ms. Avellan," he exclaimed like the old maid he was.

"*I don't know, darling,*" that familiar voice sighed beside her. Isa turned and Joan Collins was looking at her nails. Joan realized she had an audience and smiled like a cat. "*He looks like the kind that would use one of those.*"

Joan inclined her head in the direction of the doll. Isa opened her mouth to defend Bildo, but her teeth clinked when she snapped it shut. Seeing Joan Collins was one thing, talking to her would be taking it to a whole new level. It was certain: Her day had officially hit the fan and splattered the walls.

"Now before you do anything—" June said when she saw Isa's face as she burst into the main office.

Isa barely ground out, "Is he in?"

"Honey, I'm not lettin' you in because you look like you're about to shit your eyeballs."

Just then Principal Quilley happened to step out of the break room with a steaming cup of coffee in his hand. One look at Isa and he set it down with a decisive snap. "Now Ms. Avellan, I know what you're going to say and we're deal—"

"How? How the hell are you going to deal with this now?"

"Well I . . . I won't take that tone from you. Just take your students back to your class—"

Isa's voice hurt her own ears. "No! Bil—Mr. Weisshaar has gone home so he can call the union. You know why?"

June and Principal Quilley—as well as the entire office staff pretending not to listen—shook their heads.

Isa wrestled the blow-up doll onto the counter, the plastic groaning like a balloon.

"Get that thing away from me," June yelled, jumping out of her chair, which rolled into the desk behind her.

"Touch it dude," one of Bildo's students said, his voice filled with awe.

Isa slapped his hand away. "What," she challenged, "do you plan to do about that?"

Everyone's mouth dropped open, much like the doll that stared up at the ceiling.

"Well?" Isa demanded and instantly felt regret for spraying the room with her anger, especially on the man who had showed her only kindness and encouragement. "When are you going to pull your head out of the sand and realize this is a war?"

Principal Quilley's eyes flashed with hurt, but then he resumed his mantle of authority. "Ms. Avellan, I suggest you return to your classroom immediately."

"Not until someone—"

"Go to your classroom, Isa," he shouted. That knocked her speechless. Not only did he never raise his voice, he never addressed anyone by their first name. "Let the superintendent and me handle this."

Isa took a step forward to apologize when his door slammed behind him.

"Whoa, honey," June said, thoroughly impressed. "Do you need me to walk you back to your class?"

Her anger had been stripped bare and Isa stood there, aware that everyone in the room looked at her as someone who'd completely unraveled before them.

She left the blow-up doll on the counter and shoved the door open, the curious crowd pulled back in case she spit fire. The students looked at June for guidance.

"Get on out! Go to class before you get tardies." That's all they needed to spill out the door.

With a sigh and a gentle pat to her hair, June looked at a tardy student. "What are you waiting for?"

"I didn't get to touch it."

June plucked a Kleenex out of the box and pulled the doll off the counter. "What's your name?"

"Ramiro."

"Ramiro, if you don't get yourself out of my office, I'm calling your mother and that's after I have you speak with the assistant principal about who put this here item in Mr. Weisshaar's class. Understand?"

She smiled with some satisfaction when he turned heel and booked out of there.

6

Alex tapped his chin with his cell phone's antenna, debating if he should call Isa just to find out if her head was all right. But he felt bad saying to June that he wasn't interested and part of him was too chicken to call Isa.

But then his worries drifted away when Erin from HR smiled at him as she sailed by.

His eyes wandered down from her model-perfect smile to the blonde curls that pointed down to her impressive chest, which filled the wings of the glittery butterfly on the front of her blouse.

And then the most unlikely thought popped in his head. Isa didn't need all the makeup Erin wore to look pretty.

Before he could wonder where that came from, his boss, Peter, appeared in the hallway, nervously tugging at his right sleeve. "Hey, Alex . . . uhh . . . Come in and have a seat."

"Thanks," Alex said, abruptly springing to his feet and then plopping into a black leather chair in Peter's office. "I guess you want a progress report on the Anderson jo—"

"Actually no. I already got your email and so we're up to speed on it."

Alex sucked in courage, seeing the direct route to ask for his raise. But he wasn't getting a good vibe from Peter. Then again, as operations manager, Peter was always strung tight and Alex knew how to play him. He was walking out of here with the money he'd earned as their top foreman.

Before Alex could launch into his speech, Peter looked straight up at him. "We lost the bid in Vegas."

Alex felt the loss in the pit of his stomach. Construction in L.A. and Orange County slowed to the point where the firm was wrapping up the jobs they had with no other new bids going out.

Slumping in his seat, the last thing Alex wanted to plan was which of his guys to lay off. There was Jim, whose wife was having their first and unplanned baby. Then Mike, who had just closed escrow on a duplex he bought with his brother.

So if it was his raise and their jobs, well, he'd take one for the guys.

"It'll only be temporary," Peter said. "Maybe just a month or so until we get things back on track."

"That can't be the only job in Vegas," Alex said, determined to fly out there on his own dollar to get them another job. "What about the proposed office complex in Riverside?"

"We bid too high and Stefan wouldn't come down."

"But we don't have any new bids going out."

Without saying it, Peter told Alex he was just as frustrated with the partners who owned the firm. They liked their expensive toys and coming in two, maybe three days a week. They'd completely lost touch with the reality that profits were going down if they didn't lighten up.

"So I'm really sorry to do this to you, Alex," Peter said. "You've meant a lot to this company and hey, you know it'll be good for you to have some free time and go somewhere where you can get higher up into management."

Alex looked up. That sounded awfully like *he* was the one they were laying off. "What?"

Peter squirmed in his seat. "Like I said, I'm sorry. And I got the partners to give you this." He opened one of his desk drawers and planted an envelope on the desk.

"You deserve this," he said, tapping the envelope. "One hundred percent."

Alex reached for the envelope and tore it open. There were two checks: one for seven thousand dollars, and the other a payout. They even included a two-page letter of recommendation.

"We didn't want to do this. Really," Peter begged him to accept. "But we're letting almost all the foremen go."

"Almost all?"

"Stefan feels that—" Peter squirmed in his chair. "Look, they've managed this whole thing so badly, you'll want to be getting out of here."

"Who's going to manage what's left of our jobs?" Alex asked, calmly tucking everything back in the envelope, and then pressing his finger to the twitching muscle under his eye.

"I am."

"Shit," Alex hissed and Peter's eyes all but popped out his skull. Alex never lost his cool. Not on a job, not in a crisis, not even when getting cussed out by a client. Never. It gave him some pleasure to see Peter deflate with embarrassment, but that wouldn't pay Christine's tuition, much less Alex's.

"Andy really tried to keep you. He did. He wanted you to split the responsibilities between you and me but . . ."

Andy was the least important partner and oddly the one who did the most work.

"No one discounts what you've done," Peter said as fury roared through Alex's blood. "And between you and me, this place is too fucking far down the toilet to last much longer."

Neither Good Alex nor Bad Alex liked the feel of sunshine getting blown up the ass. And as much as he itched to shove that seven-thousand-dollar check down one of the partners' throats, Alex just stood up and held out his hand like the pushover he was.

Bad Alex would tell Peter to screw himself and walk away with the extra seven grand and the three-thousand-dollar company laptop.

But Good Alex prevailed. He shook Peter's hand, left his keys and company laptop, and for the first time in his adult life, walked to his car not knowing how he was going to pay the mortgage.

"You're doing it wrong! Here let me." Patty used her mumu'd girth to shove Josie.

"Hands off!" Josie's slap prompted Susan to set down her wine glass and pry them apart before Patty threw Josie to the ground.

"Girls!"

"I tell her she never puts enough salt in her *posole*!"

"You don't need all that salt."

"But it doesn't taste like anything."

"Here, let me taste it," Susan insisted. Patty was in a mood, which meant she probably got a call from her ex.

For every year that Patty fought this divorce, she gained another ten pounds until all she could wear were mumus, preferably wild tropical or animal prints. Tonight she looked like Toucan Sam.

Patty had always been, well, a "big girl." Her husband, Juan Sr., was a good-for-nothing that showed up at the beauty shop to take five twenties from the register and spend it on some girl he found in Ensenada, or, in the affair that broke the back of their marriage, Patty's next-door neighbor and Josie's sister.

How a smart, loving—albeit pain-in-the-butt—woman like Patty could keep herself tied to such a nasty little man was beyond Susan's comprehension. In the meantime, she and especially Josie paid the price.

She blew on the *posole* broth and then delicately sipped it. Perfect. But she knew Patty was in a mood.

"Maybe a little more garlic," she suggested. "Just *un poquito*."

Pursing her lips was about as confrontational as Josie would get. She threw in a pinch of garlic and stirred in hurt silence.

"I went to the *botanica* for that perfume you told me to get. Now what?" Susan asked.

Not turning from her stirring, Josie asked, "You have to get Isa to wear it?"

"That won't mean she'll use it," Patty piped in. "I'd just spray her if I were you."

Josie clanged the wooden spoon against the edge of her pot. "It doesn't work that way. The person has to agree to the spell for it to work."

Patty rolled her eyes. "You're just talking a bunch of nonsense—"

"I had nothing to do with her stealing your husband, so back off," Josie yelled, stabbing the air with her steaming spoon.

Patty dropped the roll she'd been plucking apart. "Who said—"

"I want you to stop picking on me or you can get out."

Patty's eyes rolled from Josie to Susan, begging for help. Susan fanned herself with her hand. Finally someone dared to point out the huge thundercloud hanging over them. Josie's sister, Virginia (who'd always been easy), took off with Patty's no-good husband. Good riddance, Susan had thought, but it drove a wedge between her *comadres*. After losing Yolanda as a friend when she took in Isa and Andrew, Susan didn't want to lose any more.

"Well?" Josie challenged.

"I'm sorry," Patty drawled, swallowing and then breathing as if her heart was going to fly out of her mouth. "I should go."

Josie hesitated and Susan wondered what she'd do if she really let Patty leave. For once in many, many years she didn't know what to say and the helplessness of that feeling strangled her.

"Stay," Josie ordered, lowering her spoon. "I don't approve of what my sister did but I want you to stay."

"Okay *m'ija*," Patty managed, her voice deep with emotion. "I'll be good."

"You better." Josie nodded and then turned back to her

posole. "Now Susan, I put in some extra rose oil to beef up the potion. Do you know when she's supposed to meet Alex?"

"No," Susan squeaked, reaching for her wine. "I'm still working on that."

Josie's brow ridged as she seemed to think hard about something. "Ay Susan, when are you going to learn?"

7

ALEX'S HOROSCOPE FOR SEPTEMBER 14

Considerable forces are moving against you,
maneuvering you into a corner. Do you fight, flee,
or retend it isn't happening. That is entirely up to
you. Then again, notice the use of the word
"considerable."

Caught up in a whirl of irrational panic, Isa knew she was going to lose her job. It was more than a job, it was the only thing she'd done right, that she'd loved second to her son. And all because of some stupid, unfair, heartless prank, she'd also lost the respect of Dr. Quilley.

When she found out she was pregnant in college, Isa realized she couldn't be one of those mothers who handed the baby to grandma while she struggled through medical school. First, she didn't have any grandmas she was close to and second, Isa admired women who could put their careers on top of everything else, but she knew she couldn't be like them.

So when she asked Dr. Quilley for a letter of recommendation to the School of Education, he didn't ask why she changed her mind or how she could give up medicine.

"I expected you'd see the light," he'd said as if she turned in a satisfactory paper. "And when you're finished, we'll find a position for you here."

Far cry from her father, who'd said, "Imagine what you could've done if you'd kept your legs closed." And then Isa never heard from him again until Andrew was six months old.

Not that working towards her teaching degree had been any easier; Isa never regretted giving up med school, especially when she realized her gift for working with ESL students.

Sitting at the computer station in the farthest, darkest corner of the library after school, she scrolled the Internet for Joan Collins. She couldn't change what happened this morning, but she'd be damned if she was losing her mind.

Please don't be dead, Isa prayed and then realized if Joan wasn't visiting her in spirit, then that soccer ball had knocked something loose in her head.

"Hey honey," June purred. "How ya holding up?"

According to *Hello!*, Joan was fabulously alive and well. "Not good."

"I snuck in Snickers ice cream bars," June whispered, holding open her denim jacket. "Whatcha looking at?"

"Nothing." June stopped her from switching the screen.

"Joan Collins?" she questioned, grimacing.

"What do you mean?"

"I don't know." June coughed and tore the wrapper. "She's just some old lady."

Old lady? Isa wasn't going to take to anyone putting down Joan. "Excuse me but she's the bitch that paved the way for all TV bitches. She defined fabulous."

Another cough and rip. Pointing her ice cream at Isa, June didn't give up. "No, Amanda Woodward from Melrose Place was a super bitch."

"But she never could've been who she was without Alexis."

"I still think she's better."

"Alexis would've kicked her ass."

"With what? Her cane?"

"You don't know what you're talking about."

June squinted, pressing her fingers against her temple. Good, Isa thought. She deserved an ice cream headache for putting Joan down.

"Whatever. Look, I figure it's best to tell you but I heard Dr. Quilley order up some disciplinary paperwork after you know, you ripped him a new one."

Isa took a honking bite from her ice cream. The cold pain surged into her temples.

"I'm really sorry," June apologized.

"It's not your fault." Isa's head pounded and the ice cream just sloshed around in her mouth. Forcing it down, she then noticed the look on June's face. "What?"

"Well, we got two calls today. One from an L.A. *Times* reporter and another from Rocco Ramie of Rock Hard in the Morning!" Isa couldn't imagine how June could get all giddy over the vilest, nastiest misogynistic DJ that was the spawn of Howard Stern. "Ted used to listen to him and I asked Mr. Ramie if he'd send me an autograph and—"

Isa shook her head. "Why didn't you just bring a gun and shoot me in the head? It would've been much kinder."

Remembering herself, June settled back in her chair. "Well, you have to admit stuff like this doesn't happen every day."

"And I bet Ted would've been thrilled if you were mentioned as the most f-able in the school on Rock Hard in the Morning."

"I emailed him." She giggled. "And he agreed. Isn't that cute?"

"Real cute."

"Oh, it'll all blow over. Before you know it, no one will remember."

"Doesn't matter because everyone will know. Everyone reads that stupid paper, everyone talks in this town, and hell, if some other reporter shows up, even more people will know. And if you haven't figured it out yet, no one in this town forgets."

"At least they don't know your name."

"Everyone knows that it's me," Isa nearly shouted. They looked guiltily over their shoulders but the library was practically deserted. The squeaky wheel of the book cart inched through the history section, pushed by a student with blaring headsets.

"Look I know you're trying and I'm just not . . . I just have to get through the day."

"Well I think you're the smartest person I know. Everyone thinks that way about you, especially—"

"Don't say it," Isa warned.

"Say what?"

Isa was about to say *Alex*. "Never mind."

"You were going to say Alex, huh?"

"No, I wasn't!"

June's perkiness dampened and for once she looked like she didn't know what to say. "Isa, I don't want you to take it the wrong way but . . . Well, Alex isn't as interested as I thought and I didn't want you to get your hopes up—"

"I have to go." Isa stood up and logged herself off the computer. The buzzing sound in her ears had nothing to do with the fact that Alex wasn't interested.

"I'll walk with you."

"No, I'm fine," Isa insisted. "I know what you're going to say. I should wear makeup or slut clothes or do my hair. I don't need to know how damn smart I am from you or Al— or anyone."

June stepped back and Isa saw the embarrassment shading her face. "I wasn't going to say that. I was just kid—"

"Thanks for the ice cream." Isa tossed it into the trash can against the wall. "I'll call you later."

Feeling nasty and out of sorts, Isa restacked her papers, hoping at least one of her students would walk through the door with his parents. For her entire career Isa had managed to keep her private life and her work life separate. No one knew about her divorce until she changed her last name back to Avellan. No one saw her tears fall or took the hits from her bitchiness. Now she not only alienated her mentor, but also her only friend at school.

"Knock-knock!" Susan called through the open door.

Even though Susan worked at the elementary school, Isa knew better than to ask, "You heard about this morning?"

"I did." Susan looked over her shoulder and then walked inside. "Isa, Dr. Quilley didn't deserve that from you."

Isa sucked in her breath, feeling ten years old after Susan caught her and Tamara with a *Playgirl* magazine. Susan folded her arms over her chest, leaning her hip on Isa's desk. "But I know you'll do what's right," she said, knowing full well that she was probing Isa's suffering conscience. "You will, right?"

"I don't know what I could do that—"

"Enough about this," Susan dismissed, waving her hand in front of her face as if that would simply make all of Isa's problems vanish. "Did you and Alex set a time for your dinner?"

Isa drummed her pen against the edge of a student desk, her heart accelerating at Susan's mention of his name. Even though June already told Isa how Alex felt about her, Isa wouldn't let Susan know that. One humiliation at a time.

"Alex and I aren't going to dinner," she answered carefully.

Susan's eyes landed on the dancing pen and then a subtle grin graced her lips. "You're not?"

"No." They were playing a game of high stakes and neither wanted to reveal her cards first. "Why?" Isa broke.

"Oh, I guess you didn't hear."

"Hear what?"

"You were voted team mom at practice. Oh, and did I tell you that Tamara and Will are coming down for Andrew's first game?"

Susan was a formidable opponent but Isa wasn't a kid anymore. "Good," she said evenly. "Any news if they're getting married?" Isa stopped bouncing her pen.

"*Ay*, who knows," Susan replied, her eyes narrowing that

Isa hadn't taken the bait. "They keep saying they're wait-ing, but waiting for what?"

Isa imagined Tamara was waiting her mother out on principle. But she smiled, anticipating Tamara's reaction when she came home and discovered that Susan had sub-scribed to every wedding magazine known to womankind.

Out of nowhere Susan slipped back to Alex. "So. What are you going to wear when you go out with Alex?"

Isa sucked in her breath, ready to tell Susan to back off, but she never got a word out. Some women, Latinas in par-ticular like Tamara and Susan, were born with the girly gene that empowered them with the ability to match clothes and accessories. Since Isa was nearly allergic to pink and couldn't tell the difference between lavender and mauve, she obviously lacked that gene.

"Please tell me you won't wear your combat boots or that twenty-five-cent blouse," Susan pleaded. "Not that they aren't lovely, I just think something a little more feminine would be best. Here, try this."

Something cold and flowery wet her face, smelling of roses and herbs. She coughed and waved it out of her face. "Do you like it?" Susan asked brightly, blasting Isa with more of the stuff out of a bright green glass bottle. "Josie made it for me to give you."

Isa sputtered, "Wha—what's in it?"

"Oh, nothing. Just a little something extra for your date."

"Susan, there is no date and who voted me team mom?"

"The other mamas. And I think the sooner you talk with Alex about the team, the better for the boys, don't you think?"

Out of the corner of her eye, Isa saw a woman appear in the doorway. Joan? Twice in one day?

But the woman clutching a brown purse and wearing a black head scarf was not Joan. She peered inside, waiting to be welcomed.

Waving away the crap that Susan sprayed in her face, Isa stepped forward, shedding the girlish insecurity Susan brought out and replacing it with her teacher's authority.

The woman's husband followed in a clean shirt and pressed but worn pants and then Isa's shyest student, Khadija, walked in. Even though her jeans and long-sleeved blouse were all-American, her traditional *hajib* framed her pretty face, dominated by long-lashed brown eyes.

"Ms. Avellan, these are my parents," she said and then interpreted in Iranian.

As Isa reassured them of their daughter's progress and that the school hadn't had problems with bullies, she felt as if she were stepping off a rocky boat and back on solid ground.

"At the end of each semester we have verbal presentations," Isa said. "You're more than welcome to attend."

Out of the corner of her eye she saw her student Daniel Madrang walk in with his parents, followed by Phuc Lee with her mother and grandmother.

"Thank you," Khadija interpreted for her parents. "But Ms. Avellan, I want to say I'm sorry about the uh . . ." In addition to struggling with her English, Khadija couldn't look Isa in the face. "The survey. Ali told me about it."

A chill blasted through Isa's composure. She meant to smile but probably looked like she was baring her teeth for the kill.

"You did well speaking for your parents," Isa assured her. "They have much to be proud of. Show them around."

Khadija's face reddened under Isa's compliment. "I will. Thank you."

Susan appeared beside her. "Keep this." She dropped the bottle in Isa's hand. "And I'll be happy to watch Andrew Saturday night if he's not with Carlos. Just give me a call."

"That won't be necessary."

"Oh now, don't you give me that look, Isabella Avellan. You need to not be so, so—"

"What?"

"*Estirada*, stuck up."

"I'm no—" Isa caught herself when heads turned in their direction. "You know me better than that."

Susan preened when she'd finally got a rise out of Isa. "Alex doesn't," she chirped and then slipped out the door.

8

"'Kay listen up out there," Rocco Ramie shouted over the airwaves. "I just read this story about some cheerleaders in a town called Sweetwater started this Sex Savvy Survey and had their friends vote the most uh, do-able teachers in the school."

"Dude, where the hell is that?" his partner in crime, Sal Salamie chimed in.

"I don't know. Somewhere between Orange County and L.A. Can I finish here?"

"I had a teacher I once wanted to—" Bleep.

"Shut up, as—" Bleep. "Can I fu—" Bleep. "Finish?"

"Yeah, yeah, sorry, man."

Fucking FCC, Rocco thought before he continued. "So the ones who were voted unsexiest started this big stink and got the girls suspended and then one of them, some ESL teacher, found a blow-up doll in a classroom."

"Male or female?"

"The doll or the teacher?"

"Both!"

"Female."

"They make blow-up dolls for lesbians?"

"They make anything these days. So we did some investigating and not only found a picture of the *fugly* teacher but—"

Sal held up the photo and cocked his head to the side. "Dude, she's not that fugly."

"Anything with breasts and a mouth isn't fugly to you, Sal."

Rocco saw the "f-you" about to erupt from Sal's mouth and he personally hit the bleep button and then said, "So we at Rock Hard in the Morning got y'all a present this fine Friday morning. We got the ex-husband of the teacher who was voted by her students as the fugliest of them all! Welcome Carlos Lopez."

Rocco turned to the loser sitting across from him, who said, "Yo man, what up? But, uh, my last name—"

"I'm shocked man," Rocco said. "Shocked that you were married to someone who has been voted fugly by her students. How long were you married to her?"

Carlos glanced at Sal and then the mic. "Uh, too long. So about my last—"

" 'Kay, so what was it like?" Sal asked.

Clearing his throat, Carlos leaned forward. "I mean she ain't that bad when it comes to looks and all. She put on a little weight, ya know what I'm saying?"

"I bet you have too," Rocco said, wondering if *vato* here went through an entire bottle of hair gel every morning. He circled his hand for Carlos to keep talking.

"But a man wants a woman to you know, move around or yell something when he's doing his thing, you know? Like I was saying my na—"

"I had a girlfriend like that once," Sal added. Sal had a

wife he met in college, so Rocco knew he was lying. But then this whole thing was pretty much an act. And they were stuck with yahoos like . . . Rocco looked down at the paper and realized Carlos's last name was Muñoz. Whatever, dumb shits like Carlos who wanted to be on his radio were all the same to him. But what they had cooked up for Carlos would guarantee ratings out the roof.

"Was she like that when you met her?" Rocco said, moving it along.

"She was a little uptight. But cute and you know, she let me do what I wanted." Carlos shrugged. "We won't say her name, 'ight?"

Sal and Rocco exchanged glances. This is where shit got dicey. As long as they kept her anonymous, they'd stay out of any legal crap. Rocco just hoped she really was the bitch Carlos said she was and then he could stay out of any conscience crap.

"Here's what we're gonna do, because man to man, this is wrong," Sal said, sidestepping Carlos's question.

"Thanks man, bu—"

"You're welcome. Rocco, tell him what we're gonna do for him."

"Carlos, because there're hundreds, thousands, millions of men out there who've been through what you've been through, we've selected five lovely ladies to compete for a weekend alone with you at the Hard Rock Hotel in Vegas."

Rocco hoped they'd pull this off when the girls got a look at this pasty, fat-faced wannabe in a Raiders jersey and *vato* short pants with knee high white socks and Pumas. It's a living, he told himself.

"Aw man—"

"And you're going first class all the way, especially with these ladies we've found for you."

Sal hit the switch and Guns 'N' Roses's "Paradise City" faded up.

"Isa? It's me, Tamara."

Surprised, Isa felt the first real smile of her week spread across her face. "Why are you calling so early?" she asked, looking over her shoulder before she pulled away from Andrew's school, where she'd just dropped him off with his backpack filled with clothes he'd need for the weekend with Carlos.

"Where are you?" Tamara asked.

"In the car. Why?"

"Are you driving or at a stop?"

Isa turned to face the steering wheel, suddenly aware that her friend's voice was tight with rage. "Is everything okay?" All sorts of things swept through her head: Tamara catching Will with another woman, Susan moving in with them—all of which would never happen. Well, maybe Susan moving in, but—

"Will just called me. Carlos is on the radio, and they said some kids put a blow-up doll in your classroom."

Isa breathed through her mouth, the most unlikely idea curling out of her imagination.

"He's on Rock Hard in the Morn—"

Isa flung the phone across the car as if it had sprouted needles and fumbled with her car radio. A blur of noise spat out of the speakers as she raced through the stations until she landed on KHRD just when Carlos said, "A man wants a woman to you know, move around or yell something when he's doing his thing, you know?"

Tamara's voice shouted from the shadows of the passenger-side floor. Isa could only blink as it sunk in that on the radio, Carlos just called sex with her "doing his thing" to millions of people everywhere.

She felt like God was using her head as an anvil as she bent down and picked up the phone. "I'll call you back," she said, then added, "I *did not* find a blow-up doll in my classroom!" She hit "end."

As Carlos said the nastiest things a man could say about his ex-wife, her phone rang again and Isa answered, "Hello?"

"Uh, Isa, it's me, Alex."

Oh, God. Oh God oh God oh God oh God!

"Is this a bad time?" he asked.

He hadn't heard the radio. If there was a God, he hadn't heard her ex-husband spewing details about their sex life to the entire world.

"What do you want?" she snapped.

"I wanted to see if you were doing anything tomorrow night so we could talk about the team."

"The team?"

"Yeah, you know, the one that Andrew's on." He paused. "Are you sure you're all right? You sound, uh, like something's wrong."

Yes, something was definitely wrong when she was being pulled down by some giant cosmic toilet flush.

"Tomorrow night is great," she managed.

"Isa, what's wrong? Are you hurt? Is it Andrew?"

His concern made it worse. Her throat closed up as her composure slipped away like a snake. "I need to get going. Is six-thirty all right?"

Oh God, what about her students? If they didn't hear it

on the radio, they'd hear about it from the others. Her loyal ones would be embarrassed for her. The others, well, it'd be just like high school again when everyone but Isa knew who Carlos had been sleeping with the night before.

Her phone beeped as someone, more than likely Tamara or Susan, was trying to call.

"Where are you?" he asked, brokering no protests.

"I'm on my way to work." Speaking over him, "I'll see you tomorrow."

"Are you sure because—"

"I'm absolutely sure." She ended the call and sniffled back her tears.

Isa had to prove to herself that she could *do something* rather than just endure quietly in the background. Paint her nails blinding neon green? Dye her hair copper-penny red? Wear her Hustler shirt to a bar?

"*Make him pay*," Joan advised from the backseat, stroking a fox pelt draped over her shoulders. "*Use Alex to make all of them pay. God only knows a mousy little woman like you needs an orgasm.*"

"Hey, who asked you?"

"*Listen to that foul creature. Listen to what he's saying about you*," Joan admonished. "*Darling, when will you understand that you have more power than you think you do!*"

"If you say one thing about my clothes—"

"*My dear, anyone will tell you that you could use a little sprucing up. That natural look is—*" She gave a delicate shudder and shut her eyes that were shadowed and highlighted in all of her eighties TV queen glory. "*You can do better*," she insisted. "*And while you're at it, get yourself a better hairstyle.*"

Isa shifted her gaze from Joan to her reflection in the rearview mirror. Her skin had gone ashy and the lines from her nostrils to the corners of her mouth reminded her of a hound dog. If she went a day longer without bleaching her moustache or plucking her eyebrows, she was going to look like Frida Kahlo on testosterone. And tiny wisps of hair frizzed out from the top of her head.

She looked back at Joan, who glistened like a priceless jewel. Was this how people saw Isa? Tired and well past her prime?

Joan lifted an arched eyebrow, having seen that Isa got her point. Isa twisted around. The backseat was empty.

Isa punched the radio off and then pressed the pedal down. Her tires yelped and she shot into the street amidst honking horns and shouts. Whatever screw that soccer ball had loosened in her head, Isa had to agree with Joan: she wasn't that mousy fifteen-year-old girl who let everyone parade over her anymore.

She had a date, even if it really wasn't a date. She was going to look good for herself, let Alex see what he'd dismissed that day at practice.

Her breath whistling through her clenched teeth, Isa sped past the cars that had been waiting for the green light at the intersection. Andrew was spending the weekend with his father while his mother was about to raise hell.

9

ISA'S HOROSCOPE FOR SEPTEMBER 15

The planets are pointing to a sentiment succinctly expressed by former Prime Minister Margaret Thatcher. "If you want anything said, ask a man; if you want something done, ask a woman."

The school office was quiet and the late-afternoon sun slid through the window blinds. Isa heard Lissi, the school nurse, instruct one of her kids over the phone to do the laundry and vacuum the living room before she came home. June had already taken the day off to meet her mother in L.A. for the weekend.

Her stomach felt hollow and she could feel every little hair spiking off the back of her neck. In the past, Isa had only spoken with Dr. Quilley to discuss new projects or be commended; she'd never faced disciplinary action, much less brandished a sex toy at school.

After Carlos's appearance on Rock Hard in the Morning, the embarrassment had been strung out through the entire day. She'd made a brief appearance in the teacher's lounge during lunch but quickly departed when conversations halted the moment she stepped in the doorway.

And then there was Alex. How was she going to face him tomorrow night?

She glanced at Dr. Quilley's office door. One thing at a time.

"Dr. Quilley?" she squeaked, peering around the corner of his doorway.

He turned from his game of online mah-jongg, grinning like a bashful kid. "Ah, Ms. Avellan. Please close the door behind you."

His office smelled like the smoky-sweet pipe tobacco he favored. A violin was propped up on an elaborately carved Victorian music stand and on the wall was a framed poster of Sherlock Holmes's London home, 221B Baker Street that had made the trip from the classroom where he taught honors English, to this office where he ruled the school.

"Well, Ms. Avellan, I am very concerned about the scene you displayed in the office Friday morning," he started as she perched at the very edge of the chair facing his desk. "Do you have anything to say?"

It lanced her boiling guilt. "I know it was not the most professional display and I'm not proud of dragging a blow-up doll across campus but—"

"You should've left it up to us," he said firmly but without anger. "You should've called us to Mr. Weisshaar's classroom."

"I know."

He straightened as if they were done with that particularly nasty business. "Good. I think we're quite clear on that business."

It took a second for her to realize he hadn't said, *you're fired*. She blurted, "Why?"

"I understand that you're under severe duress."

If he only knew, she thought, twisting her hands in her lap and hoping Joan wouldn't show up.

"And I've received calls from several parents who heard about your husband on the radio this morning." Even though he said it without judgment, his words caused suspicion to crawl up her neck. "You're one of my best teachers but I have to know, will this interfere with your ability to teach?"

She tried to reply but nothing came out.

"There's more," he said gently. "The district is talking about cutting back and ESL is at the top of the list."

She slumped back in her chair, her trembling hand moving up to her hair and then drifting back down to her lap. "But I have students who can't form a sentence much less understand an all-English environment. They already took away our interpreters and some of these kids only have a specialist once a month. What will they do with them?"

"They will mainstream them or send them to a neighboring district," Dr. Quilley said. "One of the school board members is a good friend of Carrie Barcus's parents and they're threatening to sue as well as make life difficult for us for suspending their daughter."

This was just too much and yet she had no choice but to hold on.

"Carlos hasn't come out and named me publicly," she said. "And it's not affecting my teaching. Actually, the students have found a new respect after I dragged the blow-up doll to your office."

He laughed dryly and some of the tension shrank. "But Ms. Avellan, be careful from here on out," he warned. "We'll back you up and your student's scores and grades will back you up, but the district is looking to cut funding and this girl's parents are . . . they're hungry for blood."

"Don't they realize they could ruin the education of students?" But she already knew the answer. Many people thought of ESL as a throwaway program, an excuse for immigrants not to assimilate and not become "American." And since the parents of these kids didn't speak English and often came from countries where they didn't speak up to authority, they were left at the mercy of decisions made by people who didn't understand or really care about them.

But she knew these kids. They had been ripped out of their culture into this bold, often confusing American one. She knew that unlike bored Spanish One students who needed a foreign language credit, these kids needed ESL to survive.

"So what are you prepared to do, Ms. Avellan?" His tone allowed for no panic or numbness.

That question haunted Isa through the rest of the day and night. It gnawed at her while she browsed the make-up aisle at the drug store, ate a dinner she couldn't taste, and then woke up from the rare moments she drifted into a sound sleep.

Isa jumped out of bed at half past ten, not having slept that late since her first week at college. The apartment was so lonely without Andrew. She stood in the door to his bedroom. She even grinned that he had shoved his things under his bed, probably trying to fool her into thinking he had cleaned up his room.

Isa walked into the bathroom, straightening the hand towels and checking if she needed to put in another roll of toilet paper. She even counted the number of Q-tips. Everything was in order but her.

"What am I going to do?" she whispered to her reflection above the pedestal sink.

Isa dropped her face in her hands and her hair fell in a ragged curtain. Where was Joan when she needed her? What happened to the fury that had caused her to drive to work like a maniac yesterday morning?

Inhaling deeply, she lifted her chin and her bangs flopped into her eyes. Joan was probably right. She needed a new look, a bold one.

Then again, she liked who she was, well, sometimes she did. The plastic shopping bag crinkled when she picked it up from the shelf where she left it last night. So maybe a little makeup experimentation and a trim was what she needed to get her mind off things. As she reached for her scissors to trim her bangs, Isa knew all she needed was just a little pampering and improvement.

She didn't, however, mean to hack off so much.

Isa lost time from the moment she realized her sink was full of hair to the moment she arrived at La Diosa Salon.

A hot blast of air and pandemonium smacked Isa in the face when she walked inside. The walls were mango orange with white Grecian molding and gold-leaf Roman-style mirrors. Over the sound of hair dryers and Thalia singing on the radio, four teenaged girls and their respective mothers screamed at each other.

Patty Covarubias jumped out from her place behind the fan clipped to her mini-TV and asked, "Isa Muñoz?"

"It's Avellan," Isa corrected.

"Oh my . . . what happened to your—STELLITA! JUANITO!" Her screech cut through the chaotic bustle and everyone turned to Isa standing there with hair clinging to her shoulders.

Stellita and Juanito rushed away from their clients. The rubber soles of their shoes screeched to a halt when they saw the damage.

"Code her. Get the cart," Juanito ordered, and everyone exploded into action but Stellita.

Patty dove for the phone. "Susan, you have to get down here. It's Isa."

Isa began to shiver in spite of the thickly perfumed heat. When Stellita's hand took hers in a sweaty grip, she felt herself walking to a chair in the far back of the salon while Juanito triaged with the other stylists.

"What happened to her?" one of the girls asked her mother fearfully.

"Don't look, m'ija," she warned, covering her daughter's eyes with her beringed hand. "Don't look."

"Hey, Isa," Stellita greeted shyly, trying not to stare at her head but failing. "What kind of scissors did you use?"

"I don't know . . . regular ones."

"How much hair loss has she experienced?" Juanito asked, parking a wheeled metal cart alongside Stellita.

"Excuse me," a woman called out. "My daughter's *quinceñera* court needs to be at the church in three hours."

Isa avoided her reflection in the mirror, holding her forehead in one hand.

Not even five minutes later the door chime ding-donged

and Susan's panicked cries echoed off the walls, "Where is she?"

Taking control of the situation, Patty took her by the arm. "Susan, it's going to be okay. You can talk to her before they put her in the sink."

"Is it that bad? I need to see what she's—"

Isa heard Susan's heels clip against the linoleum floor. A gasp and her purse clunked to the ground.

"Sit down." Patty urged Susan into the chair next to Isa. "Let me get you *un cafecito, si*?"

"Oh, my God," Susan wailed. "What are we going to do? Can it be saved?"

"Everything will be just fine," Patty emphasized with the sheen of suppressed panic glazing her eyes. "Just fine."

"But her hair—It was . . . so beautiful."

"I just wanted to trim my bangs and—" Isa tried to explain when Patty reached over and patted her hand. "There, there, *m'ija*. These things happen. My Stellita and Juanito were top in their classes. They'll fix this."

"Oh Isa! Why? Why did you do this?" Susan pleaded.

Patty leaned in close. "It was a man," she stage-whispered into Susan's ear and then lifted her eyebrows knowingly. "I can tell by her aura. Do you want me to get my Magic Eye camera?"

Susan whispered back and they nodded in secret understanding. Patty skipped away, no doubt off to her telephone in the back to call their other partner in crime, Josie. Isa slid farther down into the chair.

"You have to do something," Susan begged Stellita, who took the shortest piece of hair and used it to test various lengths and angles. "Isa has a date tonight. We don't have a lot of time."

Stellita spun Isa around. "You didn't say you had a date!"

"It's not really a date—"

"She's seeing Alex Lujon," Susan added. Stellita swung her gaze so violently that her earrings tangled in her blond-and-black-striped hair.

"Alex Lujon?" she asked in disbelief.

Susan nodded gravely.

"Juanito!" Stellita screamed.

He clipped a complicated curl in place on the debutante-to-be's head and hurried over in spite of her mother's protests.

"We have a—I don't think I can—"

"*Calmate*, Stellita," Juanito soothed. Her breath was coming in gasps as he assessed the situation. "She needs color therapy and facial hair removal from the upper lip and both brows."

He paused, shaking his salt-and-pepper head. "What time is your date, honey?"

"It's not really a—" Isa shrank in the chair. "I don't know. Six."

"There's no time for a facial," he said, his eyes narrowing with intensity. He tapped his fingers along the thin line of hair that ran from the sides of his face, along the jaw and meeting at his chin. "Prep her with a mild scrub and then wax her before the shampoo."

"Will that give us time for the swelling to go down?" Stellita panicked.

"We'll have to take that chance."

"Guys, I don't think I can afford this," Isa admitted.

"Take my card. I'll pay whatever it costs," Susan said, waving her Visa around.

"You can do this," Juanito told Stellita.

No, Isa didn't think she could.

All hopes riding on her training at Miss Elva's School of Beauty, Stellita stood bravely in the face of the greatest challenge to ever walk through the pseudo-Grecian columns of La Diosa. With a quick prayer muttered to the Virgin on the card pinned next to her three-week-old license, she got to work.

Isa wasn't sure how long she'd been under the drape. Stellita zipped off strips of hot wax from her brows and upper lip before shampooing and conditioning Isa into a drowsy state with the steady rhythm of her fingers and the warm pulse of water.

Susan selected a rich coffee color that they worked into her hair. Isa had to hold a cold compress to her lip and brows to accelerate the deswelling process.

When the color was rinsed off, they sat Isa back in the chair, turning her away from the mirror as Stellita snipped and razored away her hair. Susan held Isa's hand through the procedure, comforting her that it would be over soon.

"How much longer?" Susan asked Stellita when the clock ticked four-thirty.

"Hold on Isa," Stellita shouted over the droning hair dryer, having gained an almost grim confidence. "We're almost there."

"Can I look?" Isa asked when the dryer switched off.

Patty, Susan, and the *quinceñera* court nodded at Stellita to turn her around. But Juanito stepped in place, flipping some mechanism that sent the room flying until Isa lay flat on her back.

"Not yet, babe," he said. "We still have more work to do."

An intense light beamed into her eyes and Juanito peered

through a magnifying glass that made it seem like this giant, all-seeing eye stared down at her.

"Because you have beautiful skin, we're just using Zalia color blend in Romantic Nights to create a warm glow to your cheeks and forehead," he said, holding out his hand as Stellita slapped a brush into it.

He dusted some on her face and then impatiently tapped Isa's cheek with the brush. "Don't squint or frown during the application."

He used a palette of Peenk, Sangria, and Spice on her eyes, adding drama with a dusting of frosted Azucar in the inner corners of her eyes. He then outlined her eyes in Mexican Hot Cocoa matte shadow, frequently smudging it with a sponge applicator.

Bracing himself with a deep inhale, he loosened his shoulders. Stellita mopped his forehead with a cloth.

"We're highlighting your eyes so we're finishing the lips only with Amor lip gloss. But I'm throwing in a lipstick duet in Besame that you can mix to create darker or lighter shades during the day."

With a final dusting of French Vanilla pressed powder and a quick application of brown mascara, Juanito removed the magnifying glass and switched off the lamp. Blobs of color shifted before Isa's eyes and her stomach moaned for food.

But Juanito studied her as an artist his painting, angling his head from side to side and poking at her with Q-tips. Finally, he declared that she was done.

"Ease her up slowly," Susan warned. "She'll get a head rush."

Patty urged someone to turn off the radio and the front doors were locked. The salon was silent as a candle-lit chapel when Isa was slowly raised up from the chair. The drape was snatched off her shoulders, sending hair whirling to the floor.

Her eyelashes felt like wings and her face didn't feel heavy like she expected it to. Every eye in the salon was wide with astonishment and chests rose and fell with excitement upon seeing a miracle.

"Oh, Isa," Susan whispered, breaking from Patty's grip. Her eyes glistened with proud tears and she covered her mouth with her hands. *"M'ija*, you look like a princess."

Isa didn't want to turn around yet. How different would this new Isa be? She felt the same and she still had the same problems as the old Isa who had walked in the door.

"I'm going to turn around," she told Susan.

Susan nodded and Isa cast her eyes to the floor as she turned. Her heart thumped steadily as she raised her eyes. The crowd erupted into cheers and Stellita collapsed against her mother and brother. Isa wasn't quite sure what to say to the woman staring back at her in the mirror.

But then Joan appeared in the mirror behind Isa, her face as tender as a mother cooing to her baby.

"You see, darling," she leaned in and whispered. *"It's not a new Isa. She's the one that has been waiting inside you all along."*

10

Walking up to El Serape, Isa nearly fell flat on her face in her high-heeled boots.

"Well now, that's not ladylike language," exclaimed a nosey old woman when Isa cursed as she caught her balance.

Isa grinned with a ready-made apology on her lips but the *viejita* shook her pin-curled head as she walked away. She had another attack of doubt when she caught a glimpse of herself in the mirrored columns flanking the entrance. Catching a bit of hair that snuck into her eyes, Isa ran through her drop-out plan one more time.

She felt so, so obvious with all this makeup and hair. Alex would think she did this for him and she was another soccer mom ready to fall at his feet.

The misty wind swirled around the palm trees and Isa wondered if this was a sign for her to turn and drive home.

Double checking that the satin black bow keeping her jacket tied together was still in place, she also wished she hadn't worn this particular outfit, a jade and teal tweed suit jacket over low-rise jeans and a black lace bra. She must have become permanently unhinged to wear something like this. This was the closest she'd ever come to leaving the house without underwear.

Go in there, she told herself. And so she did.

"Hey," Alex said after he did a double take when she stood by the front door, waiting to see if he'd recognize her. As he walked over, Isa swore her heart collapsed and bounced off her stomach. He looked so tasty with a black leather coat over a red button-down shirt and black jeans. His hair was still damp from his shower.

"How's life with you?" she asked, smelling soap and clean man.

"I was wondering if that was you," he said, making her squirm under his close scrutiny. "Is that really you?"

"Yes, and if one more person asks me if I cut my hair or why I'm wearing blue contacts I'll—" She stopped herself. "Want to sit down?"

"I'm in no hurry." He seemed so at ease with himself that she truly envied him. "So when did you do all of this?"

"Today. We better sit down befo—" Alex wouldn't step back to let her pass.

"I like the hair." His eyes lazily drifted down her face, her coat, and down to the tips of her boots. His eyes narrowed like he could see right through the trusty tweed. "And I already knew you didn't wear blue contacts," he said loud enough for only Isa to hear.

She swallowed and asked herself who the hell he thought he was, coming on to her now that she looked different.

"If you wouldn't mind. I'd like to pay for tonight."

"Why? Susan put you up to it?" She knew it was a bad idea to say it right after the last word spurted from her mouth.

Alex slowly blinked his eyes like he couldn't believe what she'd said. "No."

Sensing she'd stepped just a bit too far, Isa walked over to the hostess and meekly asked for a table. The girl's eyes raked in every detail of Isa's outfit, makeup and hair—the first time any woman gave her that kind of scrutiny. Isa had to admit it felt good when the hostesses seemed to deflate.

They walked in single file as Chubby Checker sang over the speakers, while the kitchen crew banged and flashed in the kitchen.

You know, whatever, Alex told himself. He wasn't in the mood to do this, much less chase after Isa, begging for her to reveal what put her panties in a twist. She probably picked up a snotty attitude with this new look she had going. One thing he learned lately was that nice guys didn't get laid, paid, or respect.

But still, this nice guy followed her across the room, catching other guys take second looks as she passed them by.

"Hey Ms. Avellan, I didn't know you were here," a waitress greeted her from behind a tower of milk shakes.

"Hey Sajil," Isa said, a lot friendlier than she'd been with him. "Since when did you start working here?"

Sajil eyed him and then Isa, blushing when Alex caught her guessing they were on a date. "Just a couple of weeks."

"How are your classes?" Isa asked.

"Fine. Look, Ms. Avellan, it really sucks about your husband on the radio," Sajil said, taking another look at Alex. "A lot of us feel bad about that."

For a moment he wondered what Isa's husband had done on the radio. No, he really didn't want to know.

"Thanks, honey." Isa backed away from the girl. He saw

Isa rapidly blinking her eyes and he sighed. With two sisters, plus living with June, he knew that tears were on the way. Had she forgotten to take her meds or something?

Alex nodded to the girl and when he turned to follow Isa and the hostess, they had vanished. Please God, he prayed. Don't make this night last any longer than it had to.

Alex found Isa hunched in a booth, sneaking a balled napkin to the corner of each eye. Mr. Responsibility resurfaced with a vengeance, but Alex drop-kicked him back into the closet. He slid into his side of the booth, seething and waiting for Isa to break the silence.

When Alex ran out of 1950s memorabilia to look at, he gave in. "Hey, you think we should enter the Shake Your Booty Showdown?"

It crossed Isa's mind to make a run for her car, pack up Andrew, and then move straight to Ohio. But she forced herself to look up from the menu she had been hiding behind. Alex grinned at her as if they weren't on the worst date ever and now more than ever, she wanted to curl into a ball under the table.

"Shake Your Booty Showdown?" she asked, meeting him halfway.

"Says right here." He slid a menu of repulsive neon-colored drinks and fried food to the center of the table and turned the dial until it landed on the contest rules.

She laughed in spite of herself.

"Hey, you picked this place," he teased.

"It's supposed to be a family restaurant."

His eyes told her it was all right and Isa mushed her lips together, mustering what tiny bit of courage she had left and then blurted, "I know you think I'm a complete nut case but I've been having some issues at work and with Carlos so it . . . it all kind of piled up tonight and you were a convenient target."

Alex blinked like she had just started speaking in tongues but Isa forged on. "And I was wrong to throw the whole thing with Susan back in your face."

Say something, damn you!

"I'm sorry," she finished.

It was his turn to stare down at his menu as they both pretended they weren't unbearably awkward. "I want you to know that I really regret what happened the other day," he said.

"I know," she sighed. "So should we consider this a ceasefire or an all-out peace treaty?"

Her toes curled—as much as they could—in her sharp-toed boots when the laugh lines in the corners of his eyes returned as he smiled.

"Peace treaty," he offered, holding out his hand.

She took it and felt his heat shoot straight up her arm, stopping at the points of interest along the way.

"Now that you're team mom, we need to figure out all this soccer stuff."

The waitress appeared and took their orders. After she rushed away, Isa's face soured. "Funny that happened after I left practice."

"But Susan said—" He shook his head and then looked up at her with this funny grin. "Never mind. Let's just admit we've been had. So what's going on with this radio thing?"

"You really don't know?"

"I wouldn't have asked."

She started with the Sex Savvy Senior Survey, which led to Rock Hard in the Morning.

Alex shook his head, rubbing his thumb over his chin. "I'll have to see if my dad saved the *Star News*."

She narrowed her eyes playfully. "Ha-ha."

And when his mouth eased into a grin, she realized her fists weren't curled into balls at her sides.

"Frankly I wouldn't lump you in the *fugly* category."

She eyed the onion rings the waitress brought sometime during her saga of woe. If she kept eating like this he would. "I busted one of the culprits for smoking in the girls' room last year."

"No one reads the *Star News*," he dismissed and won another piece of her heart. "Everyone knows it's bird-cage liner." They both knew the *Star News* was read backwards, forwards, and upside down before it became bird-cage liner in this town. Hearing him say it made her realize that a good heart was inside his very tasty looking package.

The theme to "2001" suddenly cut off Etta James on the sound system. Alex and Isa locked gazes, each wondering what was going on. The lights dimmed as the drums bonged against the walls and a spotlight captured the DJ standing next to a girl in gold cowgirl boots, denim cut-offs, and a spangled bikini top.

"Ladies," he announced, "it's time for the Shake Your Booty Showdown!"

"You know how to pick some classy places," Alex repeated as the dance floor crowded with hoochies in tiny skirts, little girls with ribbons in their hair, and grandmas in caftans.

Isa pointed to the crowd. "See, I told you this was a family restaurant."

Alex spit his drink back into his glass and "2001" gave way to Beyonce's "Crazy In Love."

He bracketed his mouth with his hands and shouted over the music, "You could do it!"

"Excuse me?"

"If she can get up there—" Isa followed his pointed finger to the grandma who needed four men to hoist her up to the bar.

Isa glared at him and then challenged, "Why don't you get up there?"

"What?"

She rolled her eyes and then slid off her seat and pushed him back to sit next to him.

"I said, why don't you go up there?"

"They said it's for ladies only," he explained, smelling her warm vanilla scent.

"Then again, you don't have much back there so maybe it's best." She turned back to the bar.

His eyes almost bounced out of their sockets. Who was *this* Isa? As if she had just read his mind, she glanced over one shoulder and grinned mischievously. He caught himself grinning back, enjoying the way she ribbed him.

"Okay, *abuelita*," the DJ said, barely tall enough to be seen over the writhing crowd of women. "Show us what you got!"

The crowd roared when grandma started shaking the junk in her trunk to Beyoncé.

"Good God," Alex muttered, dropped his forehead into his hand, embarrassed for the woman on the bar. "I'm never going to get this vision out of my head."

When grandma was finished, Isa turned around. "You'd never win against competition like that."

"How do you know?"

"From what I've been able to see—"

"You want to go in the bathroom? I'll show you," he dared her.

She laughed as the DJ and his jiggling cohort picked the next contestant. "Chicken," she called him.

Damn, who the hell did she think she was? He took a quick glance around the restaurant and when he didn't see anyone he knew, he tapped her shoulder.

"Okay. If I got out there, you have to . . ." What punishment would be equal to doing what he was about to do? Deliberately he tortured her as his eyes took a meandering, unhurried trip over her face, her neck, and then to the sharp V where her coat took over. "You have to take off your jacket."

"What?" Her hand smacked against her chest.

He had her now. She wasn't so smug now.

"Take off your jacket," he enunciated each syllable.

He threw down his napkin and braced both hands on the table to stand up.

"Alex, don't!"

He winked and then stood up on the vinyl seat, letting out the loudest shout in the room.

"Get down!" She ripped at his coat to drag him down but the spotlight swung around and caught him.

The bikini-clad cowgirl took the mic from the DJ. "You want to come up, cutie?"

The women turned in unison and screamed their approval, reaching their hands out to him.

"I'll see you later," Alex promised a terrified-looking Isa as he stepped over her and then leapt down to push his way to the bar.

What have I done? Isa thought as the spotlight followed him to the bar. She covered her mouth with his napkin; her heart bounced in her throat like it was on a trampoline.

Alex easily got up on the bar and a fresh scream ripped through Isa's eardrums as he peeled off his leather coat and handed it to bikini girl. He motioned for her and Isa bunched the napkin in her fist, thinking he was asking for a good luck kiss. Instead she handed him the mic.

Alex pointed straight at Isa, their eyes meeting over the frenzy. "Isa, this is for you."

"Shake Your Groove Thing" boomed out from the speakers. Taunting them, Alex turned his back to the crowd and every female voice in the house surged to the rafters, begging him to give them what they wanted. Even though she wanted to, Isa couldn't look away as Alex proved her completely wrong.

Oh my God, she thought, falling back against the seat. The group of guys in the booth next door jumped to their feet, swirling their napkins in appreciation of Alex's taut backside. One of them caught her eye as his whistle pierced her ears. He held out his hand in a high five. "Girl, you take that man home tonight!"

Isa nodded, a funny quivering smile pulling at the corners of her mouth as she thought, why not?

11

SEX AND THE SINGLE MOM: Three Rules You Should Never Break. In fact, we're almost embarrassed to mention them!

1. No sex with your ex.
2. No one-night stands.
3. Never on the first date.

Alex wiped rain off his face and out of his eyes. "I can't believe I really did that," he finally said.

Isa shivered on the passenger seat beside him, clamping her hands on her thighs. Rain washed down the windshield and the wind screeched around his 4-Runner, buffeting the sides like demons wanting in.

That laugh of hers, a snorting and entirely ungraceful sort of laugh, sputtered between her chattering teeth. "Thanks for the brownie." She held up the pizza-sized container that held his prize.

He hitched his elbow on the tiny ledge of the door and

caught himself laughing with her. His stomach hurt from all the laughing they'd done tonight.

"All right Isa, it's time. Take that off."

"No!" Isa clutched the soaking coat tighter in her fist. "I never agreed to it."

Alex watched silvery drops draw lines down her cheek. With a small shake of his head, he flipped on the heater, which shot cold air against them. "You'll catch a cold wearing that thing. I insist for your health."

"I'm not that wet."

Playing with her, he tisked. "I never thought you'd welch on a deal."

"There was no deal if both parties didn't agree," she said in her snooty voice. "You took off before I could say yes."

"Ahh but there you said it. 'Could say yes' means that you intended to say yes, which means you have to uphold your end of the agreement."

He made a grab for her sleeve, stopping short of actually touching her to see what she'd do. Isa hit the other door so hard the car shook.

"Come on," he teased and then stopped. Isa was seriously spooked. He eased back, putting as much distance between them.

"Isa, I'm just kidding," he assured. An unpleasant thought tickled the back of his mind. Had some guy done something that—

He felt lower than dog shit.

"Look, it's cool," he insisted. "We'll just hang out here for a second until it heats up and I'll drive you to you car."

Without taking her eyes off him, Isa melted back into the seat.

But he couldn't help but wonder what was underneath

the coat. Nothing? Alex forced himself to stare at the windshield rather than her. Maybe it was loneliness on his part, or that Isa was wearing tight jeans and black boots designed to make a guy beg—no, it was her eyes. Whatever stuff she'd put on them made her eyes so impossibly beautiful, even more so than that day he'd noticed them for the first time.

He didn't know when or how, but this night had started as an obligation and ended as one of the best he'd had in—damn—years.

Thunder growled in the distance and seconds later the car lit up from lightning. "Looks like El Niño strikes back," Isa commented in a watery voice.

"Yeah," was all he could manage in his state of growing arousal. "The heater's starting to work."

"For God's sake, darling, just let him have it," Joan chided from the backseat. *"God knows if you keep him waiting any longer, he'll go impotent from the suspense."*

Isa didn't so much as flick her eyes in Joan's direction. *Go away.*

But could Joan be right? Alex said she didn't have to do it. Isa knew from experience that a man didn't tell a woman to keep her clothes on unless he was afraid of what was underneath. He couldn't be that great of a guy.

Then again, her hands itched to pull the bow apart and let the coat spread open to show him that she wasn't some dry old stick who lay there—how did Carlos put it on the radio this morning?

"Doing his thing," Joan offered.

This time Isa forgot that Alex was in the car and turned to the backseat where Joan gave her a careless shrug. Isa wondered where she got her boat-neck angora sweater and then realized that wasn't the point.

Just do it. Not for him but herself. Sitting here and hand-wringing was Isa's usual MO. Growing up, she'd never spun the bottle or picked dare over truth. At parties she was the one working in the kitchen or sitting in some corner watching everyone else live their lives.

She had nothing to be ashamed of.

"Exactly my point, darling," Joan said.

She had breasts that put most women to shame, even the ones who bought theirs.

"And this is the man who will appreciate them," Joan insisted.

She suddenly turned to face him. "You know what? You're right."

He glanced over. She seemed to glow in the dark, vibrating with laughter and this unpredictable wild streak he never would've guessed she had. "About what?" he asked.

"Our agreement."

"Isa, seriously, I was kidding about that."

Isa bore down on another violent shiver, but it won and Alex pointed all the vents toward her. "Where did you say your car is parked?" he asked like he wanted to get this night over with.

If Alex could shake his booty in front of screaming women and gay men, Isa could be just as wild, just as un-predictable, and damn it, a bet was a bet.

"What are you—" Alex stammered when she met his eyes and gave a hard yank on her black satin bow.

"That's the spirit, darling," Joan cheered.

When his eyes glued themselves to the parting of her jacket, Isa's heart thundered, not from fear or humiliation but from power. This was what she'd been missing out on all these years.

Alex opened and closed his mouth, his eyes pinned to the bow she held in her hands. His gaze flicked up when she stopped.

"A bet's a bet," she answered him.

"Yeah, but I'm not that kind of—"

"I know you're not." She then pushed her shoulders back to peel the coat sleeves down her arms.

Never in real life had Alex seen a tiny, black lace bra filled to the bursting point like the one he saw now. He'd seen them in magazines and certain movies, but no ex-girlfriend of his could ever hold a candle to Isa.

Was she possessed? She hadn't had any alcohol that he'd seen . . . not that he was complaining! If Isa so much as cleared her throat, her creamy breasts could tumble loose. What would he do if that happened? With the rise and fall of her breathing, they could break out at any second. He couldn't look away, not from the taut nipples straining against the filmy black material.

"Now we're even," she concluded, pulling up her sleeves and resecuring her coat in a very businesslike manner.

Alex still couldn't breathe much less tell her to wait. God damn, what was he thinking? This was Isa! Single mom whose son was on his soccer team, remember?

He planted his eyes on her chin and told them that was as far as they could go. "Sorry, but I don't think I can drive right now," he blurted.

"Do you need to put your head between your knees?" she asked sweetly.

"This isn't funny. I'm only a guy."

Her arms crossed over her chest, sending an ache right

through the heart of him because he knew her breasts were pushing up against themselves.

Gripping the steering wheel, he tried changing the subject. "So what do you think of our team?"

Keen to every movement she made, he heard her sit back against the seat. "It's great." And then she asked in that schoolteacher voice of hers, "What is it about girls and our breasts that turn guys on? I mean, they serve a purely maternal function."

"I don't know," he coughed.

She made a disgusted sound. "Please."

He felt the hot air against his cheek and watched her flip his vents toward him. She caught him looking and grinned. "Are you hoping they'll give you the answer?"

Keep your eyes up. He reached over and flipped the vents back at her. "Okay, fine but I'm breaking guy code by telling you." He cleared his throat, thinking how close he'd been to real breasts like hers. "They look like fun. They're soft and uh, you know . . ."

She laughed again and the music of it made him want to join her. "That is the saddest thing I've ever heard," she said, leaning forward to stare up at the pelting rain hitting the windshield. "This doesn't look like it'll stop soon." She flipped the vents back at him.

"Isa."

"Alex?"

They eyed each other, daring the other to move the vents. His hand shot out and she caught him. As quick as a snake he covered her hand with his free one, prying it off. Isa was stronger than he'd thought.

Smiling, she tried to work his fingers off her hand. He nudged her with his shoulder but she held firm and he found himself nose to nose with her. They stopped, caught eye to eye. He moved to kiss her and she backed off.

An explosion of lightning caught in her eyes. "What? You want to kiss me?"

His throat was so dry, no amount of water would get rid of his thirst. "I'd be lying if I said no."

"But you told Susan you weren't interested," she challenged.

He filled his chest with a breath. "That was last week. I changed my mind."

And he wished to God he'd never said the things he told June in the kitchen after that practice.

She licked her lips and then smiled, her teeth gleaming in the half light. "Why?"

Damn it if he didn't prefer this Isa over the one who'd practically spit nails at him at practice. She knew he was sitting here dying for her, ready to beg for her. Was she taunting him? What would she do if he kissed her?

"If you can't answer the question then you need to prove it another way," she whispered.

Slowly he inched towards her. She didn't flinch or run screaming out of the car. He lingered close enough to smell the sweet, almost candylike perfume of her skin. Her eyes met his, filled with dares. He paused, giving her a moment to say no, that this was crazy and stupid and they should just stay coach and team mom.

But her hand snuck up the arm he used to brace himself against her seat. Their lips met in the gentlest of kisses.

Most unfuckable teacher, huh? A fugly? A frigid wife? Isa didn't think so.

Her hands met over the expanse of his shoulders and he

breathed deeply, pulling her closer to him. A new Isa emerged out of some hidden place, wanting to fully blow his mind and make him wild just for her.

And it was working! His breathing fanned her cheek and his tongue probed more insistently until she opened her mouth and let him in.

He broke the kiss, whispering, "Backseat?"

She yanked the lever and her seat went flat. Using her legs, she pushed herself backwards as Alex crawled after her.

Rather than let him get on top, Isa maneuvered to straddle his lap. Her cold hands rasped over his rough cheeks as she took his face between them and gave him the wildest kiss with tongue and heat.

His hips pressed up against her and she moaned with approval.

When she leaned back, he surged forward to catch her in another kiss. But when he realized she was leading his hand in between the warm folds of her coat, he went rigidly still.

"Are you sure you—" Isa pressed her finger against his lips, running her tongue over her own. She released his hand and he cupped her, running his rough thumb over her nipple.

"You are so soft," he groaned.

Closing her eyes, Isa never imagined that anything could rival this rush of power that lit inside her. This was what she never had with Carlos. This was what she thought she could never do without the help of alcohol. Tonight, where they were sheltered by the white-fogged windows and the pounding of the rain, she'd be the uninhibited woman she'd been only in her most secret fantasies.

She bit her lip as his other hand fought with her coat and

then found her other breast, leaving a trail of goosebumps over her skin. He tipped her forward and closed his lips around her left nipple, teasing her through the lace.

"When do I get my turn?" she whispered.

Alex felt Isa's fingers searching for the buttons on his fly. He lifted his hips, taking over the buttons. She leaned forward, brushing the side of one plump breast against his cheek.

"Okay," he told her. She leaned back, looking him in the eye and smiling while her hand found him poking out of his jeans. "You're really sure about this?" he managed even when her fingers closed around him.

"This is pretty crazy, huh?" she whispered, driving him crazy again by drawing her teeth over her bottom lip.

"Uh-huh." His hips jammed straight as she stroked him.

His eyelids squeezed tight and he couldn't bring himself to make her stop. He barely heard the rip of her zipper and let out a shocked "ah" when she let go of him.

"What are you—" Dazed, he opened his eyes and saw her shimmying her jeans and panties down her hips. Fascinated with her smooth belly, the shadows dipping over the curves of her hips and thighs and the contrast of her dark hair against her pale skin, he could only think about sinking into her.

She got one leg free and then straddled him, her breath warming his lips. His fingers sank into the soft skin of her thighs. Their eyes were locked tight as she lowered herself onto him.

She winced and bit her lip as if she hadn't done this in a while. "Baby," he sang softly, brushing her hair back and nibbling her lips. "Take it slow."

She filled herself with him, groaned when he lifted them both off the seat, straining for more. "How does that feel?" he asked, gripping her hips with both hands.

"Really good."

"How good?" He withdrew, not letting her follow.

Her eyes fluttered closed. "Isa?"

"Don't stop."

He craned his neck, tasting her mouth like sucking the juice from a fruit. When he pulled away from her kiss, he brought her down over him and she let out the kind of moan that a man liked to hear from a woman. Alex pumped her up and down, racing towards the release that would free him from the burning tension. There was nothing tender or sweet about the way he fused her hips onto his when he came with a guttural cry that twisted out of him.

Sparks lit up in front of his eyes when she finally rested against him. A pleasant hum buzzed under his skin.

"Oh my God," he managed, his skin tacky with sweat. His open mouth left kisses along her shoulder. "Are you okay?"

"Uh-huh," she sighed.

"Did I make you come?"

She held her breath and he knew she was about to lie.

"Don't," he warned. "Just let me—" Electric shocks pulsed through him when he lifted her off of him.

She pointedly drifted her eyes down to his crotch and then cried, "Oh, shit!"

"Isa?" Thinking they had a crowd in the parking lot, he looked over his shoulders at the frosted windows. "What's—"

"You're not—We didn't—" She shielded her naked self with her hands.

"What?" he asked, seeing no one watching them.

"Oh God and I'm not even drunk."

"Did I hurt you?" he yelled over her babbling.

She jerked to a stop. "No. You didn't hurt me."

But he didn't make her come either, which he was about to rectify when she—

"Look at yourself," she said pointing at his lap. He did and the languorous haze he'd been in completely cleared. He'd not only tossed his sense of responsibility out the window, but he'd broken the golden rule of singles' sex. No condom.

12

Alex followed Isa under the trees that dripped fat drops of rain on his head. She'd all but raced away from him after she'd yanked her pants on and ran to her car. But her four-cylinder couldn't outrace superior horsepower and a stick shift.

He felt fully responsible for her now, but that didn't stop him from hoping that she was on the pill or that this wasn't that time of the month. The last thing Alex needed was to get his team mom knocked up, even if her scent burned onto his skin and he had felt those curves hidden under that coat.

With a suspicious eye cast to the twisting junipers and hedges that bordered the four bungalow-style apartments, he made sure they were alone. The diamond-paned windows were dark.

Alex stuffed his hands into his pockets even when he wanted to gather her hair in his hands and kiss her until he purged her from his system.

"You don't have to follow me," she said tonelessly over her shoulder, her keys singing as she yanked them out of her pocket. A scrap of paper fluttered to the ground but he knew if he stopped to pick it up, she'd disappear behind that door. He had to say something, even if he had no idea what.

"You really should remember to turn your light on if you're going out," he said for lack of anything else.

Isa glared at him over her shoulder, silently inquiring if she'd asked him for his advice.

"Can I call you tomorrow?"

She stabbed at the lock with her key. "That's not a good idea."

"Then can we meet for lunch or something?"

She wasn't having much luck in the dark. "I'm going to be busy—shit!"

Alex knew she just wanted him gone but he couldn't walk away. Not after the look of terror that had been on her face when she turned to him after the most amazing sex he'd ever had in his life.

He didn't know her well enough, but he'd guessed she had Andrew around eighteen, maybe nineteen, and the father wasn't on the scene. She didn't wear a ring so maybe the asshole knocked her up and then didn't have the balls to marry her. Alex should be petrified after having sex without a condom, but strangely he hovered in this misty world that resembled more of a dream than reality.

"If you're pregnant, we need to have a plan or something," he announced before he could stop himself.

Turning to face him, Isa made a sound as if she was struggling with something. Giving up, she shook her head and then shrugged her shoulders. "I don't know what to do."

"Me neither," he admitted, carefully reaching behind him for the little flashlight he'd worn clipped to his belt. "I've been with other women except—"

She looked at him and he shut up.

"Here. Let me," he said lamely, aiming the beam of light at the doorknob.

Isa had hoped she could make it to her apartment without either of them having to talk about what they'd just done.

She didn't have alcohol to blame for what happened, only desperation to prove to at least one other person that she wasn't some cold fish in the sack. Tonight, the bra would be burned.

The light he held up shivered against the lock and since no one was saying anything, the uncomfortable silence burrowed under her skin like the cold damp of the night. Finally Isa inserted the key.

"I don't know what we'll do if I'm—"

Alex didn't say anything so Isa imagined it for him: *But* she had a kid. *But* she wasn't his type. *But* he didn't want the responsibility of a kid with a woman he never wanted to date, much less commit to.

It was just sex, she told herself. No wine and roses or promises of forever. Just sex. Just the most incredible sex in which she actually came near an orgasm.

Isa paused and then turned the key. "We're both adults. I don't know about you, but I don't go around doing what we just did. Things got out of hand and we'll just forget it, okay?"

The light vanished with a snap.

"That's not gonna be easy," Alex said in the dark behind her.

She reached inside, feeling for the switch. "I can barely remember what I wore to work this week. In time, it'll be just one of those things."

His hand clamped down on her arm. "Just one of those things?"

"Yes. Now let go of my arm."

"How can you say it was just one of those things?"

"Because it—it just was—" She looked down at his hand and then back into his eyes. "You haven't let go of my arm."

He stepped up, crowding her against the doorjamb. Her breath hitched as he swooped down and kissed her.

The fine bristle of his beard rasped her chin and, instantly, all her systems were a go. Just as quickly as it happened, the kiss was over. His breath pulsed and she felt his muscles vibrating under her fingers.

"Look, you already proved your manhood, so back off." Swallowing against the pulse in her neck, she nudged the door with her back and then slipped inside. "Good night."

His palm stopped the door. "If anything happens, I want to know."

"Nothing happened. It's highly unlikely this time of the month," she lied, hoping that like all men, Alex was vaguely aware that women had periods and as far as they knew, ovulation was a bowel movement.

"But you'll tell me? No matter what, I'm responsible for what we did."

"We're both responsible."

"I know that," he said impatiently. "You know what I mean."

"Yeah. I do."

He lifted his hand and she started to close the door.

"I still—" he clenched his jaw. "I never expected what happened and it was—"

"I know," she said so he could stop struggling to say all the right words he wouldn't have meant. "This stays between us."

"That's not what I was going to say." She waited. "I was

going to say that those high school kids don't know what they're talking about."

What kind of freak was she that she was almost flattered by what he just said, that she wanted him to follow her inside and do it again for the rest of the night? Man, five years of sleeping in cold sheets and a soccer ball to the head really screwed a girl up.

Alex's shoes scraped against the concrete as he stepped down. "Lock the door," he instructed, and then disappeared from her doorstep.

Isa glared at the "Sex and the Single Mom" article Susan had clipped and slipped into her mailbox. It accused her from the other side of the dining room table, the same table where nearly four years ago Tamara had confessed that she'd made out with Will Benavides. Then Isa had felt so high and mighty that she hadn't done anything that reckless, not to mention stupid.

What if Sajil had walked out and saw them? What if Susan and John stopped by for dinner after their weekly movie date? God, what if Carlos had taken Andrew there?

What kind of mother did this make her? How would she look Andrew in the face an—

Isa jumped to her feet, remembering how Oprah Winfrey had berated Amber Frey for sleeping with Scott Peterson on their first date. But then Alex wasn't a murderer. At least not that she knew of.

And then there was the whole p-word issue. Isa tried again to count the days from the first day of her last period. She couldn't remember and she hadn't bothered to write it down in her calendar. But wait! Should she call her doctor in case Alex had—you know—diseases? Not that he seemed the type to have diseases and he smelled very clean. Her breath whooshed out and her hands shivered.

"Call him and do it again," Joan suggested. Isa spun and saw her standing in the shower, holding open the curtain like it was the stage of the Follies. *"Well, why not? You can't lie to me. I saw everything, darling."*

Isa took in Joan's white goddess gown and matching diamond cuff bracelets. "You know what? I'm tired of you showing up and—" Isa realized she was talking to a ghost, no wait, Joan wasn't dead, which meant Isa had become like that guy in that movie who—

"Don't fool yourself, my dear. You're a healthy, beautiful girl who needed some fun. Now," Joan purred. *"Go to the drug store and then call him over. Trust me, he's dying for more."*

"Really?" Isa accidentally blurted. She shook her head and grabbed the top of her head with both hands.

Joan dropped her hands from the curtains and posed them on still firm and fabulous hips. *"Men's needs are very basic. Use him for your pleasure and when you're done—"* Her diamonds winked as she flicked her hand in the air. *"Be discreet of course, but then find yourself a new toy to play with."*

Isa forced her eyes back to the mirror. Andrew's Shrek toothbrush in the holder aroused a queasy sense of guilt that her actions might endanger him in some way. Oh yeah, and she was so irretrievably nuts that she argued with Joan Collins in her bathroom.

"Seriously darling, and if I were you, which—well, obviously I'm not," she laughed. *"I would've invited him in so I could be eating strawberries off his naked chest for breakfast."*

Isa wasn't hearing this. She was upset and Joan always showed up in a crisis. And yet Isa said, "But I'm not like you. I could never be like you."

"But what about your performance earlier tonight? You took control of the situation and that, my dear, shows great promise for future conquests. You just need to refine your technique."

"Refine my technique?"

"Well, yes," Joan admonished.

"What's wrong with my technique?"

Fluttering her eyelashes, Joan seemed taken aback. *"I don't know how to put it delicately except to say that it was crude but quite adequate."*

"I was not crude!"

"Trust me, darling, in the state he was in, he didn't notice. You see the next time you're on top you should take him by the—"

"I'm not hearing you," Isa yelled, and then turned back to the shower when Joan went silent. The curtains hung there and the pipe dripped into the rust-lined drain.

Isa blinked her eyes, which felt like they were lined with sandpaper. Even though she was gone, Joan was right. Isa loved what she was doing with Alex in the backseat. In that moment she felt wild, free, and, well, completely unlike herself.

Damn it, she was tired of feeling guilty and bound by some archaic code of conduct. She'd do it again, given the chance.

No, she wouldn't. That was a once in a lifetime thing for her and it was going with her to the grave. Tomorrow, no, right now, she was going right back to the old, safe Isa who didn't do stupid things.

It's just that after being the Isa who ruined Alex for all women, Isa wasn't so sure which one she really was anymore.

13

ISA'S AURA READING

Shown in abundance is the color blue, representing a teacher, someone who is very caring and will help other people grow. The female silhouette in the background could represent strong femininity.

When Isa registered the third wolf whistle, she tossed a frown over her shoulder. She'd always been the girl with the books pressed to her chest, eyes on the ground as she scurried away.

Her hand flew up to her hair, forgetting it had been cut to barely skim the back of her neck. She felt like the only kid who showed up at school in costume on Halloween.

Clenching her jaw, Isa focused back on her first order of business this morning. After her argument with Joan in the shower—crude but adequate, her ass—she hit upon the answer to Dr. Quilley's question from their meeting last week. As soon as a decent hour arrived Sunday morning, she called him at home and he gave her idea resounding approval.

But even still, she wasn't so sure. Her judgment and sanity hadn't been in prime form lately. What if she pushed her students too far? What if she was setting them up for a colossal failure?

She unlocked the door and not even two minutes later, her students trickled in well before the first period bell. Once they settled in, she stood in between the groups of desks that faced each other in single-file rows.

When she explained the school board's possible budget cuts and the role she hoped they would play in preventing it, her doubts hardened even more.

"How can what we say change their minds?" Daniel asked as the unofficial leader of the class. "They want to care about money."

"But their jobs are to listen to the people whose lives they affect," Isa replied, even though she knew how idealistic it sounded. "Yes they care about money, but they also care about your education."

"They want us to be something we're not," Myrna protested. "I don't sound American; I don't act like it or dress like. I don't want to let go of who I am."

Although Daniel and Myrna were her strongest students, Isa read the silent distress in her other students' eyes.

"My brother, he—" Khadija halted when every head turned in her direction. Isa encouraged her to continue, especially since this was the first time she'd ever spoken out loud without Isa's prompting. "My brother tells me no one listens to someone like us."

Khadija's hands were clasped together so tight, Isa could see them trembling. "He says people who come into his computer store won't let him help them. They say he should go back to his country."

The others nodded with understanding, having heard the same thing at some point in their lives in the States.

"How can we make them understand when they don't even want us here?" Daniel asked.

"Well then, you only have two choices," Isa broke in, needing to get control of the class. "You either give up or you stand up to them and make them hear you. But either way you will be required to write a speech in English on how you feel about the cutbacks."

Myrna flopped back in her seat and she avoided Isa's reproving look.

She refused to back down even though they were pained by her intractable assignment. "If you attend the board meeting, you will receive extra credit. Your fate is up to you."

When the lunch bell finally rang, her students fled rather than linger like they normally did. Isa wearily locked her door and started for the teacher's lounge. June was approaching and she nearly walked by Isa. When she realized the woman with the shadowed eyes and snug, but not sexy, blue sweater dress and cardigan was Isa, she began screaming, "Wha—Whe—Oh my God!"

Somehow her wedge espadrilles carried June down the steps without incident. "I heard the rumors but I refused to believe it until I saw you with my very eyes. Who did this to you?" she asked reverently.

"It's a long story," Isa grumbled, feeling self-conscious as some students gathered.

June was momentarily bereft of speech. "It's beautiful." She took Isa's hand, turning her around in a dance. "And you're wearing heels!"

All female eyes were magnetized to Isa's pointy black mules. They cooed their appreciation as they walked by.

"So you like it?" Isa asked.

"Yes, but—" June loomed close as if she were going in for a kiss. "Are you wearing contacts?"

"No."

"You have blue eyes?"

How come no one ever noticed she had blue eyes? Well, no one except Alex.

"Girls," Isa said to the students. "Would you give Mrs. Lujon and me a minute?"

They slouched away with big smiles on their faces.

"I need to apologize for the other day," Isa said reluctantly, especially after the crack about her eyes.

"Darlin' please," June waved it away like what happened was nothing more than a fly buzzing in her hair. "In my family, we do worse damage than that."

"You're a good person," Isa blurted.

June softened and she squeezed Isa's shoulder. "That's one of the nicest things a woman other than my mama has ever said to me. Now—" She thrust one hip out, meaning business. "What happened with Alex?"

The reminder of Saturday night's incident drowned Isa's confidence in doubt. Just hearing his name sent off a roar that collided off the walls of her head. Snatching back some of the assurance her new look gave her, Isa straightened her shoulders. Fuck Alex. She winced, having already done that.

"I see," June murmured. She turned, "Everyone back up, me and Ms. Avellan need to chat in private." She dragged Isa back up the ramp towards her classroom. "Come on now! Get!"

Isa unlocked the door, and she and June stepped into the

room. June pushed the door closed, cutting off the students' chatter, then crossed both arms over her chest. She didn't let Isa stop to turn on the lights. "Okay. What happened?"

"Nothing." Isa plucked at her cardigan. "Why?"

"Something's not right. Alex came home Saturday night and went straight into the shower. I haven't seen him since."

Where had he been? Isa told herself she didn't want to know.

"Was he a jerk?" June accused.

"Of course not. We just talked." Isa pretended to sort through the papers she'd painstakingly organized Friday afternoon before her ill-fated weekend.

"Uh-huh." June wasn't buying Isa's explanation. "No woman in her right mind chops off her hair and buys new makeup without telling anyone first." And then June's face lit up. "Are you guys . . ."

Her tone suggested something a little more committed than sex in the backseat of Alex's car. Had Isa really done that? Standing in her classroom, it seemed like a very unlikely scenario.

"June, don't be that way. Al—" She struggled to say his name out loud, and then cleared her throat. "Alex and I had a lot of fun and that's it. End of story."

"And since when did a man like Alex get up on a bar and shake his ass in front of nearly every red-blooded woman in town?" June's eyes narrowed. "Oh yes, everyone knows about that."

"It was just a stupid contest."

"What did you offer him to make him do it?"

Isa curled her lips back, sealing Saturday night's "events" in the vault.

"Okay, fine," June sighed. "Y'all can play the game any

way you want. But it's a lot easier if y'all just come out with what you want and then get it on."

"No talking to Alex. Really June, I mean it!"

Satisfied, June straightened her sweater and then opened the door.

"June, don't you—" Isa stepped forward.

"See ya at lunch, sweetie," she chirped, leaving the door ajar.

Alex weighed his cell in the palm of his hand. A crazy idea occurred to him to drive to Isa's school and see her.

See her and then say what? Hey Isa, you may have gotten knocked-up by a guy who lost his job, supports his father, sister-in-law, and a sister in med school, and who wakes up every morning hoping the water heater doesn't explode. Gee, sorry you got mixed up with me.

Alex shoved the phone into his pocket and walked the brick path to the house. So much for being the man his mother had raised him to be. The second her coat came off, he forgot what convictions were.

"You're home," his dad said, looking up from the newspaper spread out on the dining room table.

"Yeah."

"Aren't you supposed to be at work?"

Alex stood at the end of the table, the truth burning a hole in his tongue. "Are we alone?"

Removing his reading glasses, his dad glared. "Sure. Do I need my heart pills?"

Alex sat down, threaded his fingers together, freed them, and then ran his hands over his jeans.

"Did you get someone pregnant?" his father threw out at him.

"What? What made you say that?"

His dad's laugh came out as a wheeze. "Because that's how I probably looked when your mother told me we were having you."

Alex never heard this story before. "What did you do?"

Relaxing back in his chair, the old man's memories played upon his face. "Got some extra hours at the factory and took a part-time job with your grandfather's business. It was tight but we made it just fine."

In that moment Alex decided he wasn't telling his father about work. He was going to get another job. But he needed to talk to someone about Isa, and if anyone would understand, it would be his dad.

"You know her name, right?" his dad cut through his panic.

"Yes, I know her name," he bit off impatiently. "I don't know what I was thinking. I didn't . . . I hardly knew her and then two hours later we were, you know."

His dad nodded that he knew.

Alex should've left it at that but he heard himself continue, "We don't know for sure if she's . . . you know."

"I see. Do you know if you like her now?"

"Well, yeah. I liked her from the very beginning. She's smart and she's—uh, very pretty."

A proud smile spread across dad's face. Alex knew exactly what he was thinking: *that's my boy.* But if one of his sisters were in his place right now, she'd be dead in the water. And frankly he'd want to kill the son of a bitch who knocked her up too.

"I guess we just wait and find out," Alex finished lamely.

"Get to know her then," his dad said. "Just in case if she's . . . you know and you have to get married."

Alex slumped in his seat, his shoulders knotted. "I guess I could." But Isa and her little boy deserved more than just him hanging around to make sure he was off the hook, so to speak. Also, he wasn't so sure she'd just go ahead and marry him. One thing he knew about Isa, she didn't give in without putting up a fight.

"I know you've always said you'd never get married and have kids of your own," his dad said, staring at the dinner table where so many Thanksgiving dinners and Christmases had been held. "You practically helped raise all the other kids. But think of this as a gift. All of you were gifts to me."

The emotion in his father's voice nearly made Alex spill the rest of the story. But he couldn't worry his dad that way. If he knew Alex was fired, the old man would insist on getting a job, bad heart or no bad heart. So he sucked it back in, the fear he could barely admit to himself burning the back of his throat.

"Thanks, Dad." The groaning of the chair against the tile echoed through the house. "I've got some phone calls to make."

The old man nodded as he reached unsteadily for the glasses hanging from his breast pocket. "You know where to find me."

14

Isa flinched when someone knuckled her window. As if in a daze she looked over and saw Alex standing inches from her car. With her students' reaction to fighting the school board still eating away at her confidence, Isa hardly remembered driving to the park.

"Hey," he called through the window and then motioned for her to roll it down.

She reached across the seat for her purse and got out of the car instead.

"I was wondering if that was you," he said, making her squirm under his close scrutiny. "You're coming out to watch practice, right?"

"Yes. I was just thinking about something," she said, slamming the door. "What are you doing out here?"

"Looking for you."

Isa looked for the one little tick that would give him away. But she couldn't find anything but those dark eyes focused on her.

"Thanks." Thinking he'd move if she stepped forward,

she caught herself before she ended up back on top of him. "Excuse me."

"I want to take you to dinner some night."

"Wha—Why?"

"Because I'd like to."

"But we already—" Isa almost said it.

"Let's put that behind us and start again. Isa, will you go out to dinner with me?"

She was very much aware of curious eyes from the gazebo crawling all over them. "Alex, I don't know."

"How about tonight?"

"Andrew has homework."

"We'll make it quick."

Her face flamed red with the inflection of his voice. "We really don't have time to talk about this right now so why don't we—"

He moved in and she held herself still, hoping he wouldn't touch her. If he did, she feared she'd kiss him in front of all these soccer moms who'd then tell Susan, who'd then start planning her a pink wedding.

"Tonight after practice," Alex insisted. "We'll go to Taco Mesa. All three of us."

"Let me think about it."

"You do that."

"But I need to know why." She summoned her inner Joan. "Just because we had sex the other night doesn't mean that you need to . . . pretend to get to know me or anything."

"I'm not pretending anything. If something happens . . ." he paused to look down at her abdomen and then back up into her eyes. "I want to be part of that. And if we start out as friends it'll make things much easier."

"Oh."

"So are we on?"

She wondered what would happen if she wasn't pregnant. Would he just walk away from her and Andrew? "So how do you want to explain this to Andrew?"

"What do you mean?"

She nearly asked, *are we really just friends?* But that required courage in the form of a martini glass and two garlic olives. "Never mind. Can I go now?"

He swung his arm out for her to pass. "See you tonight," he said as she squared her shoulders and saw the gang of mothers quickly avert their eyes, pretending not to watch.

Alex looked across the table at Taco Mesa and wondered once again what Isa had done to her eyes that made them so much more intense. She seemed to look right through Alex with a startling blue clarity that revealed his motives had been duty instead of desire to ask her out.

But now he wasn't so sure if it hadn't been both. Isa had intrigued him before the new hair and makeup. After that night in his backseat, he knew that a wild and unpredictable woman hid in the shell of a mousy know-it-all. God, he wished he'd never seen her naked. Eating at the same table with her and Andrew hit home that he had a responsibility for her feelings as well as that of a boy who was starved for a father's attention.

"Come on, let's go another round," Andrew pleaded, wiping his taquito-stained fingers on his napkin. The jukebox put up a good fight in the joint crowded with high school kids on dates and families breaking away from the routine of home-cooked meals.

"Andrew," Isa warned.

"It's okay," Alex assured. "Here, get started before I cream you."

"Cream me? I'll destroy you," Andrew promised as he took the quarters out of Alex's hand.

"We'll see about that."

"Andrew, what do you say?" Isa prompted. Andrew thanked him and then ran for the games.

Alex respected her gentle discipline. The way she handled her son reminded him a lot of his mother.

"You didn't have to do that," she said.

"What?"

"Put up with Andrew. He's pretty high maintenance."

"I've got nephews his age. Do you have brothers and sisters?"

"No. Just me."

Thousands of questions occurred to him at once. But he didn't know his boundaries with her. She didn't invite inquiries, or give any clues about her past.

"So what do you teach?"

"ESL."

"Yeah? My mother taught honors algebra."

"I remember her."

"So how long have you been teaching?"

"Why don't you just write all the questions and I'll email you my answers." Her tone was sharp but a smile played on her lips. She had a sarcasm that intrigued more than annoyed him.

"But then I won't get to look at you," he baited, leaning forward. "That's one of the best parts."

Her eyes darted around the room, finally landing on the napkin dispenser.

Alex felt like he'd said something wrong, but he had no

idea what. Her lips twitched while her fingers shredded her napkin. He barely made out her "Thanks."

"And thank you for letting me take you guys out," he said, backing off. "We should do it again. Just you and me."

Her face almost matched the color of the booth.

"I mean unless you've got other plans," he added, praying for the razor-sharp humor that he knew waited underneath.

"I'd like that as long as we stay out of your backseat," she said slyly.

Alex had been so careful to avoid any mention of that night and here she was joking about it. "Then that means you have to start wearing things under your coats."

"I always wondered if my chest had super powers," she mused. "Now I know it does."

"It wasn't just that. It was you." Just like that, Alex saw her confidence wilt and she blushed again. "Come on, guys don't tell you these things?"

"You were listening when I told you about my public humiliation, weren't you?" She watched him stretch his arm over the top of the booth.

"Bullshit. Seriously, would you want your students looking at you like a sex object? I never liked any of my teachers."

"Weren't you taught by priests and nuns?"

"Only until middle school, and not all of them were priests and nuns."

"Still, now that I have this new look going, maybe it'll raise my stock."

"I liked the old look," he said, meaning it. "Especially the hair. It would've made kissing you easier."

She almost backed down, but didn't. "Mexican men always want women with long hair."

"It's sexy. Especially when it's all over your shoulders and other places."

She ran her fingers through her hair and the light rippled over waves of deep brown and hints of gold.

"It's not like I shaved it off."

"I'm not complaining. It works because it leaves everything uncovered." Nodding, he reached for his soda, needing something cool to wet his throat. "Yes, I think I can definitely work with this new look."

"Okay, I've given you enough time," Andrew reappeared, resting his arm on Alex's shoulder. "Time to be destroyed."

"Give me a couple more minutes."

"Ahhh come on," Andrew groaned.

"Dude, here's more money. I need to say something to your mom."

"Mom, make him get up."

Alex couldn't admit that this sexy banter they had going had another part of him going too. Isa met the look in Alex's eyes and then a wicked grin bloomed. "Honey, let me play with you," she offered, scooting out of the booth.

"You will?"

She stood up, grinning at Alex. "Alex needs the rest."

"I should have Mom play you," Andrew challenged. "She's even better than me."

Alex arched a look up at her, his eyes trailing down and then back up. "I don't doubt it."

15

It's okay for a man to commit adultery if his wife is ugly.
Howard Stern

This guy was a frickin' idiot. Through droopy-lidded eyes, Rocco watched as the intern pointed to the seat for Carlos Muñoz to sit. The dude already put his headsets on, giving the intern a hard time when he got tangled up in them.

Irritated that he'd burned his tongue from his coffee and his wife made him get up early to take her dog out, dealing with this moron for another Friday morning was going to be even more difficult.

Where the hell did they get these people? And the women—Rocco turned and looked at three overly ripe women—were they really so desperate for a man that they'd compete for Carlos?

It's a living. But it still never ceased to amaze him what people would do to hear themselves on the radio, especially when the joke always turned on them.

His caffeine hadn't yet kicked in and with a long sigh he punched the intercom button to talk to the moron. "Yo man, you ready?"

"Yup."

"You get a chance to talk to some of the ladies?"

Carlos looked over into the booth next door, where the three girls were all staring open-mouthed at themselves in compact mirrors.

"Whaddya think?" Rocco asked.

"I think I like what I see."

Idiot, Rocco thought. But it was showtime.

"All right, we're back and Carlos Muñoz, the luckiest bastard in L.A., is with me and three fine-looking ladies— Julie, Becky and Stacy—who are competing for a weekend in Vegas with our man," Rocco announced over the airwaves.

"Now y'all saw our contestants on www.KHRD.com," Sal chimed in. Rocco sent him a glare: you're late. "But our man Carlos ain't all about looks. He's gotta have some conversation, meetin' of the minds."

Rocco caught the confused look on Carlos's face and hit mute on his mic in case he said something stupid. Rocco and the intern came up with this idea and he didn't want it to get all screwed up.

"So Carlos here gave us some questions to determine which of these three beautiful women is the smartest, and we're putting you ladies to the test," Rocco said.

"We can handle it," Becky shouted.

"Sure about that?" Sal asked, turning on the charm.

Stacy and Julie giggled, but Rocco saw the evil glitter in Becky's eyes.

"Now these are some very hard questions—" Sal warned.

"I don't like hard questions," Julie the blonde whined, fingering the tip of the microphone.

"But I bet you like other hard things, right?" Rocco teased, knowing his wife would get him for that one.

Julie frowned and shifted her head to the side as if she didn't get it.

Catching on, Carlos added, "I hope so," but his mic was still on mute.

"In each round you will gain points and then all three of you will have to fight for the date at our K-Y Cat Fight," Rocco announced.

"It's gonna be blondie," Becky shouted, snapping her hair back.

"Excuse me?" Julie challenged.

"Ladies, are you ready?"

He hit the button on Carlos's mic to cancel the mute. "Carlos, you want to ask the questions?"

Carlos's eyes widened and his mouth went slack.

"Never mind," Rocco decided. "In politics, what is the name of the intern who disgraced President Clinton?"

"Oh wait, it was that fat girl," Becky shouted.

"Nuh-uh! The president wouldn't f-*bleep* a fat girl," Julie snapped.

"Okay, ladies you need to answer the question," Sal interjected.

Rocco wondered how dumb they were when he got answers that included Marilyn Monroe, Britney Spears, and Jennifer Aniston. "Okay now, onto arts and culture. What is the title of the final *Star Wars* movie? Go!"

"I don't watch space movies," Julie whined. "They confuse me."

The other two sat there thinking.

"Time's up! Carlos, can you give us the answer?"

Carlos jerked up from staring at three pairs of breasts. Rocco held up a card for him to read. "Oh, uhh . . . *Return of the Jedi*," Carlos repeated.

"Very good. Now world affairs. What are the two countries that border the contiguous U.S.?"

"Mexico and—" Becky's eyes drifted up to the ceiling, her mouth gaping as she tried to think of the answer.

"Close your mouth please," Sal said. "You're making me think dirty thoughts."

"Wha?"

"Answer the question, honey," Rocco said.

"Okay. Mexico and Hawaii."

"England and Cuba?" Stacy ventured.

"What is contiguous?" Julie asked.

Rocco looked over at Sal, who threw his hands up in the air. No one scored any points, but the call board lit up like the Vegas Strip.

"We'll skip that one. Final question, ladies."

They perked up like little girls sitting straight for the teacher.

"What star does the earth revolve around?"

"The sun?" Becky offered.

"The moon, you idiot!" Julie screeched.

Stacy drummed her nails on the table, sticking her tongue out of the left corner of her mouth. She brightened and said, "I'll go with Julie's answer. The moon."

"Bitch, are you really that dumb?" Carlos asked. "My frickin' ex is smarter than you."

Stacy turned. "Excuse me, fat boy?"

"She might've been smart but she ain't as good as me," Becky added.

A slow grin spread across Rocco's face as the intern and the guys in the booth were sweating it out hitting the mute buttons as volleys of "f-you" and "stupid bitch" went between Carlos and the girls over the airwaves.

Isa stopped short when she overheard Stan say to one of the assistant football coaches, "Did you see the women on that website? I went to school with Carlos and man, he never scored chicks that hot."

The neanderthal chuckled, unable to pick up on the obvious compensatory remarks Stan made to maintain his cover. Sucking in that school machismo and cheap cologne, she walked into the teacher's lounge.

Just like outside the door, the jocks crowded one side of the room and those with normal testosterone levels occupied the other. Bildo looked up from his conversation with Sandy Noel, a new chemistry teacher, and smiled at Isa.

The distance to the vending machines seemed to stretch grotesquely as Isa listened to more laughter from the guys in shiny sports pants. Her face felt like it turned to wood and even though she wanted to, there was no way she could turn around and leave without inspiring talk.

Her back felt the weight of disrespectful stares as she fed the machine her dollar. Two lifetimes probably crawled by as the machine's belly growled and grumbled until her fully leaded soda tumbled out. She started to bend down but then thought they might be checking out her ass.

"Hey, Isa," Stan called when she turned back to the door, her eyes avoiding them. The guys laughed in the way that little boys did when they were about to bully cornered prey.

"Hey, Stan," she replied coolly, even when her skin burned.

He exchanged a nasty smirk with one of his cronies. "Just heard you got a new look."

"Really? Well, thanks. Juanito did it."

"I thought so. That little fag."

She waited for the laughs to die down before she said, "I didn't know Juanito was dating anyone. Hmm. Takes one to know one, doesn't it, Stan?"

His cronies sucked in their laughter as blood rushed into Stan's pretty-boy face. She left him steaming up a froth, resisting the urge to look over her shoulder to see if they'd chase her into the girl's bathroom.

When she arrived at her classroom, her cell phone was buzzing in her purse.

"I've got an idea," Alex said without preamble. "How about I bring dinner over and we hang out?"

Grinning mischievously she said, "I think you've got the wrong number."

He fell for it. "Uh, isn't this three-one-zero . . ."

"Yes, it's me!"

"Cute. So what do you think of my idea?"

The more she thought about it, the more reasons cropped up as to why she should make up an excuse not to. So she stopped thinking.

"If you don't mind playing video games with Andrew, I don't have a problem. That's our Friday night thing."

"I'm there."

* * *

True to his word, Alex showed up on Isa's doorstep with a box of chocolate and of all things, fried chicken.

"Wow, just what I need," Isa said when he handed her one of the bags.

"I didn't know what kind you liked so I got one of everything."

Her fingers slid past his warm ones and their eyes locked for just a second before he leaned in to kiss her cheek. If it wasn't for Andrew, Isa would have felt like she'd dropped into a black hole.

"You're here early!" Andrew cried.

Alex stepped inside, his heavy black coat brushing against the sides of the doorway.

"How much homework do you have left?" she asked over her shoulder.

"Just one more page."

Alex wiggled his eyebrows at her and she heard herself tell Andrew, "Put your stuff away and do the rest tomorrow."

She knew her cheeks were giving her away as she helped Andrew gather his things up from the table. She'd been fine at yesterday's practice, even though she wasn't sure how to act around him. But he brought so much noise and fun, the kind that hadn't been felt in her apartment before.

Andrew was so wound up and excited that he hadn't heard her the second time she asked him to wash his hands. When she opened her mouth to lay down the law, Alex simply laid a hand on her son's shoulder.

"Dude, your mom wants you to wash your hands." Alex nudged him. "I swear I won't touch the extra crispy until you come back."

"Better not," Andrew warned as he tripped over his own feet.

For a moment, Alex wasn't so sure he'd get to stay after dinner with the way Isa anxiously circled around him. But she gradually relaxed, watching him and Andrew slice and dice each other on the Soul Caliber video game.

As his guy lay flat on his back, broken and bleeding, Andrew handed her the controller. "You haven't seen anything yet," he promised Alex.

Isa flicked her eyes up at him and then focused on choosing her character. She picked a scantily clad warrior with pink hair and an anatomically impossible body.

"Oh, now wait," Alex said, flipping his side of the screen to select an even bigger and better character. "I'm not getting my ass kicked by someone with pink hair."

"Hair color has nothing to do with it," she said primly.

"We'll see about that," Alex said, picking a hulking brute with red eyes that glowed through a black samurai helmet.

Sure enough, Isa had moves that he hadn't thought possible. Her thumbs moved so fast they were a blur over her controller, sending the scantily clad warrior flying through the air and capturing his guy's neck between her legs.

Roundly defeated at every turn, Alex threw his controller down when she threw him off the mat and into a deep chasm. Isa and Andrew blinked simultaneously at his sudden roar of defeat.

"Do you want another round?" she asked sweetly, her eyes narrowing in warning.

"Whoa," Andrew breathed. "I didn't know that character had an energy field."

Stretching his legs and propping up one elbow on the seat of the sofa, Alex struggled to contain his temper.

"So how long will I have to hear about this?" he asked, forcing a bit of teasing in his voice.

"Oh I don't know," she said, looking at him as if she could read his mind like a book left open. "Maybe a week."

"Maybe forever," Andrew added.

"Honey, why don't you get ready for bed. It's late."

Andrew turned to Alex for support and when Alex shook his head, he gave up and disappeared down the hallway.

"I never would've pegged you as a video geek," Alex said, keeping up the teasing to break the intense watchfulness in her eyes.

Her eyes flashed. "I am not!"

"That wasn't beginners' luck. Not that move where you kicked me in the air and then stabbed me with your sword," he remembered. "That was practiced."

When Isa laughed, she did so with everything. And unlike some people, she laughed only when she meant it. She smiled at him and then shook her head, putting a damper on his totally uncalled for anger.

And then she surprised him with, "Are you sure you're okay?"

"Yeah, sure," he answered, feeling like the criminal who opened his front door to the cops. "Why not?"

Isa busied herself with switching off the game. "I don't know. You just seem different. You really were mad, weren't you?"

He wanted to tell her, just so she and Andrew wouldn't think it had anything to do with them. He wanted to tell her that he'd left the house at four-thirty this morning, pretending to his dad and June that he was leaving for work. Instead he drove to Norwalk for breakfast. Then to a Starbucks in Long Beach where he emailed his sixteenth resume and received one message.

Shame flared up when he remembered his disappointment that the email had been from Ted, rather than a reply about one of the jobs he'd applied for. Ted had thanked him again for letting June stay with him and Dad. Alex tasted the bitter acid of his dinner working its way up from his stomach when he remembered the line: *It makes me feel better knowing you're taking good care of them.*

"Why'd you think that?" he asked Isa casually.

"Nothing."

She didn't believe him. No one would believe him for much longer. So he struck back. "What would you do if I kissed you?"

She dropped the controller on top of the box. "What?"

Suddenly he felt restless, wanting to go back and play with that fire they'd started in the backseat of his SUV. When she'd been with him, all the worries had washed away.

"You heard me," he challenged. "A kiss. Would you let me?"

He crawled over and picked up the controller to roll the cord around it. "I liked coming over tonight." He looked her in the eye so she could see that he didn't just limit the comment to dinner and video games.

Isa didn't scurry away, nor did she break his gaze, which he took as a good sign. Even if his blood burned feral, he wasn't the kind of asshole who forced a woman.

Putting one fist on the ground and then the other, he eased closer, giving her time to back off. But she didn't, and at last, he brushed his lips against hers. He was just barely getting started when Isa grasped onto his hair with one hand, holding on until his scalp burned.

She moaned deep and wet against his mouth and he snaked his tongue in, daring her to keep going.

She jerked away and he nearly fell on top of her.

"Wait," she whispered, her breath warm against his ear. "I thought I heard—" She called out Andrew's name. Someone outside forced a door shut and then the lock turned over. Andrew had the water going in the bathroom.

Alex brought her attention back by tracing the side of her breast with his knuckles.

"We need to stop," she said, her voice a dash of cold water against his skin.

"Why?" he breathed against her cheek, staying right where he was. She pulled back, looking around the floor as if she couldn't remember what she'd been doing. Out of breath, he sat back on his legs as Isa shoved the game system in the cabinet, giving him a scenic view of her rear and a tempting sliver of skin over the waistband of her jeans.

"I have something to say but I don't know how to say it," Isa said, standing up and dusting off her hands as if preparing a speech. "Just so you know, Andrew worships you and I know with uh, everything, it's weird—"

"I like Andrew and I like you. We did something crazy but we're friends now and maybe with time we can be more than that."

"Oh."

Was that awkwardness because she didn't feel the same way or that she was too embarrassed to admit it?

"Thanks for having me over." He stood up and the blood rush made him dizzy. "And before I tried to, you know . . . I really had a good time just hanging out. And I'm just a sore loser." He lied about the last part.

"I didn't finish what I had to say."

He waited for her.

"I get the feeling that you're here with us because you feel responsible for the other night. And you don't have to because I don't want you to feel like you have to . . . ugh, I don't know how to say this."

"Well, I do feel responsible and I'm trying to do the right thing here, bu—"

"You don't understand," she rolled right over him, hugging her arms tightly around her middle. "If there's nothing for you to be responsible for, then you'll just drift out of our lives and Andrew will be the one who gets hurt."

He should've felt some relief that she'd seen the truth. But it stung. "Andrew and I are buddies. How am I going to hurt him?"

"This," she said, jerking her head down to the empty ice cream bowls that sat on the coffee table. "With you coming over, Andrew is probably thinking that this will be permanent." She squeezed her eyes tight. "He wants a father."

Alex took in a deep breath. He'd been so transparent. She saw right through him playing the good guy, trying to win their trust. And while that had been his first intention, he found himself enjoying the night with Isa and Andrew. They made him forget and with them, he fell right in place.

"I'm not saying this right and it's late so I—just forget we ever had this conversation," she mumbled as she brushed by him and opened the front door.

When Alex didn't move, Isa whispered his name. She wouldn't look at him as he swept his jacket from the back of the couch.

"Sorry about—" He couldn't say "the kiss" because he didn't regret it. He just regretted that it sent him right back out her door and into the night. "Tell Andrew I said good night."

16

Alex tossed his cell phone on the passenger seat, determined not to dial Isa's number or let thoughts of her and Andrew distract him from landing this job. Sunday night, Victor, a hardwood floor guy Alex had worked with on a few high-end projects, called with the chance he'd been trying so hard to get.

"See, I'm working for this guy who wants someone to manage his crews for him," Victor had said, his voice struggling through static over his cell. "I told him you were perfect."

That was all Alex needed to jump in the car on Monday morning with his resume and pray his way through traffic clogged by a four-car fender-bender down to Newport Beach.

By the time he pulled up to the job site, he put Isa and Andrew in a separate compartment. Driving under the scattered shadows of the tree-lined street, he saw the answer to his prayers in the form of a beautiful Craftsman on a street of new houses that took up every square inch of their lots. This was his chance to get back in the game. No more worrying about Christine's tuition and making the mortgage. He wasn't any closer to going back to school, but at least no one would have to know how close they'd come to disaster.

As Alex jumped out of the car, he felt something he hadn't felt in too long: confidence to talk his new boss, Daryl, into hiring him. In a market like Costa Mesa and Newport Beach, Alex imagined himself managing the crews and possibly getting his own jobs for the business. Hoo yeah, he was ready to let his resume and his experience talk for him.

Victor ran out the front door. The windows of the house were still taped and the yard was just hard dirt and piles of manufactured river rock for the walkways and chimneys. Crows squawked in a pine tree, coal black against a blue sky that promised everything and anything a guy could ask for.

"You got here in record time, man," Victor said. "Come on in."

Alex picked Daryl out immediately. He stood as big as the two-ton Chevy parked crosswise in the driveway.

"Yo Daryl," Victor called in the foyer. The plastic sheeting crinkled over the hardwood floor. "This here's Alex I was telling you about."

They shook hands and Alex thought maybe he'd seen a strange look on Daryl's face when he handed his resume over. His thick fingers made dirty prints on the fine paper while Alex pitched what a good asset he'd be to his business, how he could possibly expand the operation to build commercial spaces.

"This is like bringing a Desert Eagle to a paintball fight, man," Daryl said of his resume. "Honestly, not that many jobs like these. And with what I'm making, I can't afford someone like you."

Alex couldn't have helped it when he asked, "Then why did you have Victor call me out here?"

Victor jumped in, "Hey man, I thought—"

"Victor told me you could speak-uh the Spanish and you knew construction." Daryl hitched his jeans and raised his voice over the whine of a power saw out in the back. "I need someone who can speak to the day laborers and the soccer mom but still know how to do this stuff. *Capiche*?"

And Daryl thought because of his last name that Alex would be hard up for six bucks an hour. The blow reverberated down to the soles of his feet.

Victor shifted his weight from one hip to the other. "Uh, man, I gotta get back to that floor in the master and . . ."

Alex got more money from unemployment working on his own house than hanging drywall for cash under the table and no health insurance.

"Sorry to have wasted your time," Alex said, backing towards the door.

"Hey man, the position's open if you want it," Daryl offered, scratching his dusty arm. "Wouldn't be bad working a little while till you find something more permanent."

"Thanks," Alex said, and tried to outstep the humiliation that stayed with him for the rest of the day. He went back to the Starbucks in Long Beach, hitting the mouse key every five minutes to see if he received any email. No voicemail, no email . . . nothing.

If he could have, he'd have called off practice and then done what? As long as he kept his patience, he wouldn't snap like the night at Isa's.

"Hey Alex!" Andrew called, out of breath. "Can I help set up?"

Alex gulped down his water. He'd deliberately shown up

early to set up the cones so he wouldn't have to do it with Andrew. Dreading this, he watched Andrew jog across the field.

"I got most of it done," he said easily, even though he felt like he'd swallowed nails. "So why don't you get started with stretches?"

The more Alex thought about it, the more he realized Isa was probably right to keep her distance. Especially since he couldn't get a decent job.

So Alex figured he'd back off slowly through the soccer season. No more pizza or fried chicken or video games. But that left him feeling strangely empty.

"Wanna practice passing?" Andrew asked with a big excited smile. The kid practically vibrated with energy like a puppy come out to play.

Alex stepped back. "Uh, why don't you uh . . ."

But he didn't want to do this. Damn Isa for even making him think that his friendship with Andrew was underhanded. He liked the kid even before he got mixed up with her.

He scanned the gazebo and the park for Isa. She wasn't there. So what she wouldn't see wouldn't hurt her, he thought. "Actually I need your help setting up the goal net."

"Okay," Andrew exploded, taking off for the goal kit.

Alex didn't want to be obvious but he had to ask, "Where's your mom?"

"She had to meet with some of her students," Andrew said, happily oblivious to Alex's questioning. "Tía Susan is taking me home after practice."

Chicken, Alex called Isa.

"Do you want to come over tonight? My mom doesn't have anything going on."

"You know I better not," Alex started and then stopped when he saw a woman in sunglasses and a leopard print mumu aim a camera at them. What the—

The flash went off and she turned heel, her hands waving in the air as she ran—or more like waddled, he thought— for a baby-blue Beetle. He put his arm out protectively in front of Andrew, stopping mid-stride.

"You see that?" he asked out loud.

"See what?"

The Beetle's tires squealed and it lurched forward, took a sharp left around the parking lot, and sped up the hill to the main street.

"That woman taking a picture."

Andrew shook his head and then lifted one shoulder. "I didn't see anyone."

Alex brought his arm back. "Know anyone who drives a blue Beetle?"

"No. My Tío Memo has a red one, but he's in college."

"What about your grandma?" Alex started walking again, wondering if he should call Isa about this.

"Nope. Her car is brown."

Even more curious, Alex asked. "What about your other grandma?"

"Mom's mom? I don't know what kind of car she drives. She lives in Las Vegas. She only visited once before and she and Mom got into a fight."

Even though he wanted to, Alex decided he didn't need to know more. "Do me a favor? If you need to go to the bathroom or something, go with an adult."

"Why?"

Alex was calling Isa first chance he got to find out.

* * *

Patty's heart still rocketed when she flew through the Ricky Martin beaded curtain into the back office. She made sure a second time that Alex Lujon hadn't followed her and Juanito to the one-hour photo developing store and now, to the shop.

"Oh my God," she breathed, opening the mini refrigerator and bending down to cool off. That was close, but it'd been worth it! And that Alex. She couldn't remember what he'd looked like when Susan mentioned him, but now, she'd never forget.

Still, she couldn't quite see him and Isa together. Isa had always been a little mouse, a pretty one but still a mouse and Patty never had patience for girls who let themselves get eaten by cats like Carlos Muñoz and his mama. But by analyzing Isa's aura with Alex's, she'd see if they were meant to be together.

A twinge of guilt made her hesitate when she set the camera on the counter. The girls didn't know, but she started seeing Father Pat for counseling. Going to him made her feel weak and even more of a failure; on the other hand, it gave her some peace.

Father Pat said at their last meeting that she needed to have faith. He probably meant a different kind of faith than her auras and tiny, harmless little spells she bought at the botanica, but in a roundabout way this was faith. Patty didn't see what a hunk like Alex could see in a girl like Isa, but maybe this was a test of her faith in true love.

Humming to herself, she ripped open the envelope. She got several photos, most of Alex's back but only one of him face forward. This was bending the rules, especially the one about gaining permission to read one's aura. But this was also an emergency and no one would know.

Well, except for Josie and Susan. And Juanito, who would probably tell Stellita, which meant Patty would have to tell Stellita not to say anything.

She propped up Alex's photo, studying the colors that formed a halo around his head.

"Ay, where did I put that stupid thing," she mumbled, rifling through all the paperwork stacked on her desk. "That's where this went," she said to a Nora Roberts paperback, and then flung it aside. Finding her book, *Auras*, she wrote down the colors and began cross-referencing.

"This isn't right," she murmured, rereading her notes. She flipped through the book.

Perhaps she needed to keep going, so she did. And the more colors she looked up, the heavier her dread grew.

The book clattered to the floor. Patty couldn't breathe, couldn't move save for blinking her eyes to the screen and the interpretation she'd written on the paper.

She found her cordless phone under the Yellow Pages and called Susan's cell phone.

"Susan!" she shouted, not waiting for her to say hello. "It's me."

"Patty? What's wrong?"

Her instincts had been right. She knew it! "I have Alex's photo."

"Alex's—Oh! His *photo*. And?"

"Are you sitting down?"

"Oh stop with the dramatics. What does it say?"

"Susan, I think we're making a terrible mistake."

17

"Oh darling, these days get to be tedious," Joan sighed, fanning herself in the open doorway.

Isa nearly told her to be quiet, the students were taking a test. But then she remembered, she was the only one who could see her hallucination.

"Isn't that the same blouse you wore Thursday? Good God, my dear, please go shopping before your students think you're selling your clothes to support a drug habit."

Isa slapped her pen down, mushing her lips together until she squished any and all blood in them. She cleared her throat and mentally told Joan to beat it.

So what if she wore the same blouse on Thursday? She didn't have a lot of clothes nor did she have the money to be constantly buying them. However, she still mourned the cute skirt and lace top she'd seen on the mannequin in the mall. The skirt had cute lavender ribbons criss-crossing the front and back. The hem had a little flounce that would've looked perfect with a pair of pointy-toed sling-backs in a barely lavender satin.

"Really, darling, this is no way to live," Joan commented. *"You'll die well before your time from the ennui alone."*

Isa knew the outfit wouldn't bring her happiness. But she could picture herself perfectly in it. Then again, where and when would she ever wear it? The heels were too dressy for work and the—

Joan insisted on interrupting her. *"If you hadn't blown it Friday night, you could've worn it on a date with that tasty dish."* She stabbed Isa with a disappointed glare and then huffed as she turned to stare outside.

Isa glanced over and her class was staring back at her. She'd forgotten to call time for the pop quiz. Joan vanished and Isa went back to actually doing her job.

"Ms. Avellan, what are these t-shirts mean?"

Isa turned to Khadija, who stood by her in the doorway as a river of kids made their way out of the gates.

"What do they mean?" Isa corrected gently as she craned her neck to see what Khadija was asking about.

Khadija's cheeks darkened but she smiled shyly. "Yes, what do they mean?" she asked, carefully enunciating each word.

Isa suppressed a growl when she saw the group of boys wearing "Rock Hard" t-shirts. Those shirts were everywhere. Like roaches. "It's a radio show," she answered tightly.

"Is radio show cool?"

"For stupid people." Wincing, Isa tried again. "It's a radio show that doesn't say nice things about people."

"Oh. Like those boys?"

"Have they said mean things to you?" Isa went rigid with tension. No one messed with her students and Khadija's accent and her head scarf could make her a more obvious target among the less evolved students.

Khadija shook her head no. "Ms. Avellan, do I have to speak at the meeting with the uh, board people?"

Every time she reminded the students about their presentations to the school board at the budget meeting, she was met with more fear than indifference. Frankly, she preferred the former to the latter because at least these kids cared.

She knew that if the students themselves were to speak about how the cutbacks would affect them, they stood a greater chance of swaying the board's vote. At least she hoped they would.

"You don't have to but I think it's very important," Isa answered.

"My parents may not let me."

"Speak to them and if they have questions, I'd be happy to talk to them."

"My brother will be here to pick me up," Khadija said, clutching her books against her thin chest. "Goodbye."

After the last of her students said their goodbyes, Isa walked out the door and let the sun kiss away the damp chill from a day spent in an amped-up, air-conditioned room.

Opening her eyes, Isa saw June walking down the ramp. She left a wake of males twisting their necks to get a better look. Unfortunately most of them were wearing Rock Hard t-shirts.

"Sorry I'm late," June gushed breathlessly. "I just got an email."

"From Ted? How's he doing?"

June paused and then a smile bloomed across her face. "Tired. And he needs sunflower seeds, gum, socks." Her eyes glowed like a fifteen-year-old watching her crush cruise past her locker.

Isa couldn't resist. "I bet Alex will be happy to hear from him."

June snapped her gum, grinding on it. "Humph. That old grump? I guess."

"Is something wrong?" Isa asked guiltily. She thought of that searing kiss and her hand clutched her throat.

"Wouldn't know. That Alex wouldn't tell you if he had a shovel up his ass."

"Oh." She shouldn't have said what she'd said Friday night. And then hiding from him today at practice wasn't making her look any better. But what was she supposed to do? Let him become this temporary person in her life—no, she meant Andrew's life—and then have to explain why he disappeared?

Seriously, she doubted Alex would stick around for much longer after her period returned and the end of the soccer season. He was the kind of guy she fell in love with, not the kind who fell in love with her.

"You know, I think you were right not getting caught up with Alex," June decided. "I mean he's nice to look at but he's too damn caught up in himself."

"I don't think so. He's very considerate of Andrew and the kids," Isa defended him before she could stop herself.

"Maybe," June answered reluctantly. "I don't know what's going on with him lately."

Isa never learned. "What makes you think that?"

"You're pretty curious there, Miss I-love-Alexis-Carrington. Are you the reason why he's been so moody?"

"Doubt it." Isa hastened to change the subject. "Did Ted say when he'll be home?"

"Five more months. We're having Christmas for him in—" June's eyes drifted away and Isa turned to see what caught her attention. A group of pregnant girls chattered away, walking out of the adult education building. One girl, dressed in an oversized Raiders jersey and black jeans, stood apart.

"Those poor girls," June sighed and Isa didn't hear the rest of what she said.

Seeing them brought back a tide of memories. Memories she had shoved back as hard as she could. "I could always tell which ones will keep their babies and which ones won't," she heard herself say out loud.

"What? How can you tell?"

Because at nineteen, Isa had been the one who almost didn't keep her baby. The memories pushed harder on the door, demanding to be let out again. There was little joy when she carried Andrew. She loved Carlos with all her heart but he barely acknowledged her existence.

Well, if anything, she would always be grateful that he'd refused to let her go to the clinic and married her instead. If he hadn't, she might not have her son.

"Just an instinct," she recovered.

"I wish we'd conceived when Ted was here," June sighed. "It would've made it easier, I think."

Isa didn't know what to say so she patted June's shoulder. "You'll try again when he comes home."

"What if he doesn't? Then I won't have anything left of him." June turned, the wind blowing her hair in her eyes. "Know what I mean?"

Isa wished she did. There was a time when she felt the

same about Carlos but too many wounds left ugly scars on her heart. "Want to see if we can buy some Snickers ice cream bars at the ASB window?" she suggested, growing cold even under the warm blanket of southern California in early fall.

"*If* we'll get them," June sniffed, getting into the spirit and eager to walk away from the sadness. "You just watch me in action, honey. Closed or not, we will get them. And for free."

"How do you get them for free?"

"You just watch me. You California girls don't get much compared to us southern girls."

"This is wrong," Susan declared, throwing down Patty's notes.

"But look!" Patty held it up, waving it in the air. "See this gray? It means Alex could be dying or he's very unhappy. Either way, he's not ready for Isa."

"I've seen them together and I know attraction when I see it."

"You thought Tamara was going to marry Ruben," Patty accused.

"That was different." Yes, indeed it was, Susan thought. "And that camera doesn't mean anything."

"And this," Patty said, holding up the photo of Isa that she'd taken on the day of her makeover. Actually it wasn't just a makeover, it was a transformation.

"See that, eh?" Patty pointed to what appeared to be a red silhouette of a woman with giant shoulder pads. "Isa has mother issues. How true is that!"

"That's not her mother," Susan snapped.

"Girls, girls!" Josie backed out of Susan's living room to the backyard carrying cookies and iced tea. "This is ridiculous. No photo or love potion is going to make these two fall in love."

"I'm not giving up," Susan insisted.

"Susan, you need to let them be," Josie said.

Patty plucked two glasses of iced tea, took a swig of hers and handed one to Susan.

"You may want them to be together but what if they don't want to be together?" Josie asked.

"They've only known each other for two weeks. They just need to be alone together more and—"

"Ay you can't talk nothing to her when she gets an idea in her head," Patty muttered.

"But Susan, think about what I just said," Josie insisted. "The more you meddle, the more they'll stay apart."

Susan nearly broke the glass when she slammed it on the table. "I do *not* meddle!"

"Ohh, you hit a sensitive spot." Patty shrugged when Susan sliced a glare in her direction.

"I just don't—I don't want Isa to grow old alone. It's been four years since she divorced Carlos. Four years and no man."

"Maybe she's lesbian."

"Patty," Josie admonished.

"Well you never know. Look at Juanito!"

"My girls are almost thirty," Susan continued, ignoring the lesbian remark. "I want them to be married before it's too late. Why is that so terrible of me to want that for them?"

"Too late for what, Susan?" Josie asked gently.

"I just don't want them to be alone forever. And I love Andrew like a grandson but I want more."

"Well, it's not like the soccer season is over," Josie reasoned, peering over the cookie plate in search of the perfect one. "Don't they have till November? Maybe Alex and Isa need the time."

"But I could—"

"Find her another one," Patty suggested, pointing to Alex's photo. "This one ain't nowhere near falling in love."

Oh, maybe it was her pride that made Susan refuse to give up. Or maybe it was her instinct. She knew when Tamara first brought Will home that something was there, and she knew the same thing when she saw Isa and Alex together. They were like two ends of a ribbon that had been waiting to be tied together.

Or, it could be fear that kept her from giving up on them. What if Isa put her whole life into Andrew and when he grew up and left, she would have nothing? She would be left behind. Now that both Tamara and Memo were gone, Susan often woke up feeling the very same way.

"You just wait and see," Susan vowed to her *comadres*. "I'll bet money Isa and Alex will fall in love before November."

"You're on *m'ija*," Patty accepted, while Josie rolled her eyes and begged for divine intervention.

Divine intervention, heh. Susan didn't have time. Then again, the wheels had already been set into motion.

18

"You've been pretty quiet," Isa prodded Andrew when they passed the cereal aisle and he hadn't begged for Fruity Pebbles or Cocoa Crispies. "Is it because I couldn't come to practice?"

"No."

Man, she was leaving on the guilt train, especially since she enjoyed eating a frozen Snickers bar alongside June while they watched the football team go through their stretches. She felt bad and a little sneaky checking out jail bait, but it had been fun.

"So what's on your mind?" she persisted.

"You're not going to like it."

"All right. But why don't you try me?"

"I really want to go see Dad on his radio show."

She stopped the cart. "You understand why I don't want you to go, right?"

"Yeah but—" Andrew wilted under her gentle tone. "What if he asks me again?"

"You tell him that you're in school and I said no. Why? Did he say something?"

Andrew shut down. She needed a distraction, something to occupy his mind so that when she questioned him, he'd open up. Unfortunately he'd grown out of coloring books and he only read a book when he had to.

"Well, if he does say something—Andrew?" He looked up briefly and then went back to running his fingers over the bars of the shopping cart. "Tell your dad to call me." Even though the coward never would. "I'll explain why."

And then her guilty conscience got the best of her. "But do you really want to go?"

He nodded his head and then jerked his shoulders up. Not much of an answer, but it told her a lot about what she and Carlos were doing. Even though she swore she wouldn't, she was playing tug of war. But it wasn't out of pettiness or spite. Taking Andrew to this radio thing was wrong. What Carlos was doing was dead wrong and she didn't want her son to have any part in it.

"I'm sorry, honey, but your dad is on a radio show for adults," she struggled to explain. "They don't let kids listen to that show."

She had no idea if she was getting through to him. She wondered how Susan did it. All it took was one of her looks and Tamara, Memo, and Isa cracked open like nuts.

She and Andrew finished shopping and then loaded up the car. He regained some of his little boy exuberance but not all of it. Isa hated it when he had that look of an old man on his face. She was just about to offer some cookies for dessert when she realized her front door stood open.

"Now don't panic," Susan stated, appearing in the doorway. Holding both hands out, she said the words that never failed to inspire panic, "Everything will be all right."

It took a moment for Isa to realize it wasn't a vision, but that Susan really was standing in her doorway.

"Why?" Andrew asked.

"*M'ijo*, stay out of the kitchen."

Isa's scalp tingled. "Susan, what are you doing here?" She took a step, but Susan wouldn't let her in.

"I need you to promise me you won't panic. Everything is under control."

Since when did Isa ever panic? She peered over Susan's shoulder. This was her house and she didn't like being blocked from entering, especially if something was wrong. She walked up, forcing Susan back into the tiny foyer. "Will you please tell me what's—"

The grocery bags slipped and sank into the water-logged carpet. With a panicked look around her living room, Isa saw that water glistened off the carpet. "What happened?"

"We got here not even five minutes ago. Your neighbor called because she heard water and she couldn't get through to your cell phone and—"

"How did she have your number?"

"Well I might've given it to her when we helped you move in. Just in case."

"Guess we're going to have to order pizza tonight, huh?" Andrew said, not doing a very good job of pretending disappointment.

"Sorry, honey. We have to save our house."

He dumped his bag on the porch. "My room!" His tennis shoes made sucking sounds all the way down the hall.

"How bad is it?" Isa turned to Susan.

"John and Alex stopped it but—"

"Alex?"

"Well yes, honey. John can only fix cars and he's too old to be crawling around with those pipes."

"I heard that," John called from the kitchen.

"Now go in there," Susan urged. "And wait—" She dug into her pocket. "Where is your lipstick?"

Florida wasn't far enough away. Isa would have to move farther up north like Vermont, where it was too expensive to fly.

Seeing she had no choice, Isa sent a quick prayer for patience while Susan fussed over the same blouse Joan had criticized earlier today. "I don't know why she wears this old thing," she muttered in Spanish while following Isa into the kitchen.

Isa doubted anyone gave her neighbor Alex's number or that he'd been waiting on the stoop in case a pipe exploded in her kitchen. Oh no, she smelled a setup brilliantly cloaked in circumstance and crisis.

She felt a gentle shove between her shoulder blades, pushing her into the kitchen. And there he was, lying on her floor, his shirt tucked tightly into his shorts, one knee bent and cursing at something under the sink.

She turned to Susan, who beamed with hope.

"Looks like your pipe busted," John commented, rolling his eyes at his wife. "Made a real good mess."

"Not much left of it," Alex said from under the sink. "They've gotta be—damn—fifty years old."

"Do you know what happened?" Isa asked bravely. "By the way, thanks for coming over."

Alex squeezed his way out, sitting up with his elbows resting lazily on his knees. She nearly sighed.

"We have to stop meeting this way," he joked uneasily. "But you've got a serious problem."

"Really? How serious, Alex?" Susan asked. Isa could almost hear her thinking: serious enough to be at Isa's house every night after work and soccer practice?

"Everything needs to be replaced."

Isa thanked God she didn't own the place. But then what did that mean? Would they have to move? This was the cheapest place she could find in a relatively good neighborhood not far from her and Andrew's schools.

"Hey, Alex!" Andrew said excitedly, pushing his way past Isa and Susan. "What are you doing here?"

"Fixing stuff," Alex said.

"Can I help? Can I see under the sink?"

"Andrew, is your room okay?" Isa asked.

"Yeah, but the hallway is flooded." Andrew fell to his knees, scrambling to look under the sink.

"Don't touch anything," she warned.

"I won't." Which meant he'd probably been about to touch something.

"I'm going to the shop to get a dry vac and a couple of fans," John said, pushing himself off the counter. He hadn't even reached for his Big Gulp when Susan intervened.

"I think Isa and Alex should go get them."

"But—"

No, *but*, and *I think* were not words you used with Susan. "Alex has his truck," she argued. "Isa will know how many fans she can fit into the house."

But as her husband, John didn't give up. "We have my truck and it's my shop."

He was going to get it when they got home, Isa thought sadly.

"How about if I go with John?" Alex volunteered, getting up to his feet.

"Can I go too?" Andrew said, thumping his head against the counter.

Isa instinctively reached for her son, but Alex's large hand rested on Andrew's head, checking him closely. "Whoa, there, little man. You okay?"

"Fine."

She tensed at the way Alex handled her son. Andrew was fighting back his tears, not wanting to lose face in front of the man he adored. And then Alex was just making it worse by being so nice to him. Everything crowded in on her, one voice shouting at her to get Alex out of their lives now before Andrew got too clingy, while the other one whispered to her about making him stay.

"Be careful there," Alex said, glancing up to look at her. "If you're going to be around tools and stuff, you have to know where you're going."

Susan sprang into action. "Do you need some ice?" she hustled to the refrigerator. "Isa, don't you have any ice?"

"No."

Susan pulled open the refrigerator door and sighed.

"But I have an ice pack somewhere . . ." Isa heard herself explaining.

"No worries. You men go get the equipment and Isa and I will put away the groceries and then get started cleaning." She glared at John, daring him to even think of defying her.

He sighed from the depths of his soul and laid a heavy hand on Isa's shoulder. "What can you do when God has spoken?"

19

ISA'S HOROSCOPE FOR SEPTEMBER 25

A historic alignment occurs this week. Antagonistic influences are cleansing and clearing parts of your life and in the end, you will never be the same again.

Isa's only consolation was that this night would eventually end.

As soon as they returned with the fans and the dry vacuum, Susan whisked John and Andrew away to pick up pizza, leaving Isa alone with Alex in the apartment. Subtlety was not a key part of Susan's strategy.

And then there was everything Isa had said to Alex the other night. Mortified, she stopped scrubbing at the bathroom floor.

She and Andrew had been fine. No, actually better than fine. They'd been great. She'd never asked for, much less wanted, a guy. Now, she was literally being shoved at him.

Couldn't a woman be left single in peace, or was there some unwritten universal law that you had to be a nun or taking care of your invalid parents to be left alone?

"You okay in here?" Alex asked, poking his head into her dinky bathroom.

She took in a deep breath. "Great."

He swung his hand up towards the pedestal sink. "Can I check that?"

She lowered her butt onto her heels, resigned to (a) looking like crap in front of him and (b) having to face him always with the slither of embarrassment from the stupid thing she had either said or done the last time they met.

At least Joan hadn't shown up.

"Oh, sure." Isa pushed herself up to stand so close to the tub that it pressed cold against her calves.

He gave her an awkward smile as he eased down, his heavy tool belt sagging low on his hips. But then he didn't stop looking at her. She was about to say something when he asked, "Do you know someone who drives a blue Beetle?"

She frowned. "No." But that seemed very familiar.

"When I was setting up the field at practice, this woman took a picture of me and Andrew and then jumped in a blue Beetle. I thought you might know who she was."

Isa's eyes drifted shut and her eyeballs rolled back in her head. Now she knew exactly who he was talking about.

"No, that doesn't sound familiar," she chirped, planning to kill Susan and her gang of bumbling fairy godmothers. "But thanks for telling me."

"I told Andrew to stay close to the field just in case it was uh, I don't know, some weirdo."

Alex had no idea how weird those women were. And

strangely, she trusted everything but her love life with all of them. "Thanks. And for checking my pipes and every-thing," she said, feeling the telltale color give her away.

"It was Susan, huh?"

"Her friend."

He laughed a gentle, tumbling laugh that made her feel like they were both in on an inside joke. "I'm no expert on this stuff but—" he groaned as he peered under the sink. "You're welcome."

"But you build houses and stuff, right?"

"I built big office buildings and stuff." He sat back from the sink. "I might have to take this whole thing apart."

The frustration of her own apartment betraying her made her sigh with defeat.

"I can put it back together," he said.

"I know it's just I—" Suddenly it was like she just saw something that had been staring at her this whole time. "Where do you work? You said built. Past tense."

He was quiet for a moment and she spoke to fill in the space. "Can you tell I'm a teacher? I drove my friend Tamara crazy when I proofread her thesis an—"

"I'm in between jobs right now."

The way he said it wasn't good but she didn't want to em-barrass him. "Is that a good or bad thing?"

He grimaced as he twisted something with whatever tool he had in his hand. "Not really," he groaned and then his hand slipped and the tool clonked on the floor. "Sorry," he apologized, holding his thumb.

Isa had embarrassed him and it made her lock up. But then she crouched down and reached for the first-aid kit at the bottom of the shelf and ended up wedged between him and the shelf. "Sorry, I should—"

"No, let me just—"

"Go see if Susan is—"

"—move this way and—"

They both stopped. "You go first," he said.

"No, you."

"Wait." He held her by the waist and her resolve not to do something stupid with him melted and flowed down into a puddle on the floor. They stared at each other until he said, "I was laid off a few weeks ago. I'd appreciate it if you kept that between us."

"I'm sorry, I didn't know. June never said anything."

"She and my dad don't know."

"June would want to help out. She makes a good salary."

"She and Ted are saving to buy a house. I don't want him worrying about us while he's out there. And I don't want her to use their savings in case, I uh . . ."

"In case you don't get a new job?" Isa offered.

His gaze plopped to the floor. "Exactly."

"Why don't you put in a bid for the complex? Mrs. Lee needs some work in her apartment and the plumbing is probably bad in all the units. Maybe you could go into business yourself."

"Plumbing isn't my specialty."

"But you could contract it out."

He still hadn't let her go. "From the upkeep, no offense, but I can guess the landlord won't be willing to pay the kind of money necessary to renovate this place."

"You never know." Impulsively she hugged him and he patted her shoulders as if not wanting to get too close. And then she nuzzled his shoulder. Stupid thing to do, especially after the last time he'd been in her house, but it was like her body just took over and did what it wanted.

His arms closed in around her, fingers splaying over her back.

"Can I ask you an honest question?" he asked.

She nodded, bracing herself.

"That night when you told me about Andrew, was it because of him or, uh, do you really not like it when I touch you?"

"Yes," she whispered. "I mean no, I—I like it when you . . ."

"Me too. I can never seem to—"

"We're back!" Andrew shouted.

Isa sprang away from him, nearly thumping her head against the shelf behind her. Alex caught her by the arms.

"Tía Susan let me play some games and—" Andrew's tennis shoes squeaked to a halt on the tile.

Isa could just imagine what Andrew and Susan were thinking as Alex held her up off the floor.

Andrew's lips pulled down into a mulish line. "What's going on?"

"Nothing." Isa reluctantly let Alex go. "I was just thanking Alex for helping us."

"Were you kissing?" he accused.

"*M'ijo!*" Susan admonished, barely containing her glee.

"No man, I was just hugging your mom." Alex exchanged an apologetic glance with Isa. "We're friends."

Her son's frown refused to budge and if she wasn't absolutely mortified, she'd be proud of his protectiveness.

"Pizza's outside," Andrew mumbled, turning to walk out of the bathroom.

"We'll see you in a moment," Susan trilled in an annoying falsetto, throwing in a little finger wave to convince Isa that even Vermont was still not far enough away.

Alex caught her hand. "If you want I can cut out."

She took a deep breath and squeezed his hand back. "Stay. I'll talk to Andrew in a minute."

"I can't say you didn't warn me," he said ironically.

Isa didn't know what to say, so she got up and found her son in the kitchen.

"Andrew, what's up?"

"Nothing."

"You've seen me hug Tío John and Memo before, right?"

He didn't even nod, but she could tell he listened.

"I've hugged lots of men and I—" Oh, that didn't sound right. But she kept going. "It was out of friendship. Alex spent his evening helping us with the house and that's all it was. You have nothing to be afraid or upset about."

"But Dad's always hugging his girlfriends."

"What does that have to do with this?"

"He's always picking them over me. Is that what you're gonna do?"

"I would never pick anyone over you."

"But you're gonna have a boyfriend someday, right?"

"Maybe. But he'll know that you come first."

"Are you sure you're not boyfriend and girlfriend with Alex?"

"Yes, I'm sure. And if we were—" She paused, wondering if she should even be going there. "Why would that bother you? I thought you liked Alex."

He shrugged his shoulders.

She didn't even try figuring out his logic. "Alex and I are friends. Now are you going to be cool?"

"Yeah, I will."

And she hoped she would too.

* * *

"I've seen them together!"

"Seen who?" Patty demanded. They knew each other for so long that she didn't even have to ask who was calling.

"Alex and Isa," Susan hissed into her cell phone.

"Together *together?*"

"No, *gochina*. They were kissing in the bathroom. I was right."

Susan looked over her shoulder at Isa's bathroom door. It remained shut and everyone was still eating in the dining room. But this was a tiny apartment and the walls were thin.

"It's just an affair," Patty replied blithely. "I told you what his aura said."

"Nonsense. You owe me money."

"I do not."

"Yes, you do."

" 'Mariana de la Noche' is coming back on," Patty said. "I don't have time for this."

Click. "Patty!" With a groan Susan slipped her cell back into the pocket of her linen jacket.

Sore loser, Susan thought. She'd get her money one way or another and when she did she was going—

Stiffening, Susan had the feeling she wasn't the only person in the bathroom. In a whirl she reached for the door handle and then screamed when someone stood there on the other side.

"Were you talking about me?"

"Isa! Why would you—"

Isa bullied her back into the bathroom and then shut the door behind her. "Stop it right now."

"Why I—" Susan could hardly catch her breath.

"I mean it. Alex told me about Patty taking a picture of

him and Andrew. Why can't you guys get a life and leave us alone?"

Well! For a second Susan was absolutely speechless. But she soon caught her stride.

"*¿Con permiso?* This is the thanks I get for rushing to your home, finding someone to fix those pipes and then bringing food this time of the night?"

"Oh, knock it off," Isa snapped. This was going to stop and it was going to stop now. "If you keep doing these things, you'll drive him away."

"Away? You mean that—"

"This is my business," Isa stood firm. God help her for leading Susan to believe that she and Alex were serious. But if that's what it took to get her out of Isa's hair, than it would have to be done. And in a few more weeks, Isa could just explain that they hadn't worked out and no one would get hurt. "Or, Alex's and my business," she clarified in case Susan didn't get the point.

She gulped down the bait. "Well, you don't have to be so *grosera* about it."

"Susan, I know you mean well but just let things take their course."

Susan breathed in and then patted her perfect hair. "Fine." She gave Isa the eye. "I just don't want you to die alone."

"Thanks."

"Now listen to me. Look at Patty. Look at what a dried up, bitter old woman she's become. If you don't go out there and live, *m'ija*, you could end up the same way."

Steering Susan to the door, Isa assured her that she wouldn't die alone or end up like Patty. One, Isa couldn't quite see herself in a leopard-print mumu. Two, she wasn't bitter, and three, her twenty minutes in the back-seat of Alex's SUV proved she was anything but dried out.

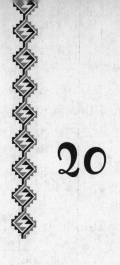

20

Alex wished Isa had invited him to stay a little longer after Susan and John left. But he couldn't blame her when Andrew hadn't warmed up to him since he caught them in the bathroom. He felt like a jerk for wanting to have Andrew's mother all to himself.

"Where've you been?" June asked when he walked through the door. "Christine's been calling all around for you. Something went wrong with her tuition check."

Alex's heart stopped beating a good two seconds as he stared at June, who had propped up her foot on the coffee table, polishing her nails.

Fascinated by the two women on television, a blonde and a brunette, calling each other bitches, June's eyes were glazed with fascination. "So where've you been?"

"Isa's."

He heard the snap in her spine when she perked up. "Really? What's going on?"

His chest was shaking. He'd transferred money from his savings just to be sure.

"Alex?" June asked. "Is Isa okay?"

"Yeah. Her place got flooded but we fixed it."

"So why do you look like something just flew up your butt?"

"I don't—never mind." He started down the hallway before he said something he'd later regret.

June stood up, balancing on the heels of her feet. "If there's something, I mean, if you need help—"

"I don't need your help just like I don't need to play twenty questions every time I come home."

June's expression told him *uh-oh*. Thrusting the little brush back into the bottle, she muttered, "Fine. Whatever. I give up."

"June, I'm sorry. I just had—"

"I'm going home."

"But you are home."

"No it isn't! This isn't my home or my family, it's yours!" She grabbed the bottle of nail polish. "I mean *real* home where people actually like having friends and call each other when they need help. No one shares anything around here with their damn secrets."

Alex wished he'd never come home. "June, this is Ted's home, which makes it yours too."

"I'm tired of waiting for Ted. I just want . . . I thought I was being . . . never mind."

He followed her down the hall then stopped himself. June was his brother's wife, not his responsibility. But he saw her lips trembling, a sure sign of tears and he'd been responsible for it.

He switched off the TV and then stood there, his panicked breathing the only sound in the room. What would he tell Christine if the check bounced? Maybe it was time to tell his dad. He had money saved away, but probably not enough to cover her tuition. Damn it though, he'd promised Christine that he would help her. He took the burden off everyone else and maybe it was just a misunderstanding or the check was late. Unless he absolutely had to, he wasn't asking his dad for money.

Alex found his dad working on his miniature train set in the garage.

"Oh hey, *m'ijo*. Wondering where you took off to," he said over the sound of tiny wheels clacketing over the tracks. Alex sniffed oil mixed with the tang of the opened boxes of fertilizer his dad kept on the dusty shelves.

"I was helping a friend."

"Ahh."

Alex watched his dad carefully take the tiny engine apart, his thick fingers somehow nimble enough to work with the parts. "Dad, did you talk to Christine today?"

His dad turned from the tiny train engine he was putting back together and leveled a look at Alex over his glasses. "No, why?"

"Nothing. June said she called." Alex shot a guilty look over his shoulder where moths flapped around the patio light, in case June hovered by the door listening. "I think it might've been a mistake to have her stay with us. We kinda lost our tempers with each other and she's threatening to go home."

"She don't have friends except that Isa girl she mentions," Dad said thoughtfully. "She's on the phone a lot with her people back home or at the movies or doing something to her face."

"You think Ted'll get pissed if she leaves?"

"Hard to tell with your brother."

"I should talk to her," Alex decided. "Maybe I'll take her out for a burger or something."

His dad sighed, setting the dismembered train on the table Alex had built for him. "Leave it be. She's not your wife."

"Jeez, give me some credit."

"I know your generation thinks men and women can be friends and maybe so, but you'd just be walking through a door you have no business going through. She's a lonely woman living away from everything she knows," he said knowingly. "And you're a handsome single man. *Comprende*?"

His dad put some ugly images in Alex's mind that he frankly could've done without.

"Well what do you think I should do?" Alex asked.

Something vaguely resembling unease and sweat tickled his spine at the way his dad grinned. "Call that Isa friend of yours. I bet she'd give her the woman's perspective because *m'ijo*, you and I don't have a chance."

Alex grabbed a shower, took a quick look at his checking balance that was still fine, and made a call to Christine before he followed his dad's advice and dialed Isa's number.

"Hey, it's me," Alex said when Isa picked up the line.

"Oh, hi," she said with surprise.

"It's not too late to call, is it? I need a favor." He glanced down and wondered if he should've put on a clean shirt over his jeans.

"Okay."

Where did he start with this? "You know June is living here with me and Dad."

"Uh-huh."

"Well, I got into a fight with her and then she started

yelling about going home because no one here wants to be her friend."

"Oh."

"So do you know anything I don't know?"

"She's lonely. Maybe I should ask her over for dinner or something."

"Can I ask you again not to say anything about my job situation? I don't want her to be any more upset."

"Of course I wouldn't. But is that what the fight was about?"

Even though he squirmed under the question, he was relieved that he had someone to talk to about this. "Yeah. Christine, my sister, she called looking for me because the school hadn't received my check. It's okay," he hastily added. "I couldn't tell June and I snapped at her."

He could hear Isa's TV in the background. It was a lonely sound.

"Alex, I really think you should tell your family. And if I know her, she was probably trying to help."

"She was."

The knot in his chest loosened and he let himself take in a deep gulp of a breath. "What else did she tell you?" Isa asked, and he didn't feel judged.

"She was going on about how people don't call for help and people who keep secrets." He wished this was one of those calls a guy made to a girl just because he missed the sound of her voice. "When she gets mad, she gets a little irrational."

"Yeah well, we women tend to do that, don't we?" Isa said dryly.

He smiled and braced his foot against the back of his chair. "I'm not answering that question."

She laughed. "Get off the phone so you can start your TV watching."

"Wait." This probably wasn't a good idea but he said it anyway. "I'm not ready to let you go."

She didn't say anything but he could hear the soft purr of her breath.

"I miss you." Too late for him to snatch it back.

Even from across town her surprise was evident. "Me too," she finally said. "What are you doing other than taking care of your sister-in-law?"

His spine bowed under the relief that she hadn't tried to politely wiggle away from him. "Just sitting in the dark trying to decide if I should read the paper or watch the news. You?"

"Making my lunch."

"Yeah? What are you making?"

"I'm not telling you."

"Okay, what are you wearing then?"

When she laughed, he could almost forget that her son had walked in on them earlier tonight.

"Do you want the fantasy version of what I'm wearing or the reality?"

A grin sneaked across his face and Alex leaned back against his pillows. "You choose."

Isa went to sleep that night feeling the unmistakable dance of giddiness in her stomach from a late-night phone call with a guy she had a crush on. It lasted all the way through the morning when she woke up before her alarm, smiling in spite of herself.

With the things they'd talked about, from her students to how they felt about the last Harry Potter book—she still couldn't get over the fact that he'd actually read all of them—she never would've thought they'd done it in the backseat of his car.

Isa didn't mind feeling cheesy but after last night, she felt like they regained some of the innocence that they'd lost. But then she remembered Andrew and her smile dimmed.

Isa shook her head, puzzled that of all the men that could enter her life, Andrew would hate the idea of her and Alex.

"What do you want?" June snapped when Isa leaned over the counter.

Isa took a deep breath. "I brought you this." She slipped a tall nonfat mocha latte with whipped cream and shaved chocolate sprinkles across the countertop.

"I don't want it." The keys clattered under the blur of her fingers.

"June, what's wrong?"

"Nothing." Her typing raced to a staccato.

"If you're mad because I didn't call you last night, then tell me."

June answered her with more typing.

"I wasn't trying to snub you," Isa tried again.

"But you didn't even *think* to call me, did you? I thought we made a breakthough yesterday."

"I had it under control and I didn't want to ruin your night."

June pirouetted in her chair and flew towards the back office.

"Well, have a nice morning," Isa said to no one in particular.

She'd come around, Isa thought as she pushed out into the jostling, shrieking stew of kids. And if she didn't, well,

Isa would have more time to grade papers and tend to her students.

That idea didn't hold the appeal it used to and she realized, belatedly, that she finally got used to the idea of June as her friend.

Isa got to the bottom of the steps when she heard her name.

"Ted hasn't written," June hollered from the top of the steps. She bounced all the way down, her voice strained from holding back her tears. "He hasn't called. I don't know where he is or anything."

"But you said you got an email yesterday."

Isa took a closer look at her friend. No eye shadow or blush. Not even mascara on a woman who hadn't left her home without it since she was thirteen.

"I lied. I know you'll never want to talk to me again but I lied," June cried. "This woman I made friends with back in Georgia—" She gulped before continuing. "She emailed me because she heard from her husband who's in Ted's unit and . . . well, I . . . I don't know. I came down yesterday to tell you and then I couldn't help but say it was from Ted because I guess I wanted it to be but I'm scared. I have this really bad feeling an—

"You think I'm terrible don't you?" June pleaded for Isa not to say yes.

"It's natural to feel worried but I'm sure he's fine. Did you ask your friend in Georgia?"

"She hasn't emailed me back."

Isa had to say something that would wash away the naked shame in June's eyes. "I've been having conversations with Joan Collins in my bathroom," she blurted.

June blinked. "Seriously?"

June took Isa's hand, her flesh solid but cold. "So I guess we're both crazy, huh?"

"Maybe Ted's on the move," Isa guessed even though the thought of ambushed convoys and car bombs flashed through her mind. "Or the mail could be slow. You never know."

"That's the worst part." June pressed the back of her hand to her mouth and Isa had never seen real fear until now. "I can't tell Alex or his father. I should, but if I do, it might seem real."

"Is there someone you can call?"

"I'm too afraid."

"We'll call together at lunch."

June nodded, catching her tears before they fell. "I just need to say something. I know you've got that good friend up in L.A. already but I just, I just need someone to go to the movies or have lunch with." Her eyes filled with more tears. "Or make up lies with and stuff."

Isa tried to smile reassuringly but it came out twisted.

"But I won't be able to do lunch or movies for a while," Isa admitted. "I have to get my kids ready for a presentation to the board."

June released her hand. "Oh. Look you don't have to be nice about it. I mean all this time, if you wanted to, you could've just said something and I would've understood."

Isa was suddenly so glad she never did. Especially in the beginning, when June showed up at her classroom door like clockwork every lunch hour.

"Hey," she said, lightly touching June's arm. "It's not like that, okay?"

Her vulnerability cracked a chink in Isa's heart. "You don't have to say that."

"Yes I do. We've become friends because you're more willing to go after friendship than most people."

June's chest swelled with indignation. "Are you sayin' I'm desperate?"

"No. I'm saying you're a better person who's a lot more generous with her friendship than I am."

"Really?" The idea so delighted her that some of June's sass and sparkle came to life.

"And by that time you'll have heard from Ted so we'll celebrate with wine coolers and a movie."

June hugged her with all her might and Isa tried to hug back with her arms pressed tight against her sides.

"You'll bring the movie?" Isa squeezed out.

"Oh, no. Alcohol is my specialty."

21

ALEX'S AURA READING

Large amounts of gray signify a person whose life force is leaking away to great unhappiness. Or you may have operated the camera incorrectly and need to try again.

The rest of the week managed to float on untroubled waters. Thursday ended with the team receiving their uniforms, but no Alex for Isa, which was okay. Really, she told herself, it was.

On Friday, twelve of Isa's students turned in drafts of their presentations to the board and Carlos wasn't on the radio. And then Isa remembered to recruit June to help her quarter oranges for today's game.

So far so good, she thought, smiling when her best friend, Tamara, walked across the street. All morning she'd been nervous for Andrew's first game, especially with the way he'd acted with Alex that night. But Andrew had just eaten his breakfast this morning and asked if he could go to the Discovery Science Center next weekend.

When Tamara showed up, Isa felt free to breathe. "You need to give your mother grandchildren," she greeted. They'd been friends long enough to dispense with the pleasantries.

Tamara stopped short of the curb and then lowered her sunglasses. "Why do you talk to that woman?"

They hugged and it felt like wearing her favorite stretched-out sweater.

"I love your hair," Tamara exclaimed, fluffing it with her fingers. "And you look . . ." She tilted her head to the side. "Different. Confident."

Never comfortable with compliments, Isa pointed to the cooler. "Help me carry this up?"

Tamara hiked her cute purse up on her shoulder and grabbed the other end of the cooler. Isa noted she still didn't have a ring on her left finger. Susan had been hinting that she had "a feeling" all week.

On the way up, Isa explained that Susan and John bought all the parents t-shirts in yellow and black with "Tigers" printed on the back over a giant paw print. They also erected a 12-foot-long banner with the boys' names written in gold glitter.

But none of that impressed Tamara. "So which one is he?" she asked when they got to the field.

She'd been talking to her mother again, Isa thought. She tugged the cooler and Tamara nearly dislocated her arm. "Over there."

"Hmmm. Not bad," Tamara assessed.

"I'll tell Will on you."

"Just making an observation. So? Anything you want to tell me?"

"No," Isa shot back.

Tamara dropped her end of the cooler, glaring eerily like her mother, who hadn't spotted them yet. Isa did a quick check over both shoulders. "I like him," Isa hissed. "And I thought Andrew liked him but now I'm not sure."

A slippery sort of grin spread appeared on Tamara's face.

"It's complicated," Isa said.

"*Un*complicate it," Tamara insisted. "By the way, he's looking at you."

Isa almost couldn't move, couldn't think; like someone snapped on the lights while she'd been sleeping.

"Look, I know you hate advice," Tamara started. "But take it from me, I know all about jumping in feet first and having no idea where you'll end up. And if I'd done what everyone else had wanted I never would've left for L.A., which means I wouldn't have a job I love, which means I wouldn't have Will—"

"And your point is?"

Tamara's eyes narrowed.

"I should just go with my feelings?" Isa asked sarcastically.

"Sometimes you don't have a choice."

"*M'ija!*" Susan cried and ran over, holding onto her huge hat with one hand. Patty was close on her heels, holding her camera.

Isa took two deliberate steps to her left while Susan and Patty attacked Tamara with hugs and comments about her hair, outfit, and makeup.

"Patty wants to take your picture," Susan said and Isa took more steps away.

"Why?" Tamara asked, sniffing out a ruse.

"Because it's been so long since she's seen you. Now stand right here."

Isa started thinking that maybe Tamara was right. Maybe she *should* uncomplicate things. Looking across the field to where Alex talked to the ref while the boys scampered like puppies on the loose, she felt his solidarity and the comfort that gave her. Why was she tied up in knots? The only, well not *the* only, but certainly the biggest complication was Andrew.

"Oh God, you have to be kidding," Tamara's voice cut through Isa's thinking and out of the corner of her eye she saw the shirt: I'M ROCK HARD.

She watched her son run hell bent towards Carlos, who stood under the trees in baggy black pants, wraparound Oakleys, and a ball cap. He handed their son a matching shirt.

Ruben Lopez walked over, barely recognizable with the extra twenty pounds he'd gained and a baby strapped to his chest.

"Watch me put it on, Dad!" she heard Andrew shout when Carlos shook Ruben's hand. He wiggled his head through the shirt, wearing it like a dress over his shiny new soccer uniform. He jumped up and down, so eager for his father's attention. But Carlos gave none of it to Andrew.

She knew that when she confronted Carlos it would be bad. Andrew might not forgive her, but she found herself walking across the field.

"Let me," Alex said, appearing beside her.

"No, I can—"

"Don't worry. I can handle it."

She let him walk to her son, clipboard under one arm as his long legs carried him with authority.

She flinched when Carlos yelled in their son's face, "Shut up!"

Andrew stopped and stumbled back. Alex appeared behind him, his hand steadying his shoulder.

Reminding himself that this ass-munch was Andrew's dad, Alex took a deep breath to keep from pummeling the guy for shouting in his kid's face.

"Hey, I'm Alex Lujon, Andrew's coach."

Carlos stonewalled him with silence and reflective sunglasses.

Alex detected some nasty vibes when he first saw Carlos walking to the field. Something told him without ever laying eyes on the guy since high school that this was Isa's ex.

"How's it going?" he'd asked, holding his hand out.

Carlos stared at it, stuffing his hands in his baggy cargo pants and rocking back on his heels. "Don't mess up with my kid," he replied. The guy with the baby didn't say anything.

Great. Alex's favorite type of asshole.

"He's in good hands, man," Alex said. To Andrew, "You ready to warm up?"

The kid looked anything but, still shell shocked from the way his dad treated him.

"Your coach is talking to you," Carlos snapped. "Listen up!"

Andrew trembled under Alex's hand and Alex knew that one day, he was going to beat the shit out of this guy. But not now, not in front of a little boy who had been working so hard for his first soccer game.

"Come on, little man," Alex said, curling his hand over the boy's shoulder. "Let's go show 'em what you got."

When they turned as a pair and walked towards the kids who'd gathered into a circle, Carlos burst out laughing. His friend said, "Hey man, why don't you cool it with Andrew?"

Andrew's head fell forward. Alex stayed alongside him, right where he needed him. "You all right?"

"Uh-huh." Andrew held on but barely.

So this was what Isa had to deal with? It was enough to make Alex almost dizzy with fury. "You know what you need to do, right? You need to get focused on the game. You know what professional athletes do before each game?"

Andrew shook his head.

"They get focused." Alex made it up as he went along. "They imagine all the other stuff stays locked in an imaginary box. And then they filter all the extra stuff out, the people on the sidelines and the guys yelling stuff out at them. That's what you have to do."

He grasped onto the back of Andrew's neck and gave a gentle squeeze. "Andrew, you know I wouldn't be saying this if I didn't think you could do it, right?"

"But my dad doesn't—" His voice climbed and then broke under the weight of his humiliation.

Alex stopped them short of the other kids. "You can do this. You can show everyone all the things we've been working on."

Andrew nodded, fighting his tears on the losing side. Hoping he'd said the magic words, Alex figured what the hell and hugged him.

Isa's jaw unhinged and her mouth fell open when Andrew clung to Alex, his face pressed into his stomach.

Kill Carlos were the next words in her mind.

"No, Isa," John said, catching her before she took the first step towards justifiable homicide. "Alex's got it."

Startled that it was John who spoke to her, Isa turned and saw Patty and Tamara restraining Susan.

"Look." John released her arm. "He's okay."

Andrew wrestled the shirt over his head, gave it to Alex and then ran to the team, who were starting their side stretches.

"Oh my," Joan sighed romantically, standing beside Isa in a black and white suit wearing a hat with a brim that rivaled Susan's. *"There's nothing like a man tending to a child."*

Something freed up inside Isa. Joan, as usual, was right. Alex was her knight in shining Nikes. Watching him with her son was like feeling the sun's warmth pushing through the clouds.

"There he is, darling." Joan turned, reflecting Isa and the park and the other parents in the lenses of her giant sunglasses. *"Everything you've ever wanted is right before your eyes."*

She dipped her chin down, looking over the rims of her sunglasses and added, *"Make sure you wear something special tonight."*

"Is he okay?" Susan asked Alex as he jogged over to them.

Alex handed Isa the shirt. She could see the rows of thick eyelashes outlining his velvety eyes. "He's cool. And you?"

For once, someone other than Susan and Tamara stood up for her. Alex didn't do it out of loyalty, he did it because he cared.

"Thank you," was all Isa could manage in that gauzy moment.

The corner of his mouth quirked up. "For not kicking his ass?"

She squeezed Andrew's shirt in her hand. "Something like that."

22

"Well hi there!" June said when Andrew opened the door. "Is your mama home?"

He jerked his thumb over his shoulder. "In there."

She smiled, seeing Isa in the shape of his eyes and eyebrows. "Don't you worry. I'll get her all fixed up."

Unconcerned he shouted, "Mom! Your friend is here."

Isa groaned, throwing a Mandarin dress on top of the pile of discarded outfits. "How many times do I have to tell you not to yell?" she yelled back.

She had nothing to wear and only thirty minutes to get ready for the team's pizza party. Why she decided this night would be the night she'd "go for" Alex, she'd never know. Suddenly, she felt possessed by the same anxiety that drove women to come to blows over G-strings at a post-Christmas Victoria's Secret clearance sale.

Her objective ruled out her typical outfit of jeans and a shirt, but then a skirt and heels at a soccer team's pizza party advertised, "desperate single mom." The black lace bra under the coat was obviously out of the question.

"All right young lady," June announced from behind a

mountain of purses, heels and various clothing. "Get ready to be MILFed!"

"Wow! It's even worse than my room. What happened in here?" Andrew's amazed voice called out through the curtain of clothes.

Isa hadn't seen him behind June. "Nothing!" she protested.

He hitched the corner of his mouth, unfortunately, looking a lot like Isa did when she caught him doing something he wasn't supposed to be doing.

"Why don't you go play with your toys," June grunted when she dumped her loot on the bed. "Oh, my poor back."

"Mom, it's just a pizza party."

Assuming some parental authority, "Is there something you need, honey?"

"No. But how come you didn't ask for my help?"

"Because sweetie pie," June chimed in, "you're a man and men don't help ladies dress unless they're ga—"

"Need to get dressed themselves," Isa interjected, giving June the look. And she didn't think men had to be gay to help women dress. Maybe with more time in California, June would become more enlightened.

Then again, Isa took another look at Andrew's black soccer socks sticking up from the top of his Ugg boots, red board shorts, and his jersey. "Go get changed," she told him.

"But I am changed."

"Why don't you put on some jeans and a clean shirt?"

He pulled the jersey from his neck and sniffed. "But I don't smell bad."

"Did you close the front door after June?"

His eyes widened before he spun and sprinted out of the bedroom.

"You got yourself a nice little boy there," June remarked kindly. "Now. Let's get you dressed."

"I was thinking—" Isa began, but June was in her zone.

"I thought about that whole uh . . ." June's eyes tick-tocked from side to side and then she lowered her voice. "Joan Collins thing and realized we need to create a new you."

Isa wasn't following but she had to explain, "Joan isn't a ghost."

"I know but I don't want to talk disrespectful of her an—" Excited, she stepped forward and hissed, "She's not here is she?"

Feeling like an idiot, Isa shook her head but glanced over her shoulder just in case. She hadn't seen Joan since the game. She winced. How much longer did she have before she had to be put on medication?

"Anyway, Joan is your sexual self speaking out against your more uh, uptight self."

Uptight was better than crazy.

June held up her hands, anticipation shooting out her French-manicured tips. "Be prepared," she announced.

She whipped around and like magic was holding up a black-sequined halter top and a black leather mini skirt that doubled as a napkin.

"We're going to Napoleano's not White Lotus," Isa reminded her.

"Oh, right. Okay." She flung that down and then clapped her hands. "What do you think about this?"

Isa looked at the denim mini-dress and thought, *"Daisy Duke Does Dallas."*

Several outfits went into the reject pile until they had nothing left to work with. Isa fell dejected on the edge of her crowded bed.

"We can do this," June said, fanning herself with both hands. "Men are very basic. And I know Joan won't leave us in our moment of need."

"Will you quit," Isa muttered. "Joan is just . . . just a figment of my imagination."

"Don't say that! You'll hurt her feelings."

Isa stood up, realizing she was becoming her mother: desperate for a man and willing to do everything but be herself in pursuit of one. "This whole girl thing isn't me." Defiantly, she rammed her foot into the leg of her favorite pair of jeans.

"Isa, what are you doing?"

"I'm just going to be me. Clearly I'm not cut out for this."

"Put the jeans down. Now!"

"I'm going like this."

June took a threatening step forward. "Don't make me go over there and pull them off! You can do this and you're going to do this right!"

"I'm sorry but—"

June lunged forward and caught her jeans by the back pocket. "Off!"

"Let go!"

"The perfect outfit is here! I can feel it," she cried, tugging them down. "Joan is with us."

Clutching onto them for dear life, Isa batted at June's hand. "No, she's not. Hey, let go!"

"So help me I'll rip these jeans off you." June's eyes had an evangelical glow.

They looked like Alexis and Krystal duking it out, or worse, the stars of a porno.

The pocket made a tiny rip and Isa gasped. June released the jeans. Isa leapt back. "Okay, okay!"

"I have a compromise," June declared.

Isa twisted around to try to see the damage.

"What about those jeans—" June fished through the pile and yanked out a vivid blue top with a sheer overlay embroidered with lace. "This and these shoes?" She held up a pair of heels with turquoise stones threaded through invisible straps.

Isa felt the glory of the immaculate outfit flow through her. Her jeans were casual, but the top was sexily romantic but not too sexy. And the shoes . . . She looked down at her feet. Uh-oh.

"It won't work. I have to paint my toenails."

"No worries. I have polish!"

Damn, the girl had everything.

"So?" June asked expectantly.

Isa only had to nod. They were five minutes late by the time they painted her nails, redid her lipstick, and debated over earrings. At the end, June ceremoniously made her stop one last time in front of the mirror.

"Look here honey, you're a real girl."

And once again, Isa felt like one.

The sound of crashing cars, firing guns, and cops warning everyone to "Get down! Get down!" competed with the parents laughing over pitchers of beer and margaritas. When the video games ended, kids groaned and begged parents for additional quarters.

But there was a noticeable pause in the noise and confusion of Napoleano's when Isa walked through the door.

Some women's eyes scanned then narrowed with envy; a few widened when they recognized her. The men surveyed Isa's geography and wondered if her cleavage was smoke and mirrors or the real thing. The only man who didn't notice was Alex because he was in the bar with the fathers, ordering beer. Andrew disengaged from her side, running off with his friends. With a dispirited sigh, Isa watched the restaurant resume as normal.

Napoleano's looked very much the way it did in 1946 when Grandpa Nico was discharged from the army and opened the place with his wife's tomato sauce recipe and all their savings in the pizza oven. The checkerboard floor was scarred, and sticky red and white checkered tablecloths were stapled to the undersides of the tables. Nico Sr. refused to let Nico Jr. install air conditioning, claiming it would ruin the dough, so tired ceiling fans twirled the scent of oregano and baking dough over the sweating crowd.

Isa took her place at the tables with the mothers. After ordering pizzas and vats of soda, they settled down to discussing everything from clothes to babies to how much longer Jennifer Lopez would stay with her current husband. The men congregated at their end of the table, talking about everything they didn't want their wives to overhear.

The gender segregation was well and good when you wanted to get away from your spouse, but for a single mom who fussed over her outfit, her hair, and her nails, it was an exercise in frustration.

Isa hadn't budged from her place on the women's side of the table, sneaking looks at Alex, who had only told her, "Nice shirt," before getting monopolized by the men.

She warred between pouting and all-out fear. She'd never pursued and she'd expected he'd get the hint and come to her. Except he hadn't and she wasn't completely sure if it was because of the men, or if he'd given up on her.

"So what's going on with you and Alex?" Lydia asked. Her son, Danny, had gone to Tiny Tots with Andrew. "Are you guys dating?"

As the only divorced and nondating single mother, Isa realized the conversation turned to her. "No, we're just friends."

The other mom, whose name Isa couldn't remember, fanned her face with a menu. All night Isa hoped someone would use her name again. "I'm telling you if a man who looked like Alex looked at me? Hell, I'd leave my husband."

"Don't you think Alex looks like that Freddie Prinze Jr?" Lydia asked.

"Hmm, you're right. But Alex isn't skinny like him."

"I think he looks like Angel from Buffy the Vampire Slayer," Aracely chimed in. She had been Tamara's chief rival for homecoming queen.

Their faces lit up and then whipped around to see if Alex was more Freddie than Angel. To Isa, he was perfectly Alex. In unison they turned back and leaned forward.

"But seriously, Isa, you've gotta admit Alex is hot," Lydia said, sipping her margarita.

"Yeah, but . . ."

"What?"

"Alex is a good man," the no-name mom said, as if Isa were completely transparent. "Lydia and I were just talking the other day that he'd make a good father to Andrew."

As if she'd been woken up in the middle of night by the smell of smoke, Isa realized she had been the topic of many secret conversations.

"You need to do what's right for you," Lydia added. "And if you need anything . . . like us to have a sleepover?"

They laughed like mob bosses bribing the mayor.

"Oh-oh-oh! We could let the air out of your tire so he'd have to give you a ride home," no-name mom said excitedly.

"Men like it when they think you need them," Aracely added, and the group nodded their heads sagely.

"Whatever you need, you just ask one of us," Lydia finished.

Over the radio a commercial came on for Rock Hard in the Morning and on hearing Carlos's name, a group in the back bar howled and cheered.

The women pressed their lips into flat, disapproving lines. Isa sat there like a day-old balloon, soft and gushy with no more bounce or brilliance. She'd endure in silence, but not without drilling her nails into the palms of her hands.

The commercial continued and everyone looked at her with pity and relief that their exes weren't on the radio. But then a chair scooted out. Collectively, the room looked up and watched Alex stride to the jukebox. Conversation weakened as curiosity piqued and out over the speakers, a drum roll sounded followed by a guitar twang. John Lennon's voice sang out, "Something in the way she moves . . ."

Isa audibly sucked in her breath as the song lazily continued like a man taking his time with the woman he loved. Men were not yet aware of the charge that shot straight from Alex, who turned away from the jukebox, to Isa, who literally held onto the edge of her seat. But the women honed in on his declaration.

Isa tingled in a way she hadn't since she was fifteen. Mesmerized by Alex advancing on her, she was vaguely aware of the roll of chatter that rose up around them. He bypassed the guys who were slowly becoming aware that something was happening. Locked into his dark gaze, Isa held her breath until his hand claimed the back of the empty seat next to her.

"How's it going?"

Lydia, no-name mom, and Aracely popped out of their seats. "We need more margaritas," Lydia announced. "Isa, you stay here and hold our seats."

Something in the way Alex's eyes glittered kept her right where she was.

23

WRITTEN ON THE WALL
OF THE MEN'S ROOM AT NAPOLEANO'S

Number of proposals in the dining room: 157
Of those proposals who were married: 100%
So men, if you're not sure, get her a beer.

Alex sat with a long sigh, seemingly unaware that everyone would be talking about how he played Isa a love song on the jukebox at Napoleano's. No one would be this excited since . . . well, nothing really exciting had happened in Sweetwater for a long time.

But all Alex had to say was, "Good game, huh?"

"What?" Isa managed.

"The game. Andrew played pretty well."

What did Andrew or the game have anything to do with the Beatles serenading them from the jukebox?

"So how's Andrew doing?" Alex continued.

"He's great," she said, pulling all the right words in the

right order while she analyzed everything he hadn't said. "Nothing like scoring three goals and a pizza party to pull a kid out of the dumps."

"Yeah I uh, I was afraid I might've overstepped with Carlos and—"

"You're his coach and his friend," Isa insisted. "He probably wouldn't have played or might've wanted to quit if you hadn't stood up for him. So uh, thank you."

Alex looked floored. "I hope he stays. He's good. Maybe he'll be on a Wheaties box."

Isa gave up. She had no idea what just happened between Alex's playing the song and him sitting here talking about her son growing up to be on some stupid cereal box.

"Let's not get ahead of ourselves," she ground out as the song gave way to Nirvana's "Teen Spirit."

His eyes lingered on the coy amount of cleavage her blouse allowed. "You look really nice tonight."

Took him long enough. "Thanks," she murmured, her gaze falling to the floor.

"I was—"

"What are you two talking about down there?" Big Danny, Lydia's husband and the assistant coach, bellowed from the other end of the table.

"How ugly you are," Alex shouted back.

"Naw naw naw naw." He fell on his elbows before he went face first into his beer. "You two're talking about something serious."

"Lydia, I hope you're driving tonight," Alex shot back. "Looks like someone's ready for bed."

The group made a long ohhhhh. "Good idea," Isa murmured and Alex nearly broke his neck when his eyes shot back at her. Isa realized June was right: men were pretty basic. They didn't get it unless you stripped off your top and sat in their laps.

Big Danny stood at the head of the table, blinking his eyes as he tried to come up with something to toss back at Alex. Lydia appeared with a you-go-girl wink at Isa and unhooked her purse from the back of her chair. "Come on, papi. Take me home."

"What?"

Everyone stood up making noises about the time and how they needed to go to church or Home Depot early tomorrow morning. The husbands formed a circle of their own while the wives pried children off the video games.

Alex watched those bonds between husbands, wives, and children. He'd always seen them as yokes that brought responsibility and tied a person down from accomplishing important things. But for the first time he saw that those bonds gave you people to hold onto, to take care of.

Even though this was the worst time imaginable, Alex wanted that security, the sense of place with Isa and Andrew. And when he heard that stupid commercial and the guys bleating in the bar, something dark and angry got him out of his chair and to the jukebox. "Something" had been his mom's favorite Beatles song. Every now and then she'd make Dad dance with her in the living room while he and his brothers and sisters pretended to be grossed out. He felt like the song could say something to Isa that he could never put into words by himself.

He started when Isa stood up behind him and then he took her hand to keep her from walking away.

In the center of the clamor for coats and purses, while the kids pleaded with moms for just one more game, Alex tried to put the indescribable into words. But he turned his hand under hers and she answered when their fingers threaded together.

"Mom!" Andrew appeared at the table between them, his hair sweaty and his eyes high on soda and make-believe gunplay. "Danny said I could spend the night at his house. Can I?"

"You don't have any of your things," Isa said, transforming from hot mama to mom in an instant.

"That's okay," Lydia, Danny's mom said, her eyes zeroing in on their joined hands. "He can borrow some of Danny's clothes."

"I don't want you to go—" Alex squeezed Isa's hand and she shut up. "Are you sure?" Isa asked Lydia.

"No problem. We'll bring him home at eleven tomorrow, or—" Her eyes linked the two of them. "Later if you want."

"Okay." She freed her hand from Alex's hold and caught Andrew when he made for the door. "You do what Mrs. Alvarez tells you and you eat what she makes for breakfast, okay?"

"Yeah, mom." He leaned to give her a kiss, but remembered his buddies were around. "I'll see you tomorrow."

"Good night, little man," Alex added, but Andrew pulled away.

Andrew didn't answer back.

Isa gave him what looked like an apology in her eyes and Alex knew he was spending another night alone. He had to be cool about this. Andrew was her son, he came first. While Alex knew those things intellectually, he felt the plunging disappointment that he'd come so close.

"Good night. Love you," Isa murmured to Andrew.

Lowering his voice, Andrew said, "Love you, too." He turned away and walked around the table rather than by Alex.

Isa pressed her lips together.

"I should get going," he said, saving her the awkwardness of apologizing for Andrew.

She hesitated and then nodded.

He went to say good night to the rest of the parents, carrying an emptiness he'd never felt before.

About an hour later Alex sat alone in his car and wondered if he missed something?

He cycled the clues through his mind: the outfit, the flirting, and Andrew staying the night at Lydia's house. But then there was the whole part where Andrew gave him the cold shoulder and Isa left Napoleano's without him. Now he was parked across the street from her apartment.

Alex was pretty certain that there was something between him and Isa. He'd made it pretty obvious with the song but not too obvious because she wasn't comfortable with public displays of affection. And he thought she gave him the green light with the looks and the hand holding. He knew he hadn't said anything wrong. Then again it could be something he hadn't said.

He should go walk across Isa's street and knock on her door. No, he should call and pretend he wasn't staking out her place. No, he should—

If he called, what would he say? He could invite her to get an ice cream but he knew that at a quarter to eleven the only shop in town had already closed its doors.

Alex stared straight ahead. The street appeared like a still frame as the fog diffused the lights and the houses stood dark while people slept or watched TVs in bed. He laughed, thinking of the crap he and his buddies pulled on these dark, quiet streets in high school: sticking fireworks in pumpkins on Halloween night, busting mailboxes apart with baseball bats, or toilet-papering cars that belonged to their buddies. That was some good stuff.

He jumped when someone knocked on his window. Holding a thick sweater up around her chin, Isa circled her fist for him to roll down his window.

"What are you doing out here?" he asked when he got the window down.

"Shouldn't I be asking that question?"

"Yeah I was thinking that uh, maybe you'd like to get something to eat, I mean some ice cream or something."

"It's almost eleven."

"I know."

She stepped closer to the window and Alex laughed at himself, feeling like that stupid kid he'd once been who blew up pumpkins and destroyed mailboxes for fun.

"What's so funny?" she asked.

"I uh, I don't know what I'm doing here," he confessed. "I mean with Andrew mad at me and—I'm really screwing this up, aren't I?"

She shook her head, that serene smile never leaving her face. "I'm scared too."

"Of what? Me?"

"Of making a mistake." Her eyes faltered, but after a moment she looked back up at him. "But I'm even more scared of losing what I want."

"Me too," he told her.

She took in a deep breath, gathering all of her courage and it made him swell with pride that she was doing it for him. "Do you want me to tell you what you're going to do next?" She said it in such a way that excited male fantasies of porno-style sex.

But this was Isa. They'd already had porno sex in the backseat of this very car and now they were facing each other honestly about what they were intending to do. He wanted this second time to be what the first time should've been.

Isa leaned forward, smoothing her hand over his cheek and moving in for a kiss. "Isa, wait," Alex said.

She froze. "For what?"

"Let's go inside."

"No one will see us."

"I'd rather go inside."

Isa's fingers felt good moving through his hair. "Do you not want to do this?"

"Yeah—"

She shocked him by striking out and taking his lips. He groaned as the heat of her moved under his skin and wound its way to the very heart of him. He tasted mint and the warmth of her tongue, slightly sucking it into his mouth until she shot up to her tiptoes.

"You like that?" he whispered against her cheek.

"Do it again."

He reached down and unbuckled his seatbelt to get out of the car and take her across the street and into her apartment where he could lay her out on her bed and—

"Are you in your nightgown?" he asked, looking down at her bare legs and her feet shoved into a pair of black flats.

She opened her sweater to reveal the top of a white cotton nightgown. He dropped his keys twice in his struggle to get out of the car and slammed the door so hard, the sound ricocheted down the street.

Taking her hand, they ran across the street, the misty cold feeling good against his hot face. She stole ahead of him, flashing her sweater open and laughing when his toe caught on one of the uneven bricks.

"I'm going to get you," he threatened, chasing her up to the door and catching her around the waist when she shoved it open.

They spilled into her small foyer and he kicked the door shut. Spinning her to face him, he ripped the sweater open and took her mouth mid-laugh, making love to her tongue while he peeled the sweater sleeves off her arms.

His breath went shaky in his chest and he told himself to slow down but that cautionary voice faded away as his need to touch, taste, and see all of Isa swelled. Her nails scraped against his sides, sending shivers over his skin as she balled his shirt in her hands and tugged him towards her. She broke the kiss, smiling up into his eyes with the most beautiful smile on her face.

Getting down on his knees he buried his nose in between her breasts, inhaling the scent of Hawaiian flowers. Did she choose this lotion for him? Had she rubbed it into her skin, still wet and hot from her shower, imagining his hands greedy to touch and his tongue eager to taste?

He eased his hands up the sides of her body, dipping at her waist and then spreading against the sides of her breasts and up the soft slope to the top of her shoulders. Hooking his fingers under the straps and slowly riding them down her arms, teasing them both by stopping just over her breasts and then pulling it so they came free.

"Alex," she whispered.

His heart thundered all the way to his throat, but he looked up from her bare breasts to her face. She swallowed, and out of the corner of his eyes her hands moved to cover herself.

"What?" he asked, gently stopping them and pressing a kiss against her wrist.

"I want you naked, too."

Her frankness shocked him. "How much?"

With everything she had. Unlike her body, his was athletic, sculpted and shaped by sweat and exertion. Alex quickly unbuttoned his shirt and then hiked it over his head. Her mouth watered, taking in his solid torso and the green plaid boxers that peeked up from the waistband of his jeans.

Shoes were off and then he pulled everything down so all he had on were the lights.

"Not bad," she said, watching him harden under her admiring eyes.

He got back to his knees and snuggled against her breasts.

"Hmm," she hummed, stroking his hair and then whispering all the places of his that she wanted to feel and kiss. Alex breathed in strongly, nuzzling one breast with his cheek.

"Kiss me," she said, fisting her hand in his hair.

His eye strayed up and his mouth quirked into a grin. But his tongue flicked out and tasted the underside of her breast. "Unh-uh."

He sucked her nipple into his mouth and she sank against the wall. His mouth worked as if he could swallow her whole.

He took her other breast, humming warmly against her skin. With his free hand he tried to work down the rest of her nightgown. She caught it. "No," she said, feeling more powerful with each breath. He looked up at her, planting kisses around her tight nipple.

Feeling bold and wild, she lifted her dress up, ticking him with the eyelet hem, and then draped it over his head. "Oh, man," he murmured, edging forward and parting her knees. "Your skin is so soft."

She shivered as he ran one finger down the center of her stomach and dipped into her belly button. She closed her eyes and lifted one knee to rest on his shoulder, urging him on.

He hummed his appreciation as his fingers snuck up her inner thigh and found her ready for him. "If I'd known—" she thought she heard him whisper.

"If you—oh!" she bit back when he bit her stomach ever so lightly while his fingers danced over her.

"That you'd be this wild," he whispered as a finger spread her open.

She coiled tight, eyes squeezing shut as her orgasm threatened to rip her to pieces. No one and nothing intruded on this moment between her and Alex.

He hummed against her flesh and before she could even think to hold back, she exploded, filling the room with her cries. He laughed again, pressing his cheek against her liquid thighs. "Now I know what to do next time," he teased, ducking out from under her nightgown and, as slowly as a candle burning a wick, standing to his feet. She knew that he was going to pick her up and take her to the bedroom.

"No, don't," she managed, holding her arms out.

He pressed his erection against her and she jumped as if licking a live wire. "We can't go in my room," she explained.

"Why not, babe?" he asked.

"There was a uh, wardrobe explosion in there."

He stilled and backed up to see if she was serious.

"June came over before the party with some clothes and I was just starting to put them away when I heard your car outside."

The look on his face changed from teasing to indescribably tender. "My beautiful Isa," he breathed, cupping her head with both hands and kissing her. "You did that for me?"

Her nipples beaded hard against his chest and his erection searched through the folds of her nightgown.

"Alex," she begged, reaching down and cupping him in her hand.

His breath hissed out but he let her stroke him, his eyes locked with hers while he braced himself up with one hand planted by her head.

"I want you back inside me," she whispered.

He grabbed her hand and her fingers fell open, releasing him. The light played over his muscled back as he reached over and yanked his pants over to search through his pockets. He was everything she'd imagined, taut lines and tanned skin. Ripping the package open with his teeth, he pushed her higher up against the wall, reached under her legs and spread them wide.

"I've been wanting this for weeks," he said as he joined with her, finding his way deep into the heart of her.

All she could do was hold on, sighing at the feel of him so thick and hard inside her.

Even with her so tight around him, he kissed and caressed while he moved in and out of her, working into a wild rhythm. Under her hands his shoulders tensed and he jerked tight against her, clutching her hips in both hands as he ground out her name, strung tight as a wire and then collapsed.

Feeling warm and secure with his heart hammering against hers, and him still warm inside her, she crossed her ankles over the backs of his iron thighs and held him, never wanting to let go.

"Isa," he said, still out of breath. "The third time will be—"

She hushed him with a kiss. "How about if we just try to do it in a bed?"

24

When Alex woke up the sun hadn't even made a dent in the sky. He'd fallen asleep with Isa draped over him, too tired to even brush aside her hair, which tickled his nose.

Her sheets smelled faintly of her and sex and his eyes shot open to find her gone.

Aching with exhaustion, Alex counted the condom packets littering the floor like bread crumbs. He took a moment, feeling an odd mixture of embarrassment and pride in himself. He'd always heard of people who had sex more than two times in one night, but he'd thought they were lying or just urban myths. Snickering, he searched for his clothes and then remembered he'd left them in her living room. Well, he thought as he stood up, it wasn't like she hadn't seen him naked.

Rubbing sleep out of his eyes, he made his way into the kitchen.

"Why are you sitting in the dark?" he asked when he found her perched on the very edge of a chair, her knees hiked up to her chest. She didn't hear him until he stepped onto the linoleum and hissed out a curse at the cold.

"Just thinking," she said.

So what do you say to the woman you had wild crazy sex with? "Are you okay?"

"Couldn't sleep. You snore, by the way."

He grinned, wanting to touch her hair. He'd never touched softer hair than hers. She looked back out the window and she reminded him of those moon-faced goddesses that commanded respect through silence rather than words.

"What are you thinking about?" he asked.

He heard her make a sound as if she started to say something and then decided not to. She shook her head and then shrugged her shoulders.

"Me too." He pulled a chair back, careful not to make the slightest bump against the fragile silence. "And even though I feel like I got hit by a truck, I'd never take it back."

She laughed softly, reaching for his hand. "Are you telling me that I wore you out?"

"I wouldn't say that."

She held her smile but he saw it fade. "I'm worried about Andrew," she confided.

"Me too."

"But I still want to see you."

He rested his other hand on top of hers. "Good, because we've only done some of the things I had on my list."

She let that comment go with only a skeptical lift of her eyebrows. "I only have one condition. We need to keep this between us."

Even though she was sitting there, warm and beautiful with him, he felt her pulling back. "Like when Andrew's at his dad's place?" he prompted.

She nodded.

"You know that everyone at the party last night knows I'm here?"

She dragged her teeth over her bottom lip and Alex felt something stir to life in his lap. "We left in separate cars," she said.

"Lydia lives two blocks down from you and my car is out front."

"I just don't want to do this in front of Andrew. I mean, going out together or you spending the night. At least not yet and I won't ask anything from you."

"This sounds like we're prenegotiating our divorce settlement."

He backed off when she leaned in for a kiss. "And? There's more behind those eyes. I can see it."

Isa blinked and then looked down at their joined hands. "My mother flaunted her men right in front of me. Every time I went to visit, I either had to listen to her moan about the last guy who left her, or hang out at the mall with the ten bucks she gave me while she 'visited' with the current one. I won't do that to Andrew."

Alex looked past her where the fence, the rooftops, and even the mountains appeared out from under the shadows of night. Just like that, time slipped from darkness to morning and he wondered if, like the darkness, Isa would eventually slip away.

"And I don't want to pressure you right now, especially when you don't—" She stopped herself and then dropped her chin to her chest. "This isn't very romantic, is it?"

Alex cleared his throat and meant every word. "It was honest and I never want us to be anything less than that."

Her legs slid down from her chair and onto the floor.

"Now that we've skipped the formalities, we can get back to your list," she purred.

"Wow, when you put it like that I—" Her breasts swayed as she leaned forward and the glass in the window reflected her generous behind.

"You what?" she asked.

"Sorry, lost my train of thought." Of their own accord, his hands went to her breasts as she straddled his lap.

"I don't know what it is about these things that get you all worked up but I—" His mouth clamped down on her, sucking her hard.

"Hmm?" he inquired.

She scooted up against him. "Never mind."

Isa knew that she looked like a woman who had had great sex, but only to the trained eye. So she avoided the front office this morning and hoped June would keep her mouth shut when she showed up for the lunch break.

June came in, fixing an earring of dangling mini lemons. "You little—" She caught herself when she remembered the students. "Look at you! I knew it!"

"Can we go outside for a second?" Isa said, zipping over and pulling her back out the door.

Bursting with pride, June clapped her hands together and held them up to her chin. "Now I can't betray my sources but a little bird told me my brother-in-law's car was parked outside your apartment," she sang.

"Really?"

"And since he came home yesterday afternoon wearing the very same clothes he had on when he left the house Saturday night, although they were a little wrinkled, I figured that two people had a very good time together. So?"

Isa took in a deep breath and saw no sense in lying. "We slept together."

June's eyelids flapped like a loose window shade. "Isa!"

"That's what you wanted to hear, wasn't it?"

"You don't have to be so blunt. He is my brother-in-law, you know."

"What did you think we did?"

"Well I . . . I just . . . was it at least romantic?"

Isa thought about it. Could she say a mutually agreed-upon sexual relationship was romantic? "Yes. At times."

"At times?"

"June, we're not in love. We're attracted and as two mature adults we did something about it." Why did the words feel like she'd just tossed a handful of rocks in her mouth?

June mouthed "something about it" and then her face squeezed into a perplexed expression. "Are you insane? We're in a school!"

"I'm practical and I need to get to work."

"Now I wish I'd never asked, I tell you. You both are sick."

"Excuse me?" If ever there was a moment when the pot called the kettle black, this was it.

"It's true. Just having sex? What a waste of time."

"But didn't you—"

"Absolutely not! I loved every man I've been with. It's the God's truth."

So had Isa. "You're a romantic," she said to save face. "And I'm a pragmatist."

"But Alex is romantic."

"How do you know?"

"I live with him, don't I?"

"Do you know how bad that sounds?"

Rolling her eyes as if the concept were just too obvious, June leaned forward. "Honey, I grew up with seven brothers. And I know when a man is getting ready for someone special, or just to get some. Saturday afternoon, Alex was getting ready for someone very special."

Curious, Isa leaned in closer and June grinned smugly. "When a man cuts himself shaving, he's thinking of what he'll say, or how he'll try to kiss her," she explained. "If he doesn't cut himself, he's got nothing weighing on his mind. Unless he's inexperienced, but I bet you now know that our Alex is very experienced."

And June would be very right. Straightening up, Isa needed to get going. "So that's it?"

"That's exactly it."

"Did Alex cut himself shaving?"

"Three times. I heard him cussing through the bathroom door."

A smile touched Isa's lips. He'd cut himself shaving for her? Maybe she shouldn't hold it against him that it took him hours to notice her outfit Saturday night.

"As always, it was enlightening," Isa said, making ready to return to class.

"Good things are about to happen. Says so according to your horoscope," June trilled. She slapped the sides of her hips with her hands when Isa kept going. "Don't you want to hear?"

"Ms. Avellan," Dr. Quilley greeted and the girls jumped. "Mrs. Lujon, how are you both?"

They murmured that they were fine. "How is your new lesson plan working?" he asked as if he were back in England taking a turn through the park.

It took Isa a few brain cycles to catch up. "We're starting

our first practice today. Mrs. Lujon is going to help coach them," she lied so June wouldn't get in trouble.

He looked from June in her lemonade-colored outfit with lemon earrings, to Isa in her khaki pants and blue school shirt. "I see."

Isa took a protective step forward. Even though she once questioned June's intellectual prowess, she didn't want to hear anyone else doing it.

"Mrs. Lujon is going to work with them on presentation an—"

"Excellent. I hope you'll invite me to see the presentations," he said. "Tuesday the twenty-eighth would work best for my calendar."

He'd just reminded her that the school board would discuss the budget cuts in three weeks.

"I'll let them know," Isa said.

Dr. Quilley leaned forward, his eyes dead serious. "I'm counting on you. I have absolute confidence in your abilities to understand and handle this situation."

He hadn't taken more than three steps when June asked, "Was he speaking to us in secret code?"

"Something like that."

"Well, stop standing around. When do you want me to come in and help?"

Isa stopped short. "What help?"

25

From the Magic Eye Camera Instruction Booklet

We do not guarantee the accuracy of this camera's functions. It is constructed purely for entertainment purposes and we cannot assume liability for improper usage.

"I want to help."

Isa almost explained that she'd lied to Dr. Quilley so June wouldn't get in trouble for chatting, but then she realized June really wanted to and . . . Isa should've kept her mouth shut. "You don't have to," Isa hastily started.

"But I could help," June exclaimed. "I know how to stand out from the crowd and make a good impression. I've won twelve beauty contests."

"What contests? You never said you were a beauty queen."

"Uh, just some back home."

"Name one."

"Dirty Dan's Wet and Wild T-shirt contest," June admitted frankly. "That was, of course, before I was married."

Isa wondered if June was somehow related to her mother, Dara. "I knew I shouldn't have asked."

"And I know how to talk in front of people," she insisted. "Come on, I'll just sit and watch today and then we can work like a team."

More like Lucy and Ethel, Isa thought. But then if her students practiced in front of one stranger, they might get used to the idea of talking in front of a room full of them. In spite of June's dubious professional past, she'd be a friendly face to her kids.

"You can watch," Isa warned, every protective cell in her body prickling. "If you have suggestions or comments, write them down and then give them to me."

"How come?"

"Because some of these kids are very self-conscious. Some of them won't read out loud in class in front of me and their friends, much less someone they don't know."

June nodded soberly. "I didn't think of that."

Isa reached for the door, gesturing to June to go in. By their fourth and next to last practice session the kids warmed up to June and made it a point of pride to attempt an accurate imitation of her Georgia accent. But when June first walked through the door that afternoon, the kids capped their chatter, watching her warily as Isa made the introduction. All but two students refused to take their turns, even though June quietly jotted notes on a notepad Isa gave her. And her notes were surprisingly on target for a wet t-shirt champion.

At the second meeting, only three students had the guts to stand up while June consumed three chocolate cookies, a pack of M&Ms, and a diet Pepsi. Just sitting next to her, Isa felt like she'd gained ten pounds.

By the third meeting, June announced that she was taking the hour to coach the students how to approach the podium. "I can't see y'alls faces," she'd said. "Look at the board sittin' there like you know exactly what you're there to ask for but friendly like. No one likes someone who's stuck up."

"Uh, can I ask you a quick question, Mrs. Lujon?" Isa asked before they got a lesson in selling their assets to a crowd of roaring drunks.

"These are my kids," she said with the roar of imaginary drunk frat boys in her head. "I don't want ZZ Top. I want 'Pomp and Circumstance.'"

June stiffened with offense. "Give me some credit. This is me you're talking to."

Before Isa's eyes, the Marilyn Monroe wiggle was replaced with a dignity that would've been worthy of Madeleine Albright addressing Congress. The girls giggled, but they soon stood up and followed her lead. Some of the boys outright refused, but Isa knew never to underestimate June again.

But the week before the board meeting, only three of the twelve students showed up for lunch.

She'd pushed them too far, too hard, Isa thought, waiting by the door. Some couldn't read a sentence out loud in class, much less address the school board. Isa thought they had lost before they'd even left for battle.

"This can't be," June declared, looking around the room. "We have less than a week."

"But that will give you three an advantage," Isa said to Khadija, Phuc, and Daniel.

"I'll be right back," June murmured as she swept out the door. "I don't take to no quitters."

Isa couldn't leave her students in the class alone and waited with them by the door while June in her red knit dress and hippie-girl braids disappeared into the sea of kids at lunch.

"What do you think she will do?" Phuc asked.

"We'll see," Isa answered.

Ten or fifteen minutes later June returned with the remaining nine students like they were wayward ducklings swimming in the wrong pond. The kids looked okay, maybe a little abashed, but they understood the universal language of the pointed finger aimed at a desk.

"Now let's get to work," June announced.

When the kids realized she meant it, they got to work, hands shooting up when Isa called for the first speaker. The only one who didn't raise a hand was Khadija.

Of all her students, Isa worried about her the most. She was painfully shy but exceptionally smart, reminding Isa so much of herself at that age. And while she progressed quickly in her written language skills, she still stumbled when asked to speak out loud. But she attended all five sessions, eating quietly yet listening.

Finally Isa gave her a nudge. "Okay Khadija, you're next," she announced.

She looked up bewildered, holding a chip midway between the bag and her mouth. "I don't have anything prepared."

"Come on," Phuc pleaded, followed by the others.

"Yes, you do."

"Just go up."

"We all did it."

Khadija studied her notebook. "They won't listen," she said in barely above a whisper. Her reply reverberated through the room and eyes fell to their desktops. Even though they had gone through the motions, practiced their speeches and agreed to show up next Tuesday, they couldn't shake the belief that they were bound to fail.

And Isa had no idea what she could possibly say that would make them believe otherwise. "But what do you want to say?" she asked. June sat quietly, waiting for the right signal from Isa.

Khadija shook her head.

"Okay, but what do you think about what they want to do?"

"Maybe you should leave her alone," a student murmured.

"Then why are you here?" Isa asked, keeping her voice level even when she wanted to scream the consequences if the board passed the measure. "If you don't think they're going to listen, why did you spend your lunch in this class-room rather than outside with the band playing on the quad?"

Heads hung in the hot silence that smelled like old carpet and potato chips. June opened her mouth to speak but Isa held up her hand. "How many of you will even be there?"

Applause ratcheted through the walls even though their class was as far from the center quad as possible. A guitar chord throbbed and then the band struck up a new tune.

She took a different tack. "Remember what I said about what it means to be here in America?"

They looked at each other, wondering who would be the brave one. Daniel reluctantly raised his hand. "You say— said," he corrected himself. "That it's about having freedom to ask what you want."

"If you decided not to speak at next week's meeting and they decided to send everyone back to mainstream classes, what would you do?" she asked, hating herself for making them see the reality of their situation.

Daniel waited for someone else to speak but continued. "My grades would go bad again."

"Then stand up for yourselves. No one else will."

Isa let them think about what she said as she opened the door, letting in a rush of wind that circled through the stuffy room. The bell shrilled and the laughing voices of kids rippled out from the quad. Behind her, the students rustled with the business of packing up bags and shouldering backpacks. No one spoke.

"I'll be there, Ms. Avellan," Daniel said before he ducked out.

Isa thanked him. But the others tried to make themselves smaller as a hulking silence entered the class.

"*Say something now, darling,*" Joan hissed from an empty seat at the front of the class. "*This is your moment.*"

Now more than ever Isa needed to say something movieworthy to light the fires within them. The second hand on the clock ticked apathetically.

She opened her mouth.

"*Good Lord,*" Joan heaved and slid out of her desk. "*Repeat what I say.*"

"What?" popped out of Isa's mouth.

Her students turned to each other and then cautiously stared back at her.

"*Now pay attention,*" Joan started.

When Isa waited for her to say something, Joan rolled her eyes and gestured impatiently for Isa to repeat, "Now pay attention."

"Think about what you really want," Joan prompted.

Isa repeated it.

"And whether you can live with or without it."

Her students were actually listening.

"We are approaching the time when you won't have a choice. While it's available to you, stand up for what you want because at least you'll know that you did everything you could. So those of you who want a choice, raise your hand."

When she was done, Isa was a little out of breath. June's lips were crinkled with emotion as she wiped at her eyes.

One by one, every student raised their hands and Isa knew that no matter what happened, she had won the most important battle.

26

"I need you to come down here," Isa said when Tamara answered her cell phone.

"What's wrong?"

Isa couldn't stop the shivering ever since she looked at her calendar this afternoon after class and realized that— she had to be calm. "Nothing's wrong."

"Is it Andrew?"

"Andrew's fine. I just really need you here."

"Isa, you're scaring me."

"Just come down quick."

"I'm finishing an appointment now so I can be there in an hour," Tamara promised even though she had to drive all the way down from L.A. at three in the afternoon.

But Isa couldn't do this alone. She tried, but she circled through the parking lot in front of Longs Drug Store and then parked on a shady street.

"Do you need to go to the hospital?" Tamara asked.

"Just meet me at Longs."

Isa uncurled her fingers from the steering wheel when she hung up and placed the phone on the empty seat beside her. With all the stuff going on, Isa hadn't noticed until she looked at her calendar today. When she couldn't remember the last time she'd packed tampons in her purse, she knew she was in trouble.

She survived the wait by eating. Cookies, M&Ms, full-leaded sodas . . . anything edible that crossed her path. She even pushed Andrew to go play at his friend's house so she could—

God, this couldn't be happening again.

In record time, the tires of Tamara's Karman Ghia screamed into a parking spot. Isa stood up from her table at Starbucks and walked outside.

"You got here fast," Isa managed through the panic that had been strengthened by caffeine.

"Miracle of all miracles, there was hardly any traffic." Tamara unbuttoned her silver-gray suit jacket. She rested it on the seat and then slammed the car door. Isa felt a little guilty for making her come all the way down but she couldn't call June in on this one. She was too close to Alex.

Stabbing her fist into one hip, Tamara cut to the chase. "What's wrong?"

"I don't know how to say this so I'll just spit it out."

"Do I need to be sitting down?"

"No," Isa turned and walked through the automatic doors into the damp chill of the drug store.

"Okay. What?" Tamara asked behind her as Isa weaved her way toward the back of the store.

"You're going to kill me."

"Isa, I drove down through Wednesday traffic and ditched dinner with Will, whom I haven't seen in a week, to get down here. Please just spit it out."

Isa stopped and Tamara rose up on her toes to stop from

colliding into her. Isa couldn't cross the divide between the greeting cards and the feminine hygiene sections.

"I shouldn't have called you," Isa babbled and she never ever babbled, "Oh God, I'm so sorry for calling."

"Hey, hey." Tamara put her arm around her and pulled her in for a tight hug. With a sigh, she took off her sunglasses. "You can call me whenever you need me but right now, you're scaring the crap out of me."

"Just follow me and don't say anything."

Wiping her hands on the front of her jeans, Isa led Tamara past incontinence pads, tampons, K-Y, suppositories, and then stopped.

"Oh, Isa, no," Tamara groaned, covering her mouth with both hands.

"Don't say anything. I just need you here for this." Isa took a brave step towards the shelves loaded with pregnancy and ovulation kits. They tilted at an odd angle and her vision blurred.

"How could you do this? *Again*?" Tamara begged, her voice climbing an octave. "Don't you remember—"

Isa whipped around so hard she started to sway on her feet. When her balance righted, she spat, "I didn't exactly plan it."

Tamara dropped her hands. "Same with the first time!"

"You know what? Go back to your dinner with Will. Oh, and keep your mouth shut."

"Isa," Tamara said in a small voice.

Isa threw Tamara's hand off her arm. "You're not the one who has to live through this again. Think I forgot? Am I that stupid to you?"

"No, you're not," Tamara sighed, yanking a test off the shelf and reading the back of it. "I'm not mad at you, I'm just—"

"Disappointed?"

"No. Worried and—" She took a deep breath, looking over her shoulder. "This place brings back really bad memories."

Tamara stepped closer and lowered her voice. "I came here when I thought I was, you know."

This was news. "You were? With Will?"

Tamara shook her head. "Ruben." Her lips curled. "Before Mireya's wedding. I was too scared to buy one and then I found out I wasn't."

They were quiet while a voice on the PA called for a cashier on number four. The harsh lights bounced off the shiny white linoleum floors, and Isa smelled a nauseating perfume of Epsom salts, mothballs, and medicine.

With a sigh, Tamara walked to the pharmacy, grabbed a hand-held basket, and returned. "Well, let's get this over with," she decided, tossing the test in a basket. "This one says two for one."

"But that one's on sale," Isa pointed out.

"Get that one too. And we'll need some water."

"Thank you." Isa meant it more than Tamara would ever know.

"You're welcome. Although, if you're not—" Tamara looked around. "You know—" She mouthed *pregnant* and then continued, "You owe me a drink."

"I'll buy one for you even if I am."

"How certain are you?"

"Pretty certain."

Tamara rolled her eyes. "Dude, how could you miss—"

"I lost track! What? Do you know when your last period was?"

"I'm on the pill." Tamara would be the perfect friend if she would just shut up. "Am I right in assuming who *he* is?"

Isa thought about playing dumb, or just ignoring the question. But this was Tamara, so she admitted, "Yeah, it's *him*."

"Are you going to tell *him*?"

"Tell him what?" Alex asked behind her.

Isa spun and found Alex standing there with an older man who looked a lot like him. What happened next was a blur.

For a second, while his eye muscle danced, Alex knew Isa nearly told him the pregnancy tests were for her friend. But when her gaze refocused from his dad to him, Alex knew she couldn't lie. Nor could she tell him the truth.

From total numbness he bounced right into action. "Dad, would you give me a second?" he asked.

"Of course. I have some things I need to get," he said, clearly hearing the "no questions" in Alex's voice.

Ignoring her friend, who took a protective step towards Isa, Alex put his hand between her shoulder blades. "Let's go next door and talk."

Isa told her friend it was okay and she left with him.

After he got her settled at a corner table in the far back of Starbucks with a coffee for him and a bottle of water for her, he sat down and tried to think of where he was supposed to start.

"Were you planning to tell me?" seemed like the best place.

"Yes," she admitted. "I never planned this."

"I didn't say you did."

"But you think so."

He shook his head, oddly calm even as both their lives teetered precariously on catastrophe. "It was that first night, huh?"

She kept turning the bottle in her hands. "I still don't know for certain. It could be a medical thing or stress."

He didn't dare give himself that hope. "We should find out."

"Yeah, that's what I was about to do."

"I want to be there when you find out. Is that okay?"

She stopped playing with the bottle and looked up at him as if he'd surprised her. "Why?"

"Because we got into this together." His mind blipped the possibility that maybe he wasn't the only one but he pushed that thought away.

"You're the only one," she answered, seeing his thoughts so clearly.

"I wasn't going to—"

"If I were you, I'd wonder the same thing."

"But you're not me and in case you're wondering, I'm not like Carlos. No matter what, I won't walk away from you or the—" He couldn't quite say *baby*. If he just thought of her as "possibly pregnant," it seemed he'd have an easier time getting through this. "Or what happens next."

She looked away.

"Are you planning to—" He couldn't wrap his lips around the word "abortion" either.

"No. I couldn't."

"If you are—"

"Let's not talk about this right now. This could all be for nothing." She straightened up and twisted the cap off her bottle but she didn't drink.

But this wasn't for nothing. Somewhere deep in his gut he knew this wasn't for nothing, and when they found out for certain, he knew he'd never look at Isa the same way again.

It struck at the core of him that she could be the mother of his child, that he could be a father right this very second.

His old job had trained him well for any and all disasters, so he went back to what could and needed to be done right now. "I need to drop off my dad. Can I meet you at your place?"

"Yeah."

"Where's Andrew?"

"He's at Little Danny's house."

Andrew was another problem. Alex hadn't been able to bridge the distance the kid firmly put between them.

She looked up and he turned to see her friend walk over with two bags.

"Hi, I'm Tamara," she said to Alex.

"Alex Lujon."

"We met. Isa, are you ready?"

"I'm going to . . ."

"I'll take her home," Alex said, suddenly overwhelmed with protecting Isa.

But Tamara was just as protective. "Your dad told me he was walking back," she replied, assessing him coolly. "Isa, do you want me to meet you at your place?"

Isa shook her head. If this were any other situation Alex would appreciate Tamara's loyalty, but right now he needed to be in control.

"Isa, let's go," he said, standing up.

Tamara didn't back up. "If you hurt her, you have me and my mother to deal with."

That pissed him off. What'd he do to be spoken to like that?

"Tamara, it's okay," Isa said before he said something he'd regret. "Thank you for coming all the way down here."

Sizing him up again, Tamara thrust the bags at him. "Call me tonight, okay," she asked Isa, her eyes promising cruel and unusual punishment if Alex hurt her friend. She then turned on her heel and walked out, making other people move out of her way.

Alex turned to Isa. "Are you ready?"

"How am I going to pee for all of those tests?" she wondered, staring at the bag.

He grinned, holding up the second bag with two large water bottles. "Looks like we better get started."

27

ALEX'S HOROSCOPE FOR OCTOBER 16

Embrace the unexpected. After all,
what other choice do you have?

"What does it say?" Alex asked through the bathroom door. Even the dark apartment seemed to hold its breath.

"It doesn't say anything," she said.

"I know but is there a line yet?"

"No."

He looked back at the box in his hand and then his watch. It said she was supposed to take the test in the morning because the hormone would be more concentrated. But he didn't think he or Isa could wait till tomorrow morning.

"Would you go do something?" she asked. "You're freaking me out."

"I agreed to wait in the kitchen while you . . . you know

in the cup, but I'm staying here," he insisted, laying his hand on the door.

He heard her mutter.

Josie slowed her van when they turned the corner onto Isa's street. Creeping along, Patty and Susan scanned the cars for Alex's 4-Runner.

"There it is!" Susan pointed out. "I told you!"

"It's not going to work, Susan," Patty warned. "I told you the auras do not lie and I double checked, then triple checked."

"Can I speed up now?" Josie interrupted, her heart beating for fear that Isa and Alex would catch them.

"No!" they both shouted.

"This is the second weekend he's been here and I know in good time, he'll propose," Susan insisted.

"You're setting yourself up," Patty sang.

"You know what?" Susan twisted in her seat to point her finger at Patty. "You don't know love anymore. When Roberto left, you let him win."

Josie sucked in her breath. Here they go again.

"Excuse me?" Patty drawled, the whites of her eyes glowing lividly. "Miss I-read-those-trashy-romance-novels with those, those women flaunting their chests and those men with those big pee-pees—"

"They do not flaunt their—"

"You live in a Snow White world, *m'ija*," Patty yelled over Susan's sputtering. "You think the real world has those fairy godmothers and dancing midgets and shit. I know reality."

"You're just a dried-up old woman."

"You're some silly old woman who hasn't realized she's old!"

"Well maybe if you read some of those books you would've had more fun in bed!"

Josie slammed on the brakes and the girls screamed, throwing their arms out to stop from flying out of the captain's chairs in the back. "Stop it! Now I'm driving away and we're going to the movies."

She stomped on the gas pedal, throwing them back into their seats. It was like she had the kids all over again, except these two sounded like a couple of cackling old hens.

"And if anyone should be giving advice it should be me," she added breathlessly. "Between the three of us, which one has two married children and grandchildren on the way?"

Susan and Patty stiffened in their seats.

Eyeing them in the rearview mirror, "That's right," Josie said, her heart racing. "I didn't think either one of you had anything to say."

Alex was about to rap his knuckles on the door when Isa opened it.

He prepared himself to know once and for all if he was a father. He didn't want the first thing Isa saw on his face to be disappointment.

"It's pink," she said simply, holding out the test.

His hand shook as he reached for it and took the plastic stick. Sure enough, two pink lines stared right back at him.

"What are you thinking?" she asked. "Say something."

He didn't know what to say. He didn't know how to describe how he felt. It was like ice-cold water rushed through his veins and left a tingling wake. Alex had always imagined that if he'd ever become a father he'd feel a joy too large for his body. But he wasn't even sure if what he felt was fear.

"Do you want to keep this?" he asked, holding up the plastic stick.

Her eyes were huge and she mutely shook her head. He tossed it aside and gathered her in his arms, holding her tight against him. Tears smarted his eyes and he felt her face crumpling against his chest and her eyes wet his shirt.

"Isa," he whispered into her hair. "Isa, don't be scared." Even though he was cold with shock, he couldn't bear that she was.

"Baby, here," he pulled her away and tilted up her chin. "No, no more." Gently he kissed her, taking his time as he soaked in her fear and her doubt until she began kissing him back.

"Unh," he groaned, breaking the kiss and pressing her tight against him again. She left shy kisses against his neck and her hands traveled over his back and dipped into the waist of his pants.

He picked her up, hiking her legs around his waist and carried her into her bedroom. As if she were a delicate treasure he laid her on the bed and with his kisses pushed her onto her back, letting his hands explore the velvety skin of her waist.

"Are you sure?" he asked, unbuttoning her blouse.

He wanted to be warm again. He wanted to forget for just a moment that their lives had just changed forever and nothing would be the same again. He wanted to chase away the haunted, desperate gleam in her eyes.

But she still didn't answer his question and he paused, wondering if he was doing the exact wrong thing to do. Her hands came up and she pulled her bra down for him, inviting him to take more. "You're so beautiful," he said against one breast before he licked it. Her legs spread open for him and he settled into the nest of heat radiating through her jeans.

Isa lifted her hips, teasing him. "Come inside me," she said. "I want to feel you."

His tongue stopped dancing over her nipple and he lifted up on his elbows. "We don't have any—" he stopped himself.

She knew he slipped but it brought back all the darkness that suffocated her.

"Sorry," he apologized, closing her blouse up. "We probably should talk about this and . . ."

Isa didn't want to talk because that meant facing the reality that she'd made the same mistake she swore she'd never make again. She pushed her elbows back so she could sit up. "I want to see you going inside me," she heard herself say.

Alex's mouth dropped open. She cowered back, knowing he was going to pull away and pretend he hadn't heard her. "The sun is setting so we better hurry," he said thickly.

They didn't speak as they whipped their clothes off, letting them fly off every which way. She crawled towards the center of the bed, touching herself without embarrassment as he drank in the sight of her.

On his knees, he stopped her hand and parted her for him. She watched his face as he entered her, alert and tense with purpose. When he rooted himself, she looked down and saw them joined together. Tears of a different sort stung her eyes.

"Do you like that?" he asked, nudging down for a kiss.

She linked her legs behind him, opening her mouth to receive his tongue, which he thrust in rhythm with her hips.

For the first time with Alex she made love to him with hope in her heart. Hope that he wouldn't leave her. Hope that he wouldn't stay for the wrong reasons. That was all she could do for now—hope.

28

When Alex pulled up to the giant Craftsman in Newport Beach, two men rolled sod on the ground. With the gray sky and the mist in the air, the tinted windows reflected Alex's grim expression as he took the steps up the wide porch.

It would only be temporary. He needed something, anything to pay the bills until he found a permanent gig. One step at a time, he kept telling himself after he left Isa to go lie in his own bed and stare up at the ceiling all night.

He found Daryl barking into a cell phone in a kitchen that was the size of Isa's apartment. Alex laid his hand on the cold, impenetrable granite counter and waited.

Daryl turned and then did a double take when he saw him standing on the other side of the island. "Get back to me no later than eleven-thirty," Daryl demanded, and then flipped the phone shut in his meaty hand. "Hey, how's it going, man?"

"All right. Have a minute?"

"Not really. Project in Laguna Beach got all screwed up by the frickin' neighbors. So what's up?"

Alex swallowed like he'd just taken a bite of moldy cheese. "Is that job still open?"

"Things didn't work out, huh?"

"It's been real slow."

"I've got someone in there now. He's doing an okay job." He hefted his pants and then came around the island. "Sorry things didn't work out."

There had been a time when Alex could name his price. But that time was over. His parents raised him to believe that a father provided. "Do you have room for another guy?"

Daryl chomped on his gum, studying Alex through pale blue eyes that didn't blink. "If you can take over the Laguna job and get those assholes back online, you have a job."

"I might have another job for you," Alex offered, hoping to up his pay. "Up near Montebello. A little four-plex needs new pipes, electrical, and some other work."

"You offering to partner up?"

"You specialize in homes, I specialize in commercial. We could do pretty good."

Daryl hacked his two-pack-a-day habit in his fist. "I only work independent."

This wouldn't last forever, Alex told himself. "You got a deal. What's down in Laguna Beach?"

"Hey mom," Andrew yelled. "Mom!"

Isa realized she'd been reading the same sentence in her novel for the duration of a sitcom bleating from the TV.

"Stop yelling," she snapped.

Andrew pressed his lips together. "Dad is on the phone and wants to know if he can pick me up from school on Thursday."

The phone rang? Isa sat back in her chair, her butt and back sore. The whole house could've been on fire but she wouldn't have noticed, having replayed that night with Alex in her head.

Pulling herself together with a deep breath, she reminded Andrew, "You have soccer practice after school."

"I know but . . ."

"What?"

"He wants me to see his radio show in Hollywood."

"Is he on the phone now?"

Andrew nodded. Isa heard the battle drums in her head.

"We've discussed how I feel about this."

"I know, but he's asking again," he pleaded. "Don't be mad."

"I'm not mad."

"You're mad, I can tell," he cried.

Her son was perilously close to tears and she would be too with all the uncertainty weighing on her shoulders. "Andrew, do you want to go?"

He shook his head no. But he didn't want to admit it to his father. She couldn't make him do it. Even though the last person she wanted to speak to was Carlos, she still braced her hands on the table to stand up and then hobble over on numb feet.

"Carlos?"

"Hey, I was waiting for Andrew."

"I know. You wanted to take him to the station?"

"Yeah. I thought it'd be cool."

"Carlos, I can't imagine that you would think I would let him go."

"It's not your decision," he sneered. "Put him on the phone!"

"As his mother, yes it is."

"Put him on the fucking phone," he shouted.

She looked over her shoulder. Andrew stood behind one of the chairs, clutching to the back with white fingers.

"God damn it, I'll pick him up from the school whether you want to or not—"

"If you do—" She remembered Andrew was listening and switched to Spanish. "I'll call the cops and then I'll call the radio station and tell them you tried to kidnap your son to go with you."

"What?" She heard the fear in Carlos's voice. But he always had to save face. "Did I hear you right? Did you jus—"

She hung up the phone. For good measure, she switched the phone to silent so if Carlos called back, which he wouldn't, it wouldn't scare Andrew.

"What did he say?" Andrew asked.

"He's just disappointed, honey," she said, composing her face so Andrew wouldn't see the fury burning through her. "Can I ask why you don't want to go?"

"Because Danny played some of it on his computer. He said mean things about you."

Her breath was coming out in dark snorts. "Did you understand what he said?"

"Kinda. You don't say things like that about him."

"Andrew, there are times when I want to say mean things about your father. But I want you to know that I never would."

He mushed his lips together and relaxed his grip on the chair.

Since she had him, Isa ventured, "Andrew, I need to know something."

His eyes flicked up warily. "Okay."

"Are you mad at Alex?"

He shook his head.

"Then why have you been so quiet with him? You're not in trouble," she hastened to add. "It's just that you guys used to be good friends."

Andrew stared at the rungs in the chair. "He embarrassed me."

"When?"

"With Dad. At the game that time."

Isa should've done something rather than let Alex do her job for her. And she had no idea what to say to her son to erase the tortured look on his face.

"Baby, Alex was just trying to help. You have nothing to feel embarrassed about."

"Can I play my X-box?"

If someone could invent a device that allowed mothers to look into the minds of their eight-year-old sons, there'd be a lot fewer terrified parents in this world.

"Not until you explain why you were embarrassed."

"I don't know," he pleaded, his voice straining.

Let him go, she told herself. He'd had enough for one night, and frankly, she did too.

Alex walked up to the door with the plans for a seven-million-dollar mansion in one hand, and an agreement for a salary of eleven dollars an hour. The door opened and his dad held out a beer. "Here. Thought you could use this."

"Sorry I'm late," Alex said, taking the bottle that his dad uncapped for him. It went down ice cold and completely tasteless.

"Nothing like liquid courage, eh?"

Alex turned to shut the door behind him, about to ask where June was. What he had to say he wanted to do in private. He took another swig.

"Do you love her?" his dad cut to the quick.

Beer seared down the wrong tube.

"She's real pretty. And nice too," he continued pleasantly, easing down into his green chair.

"Thanks," Alex wheezed.

"But you didn't answer my question."

Coughing until he could take in a full breath, Alex cleared his throat and fell into the sofa. "Can I ask where June is?"

"Movies."

He digested that and tried to regain normal breathing. "I do—it's complicated."

His dad pursed his lips, shaking his head. "Well, sometimes love comes later. You getting married?"

"We haven't talked about that yet. But yeah, it looks like we will." Alex should've called her from the road. He'd spent the entire day in the Laguna Beach city hall getting one answer from one clerk and then a completely different one from another on permits and hearings with design review.

One step at a time, he told himself.

"I don't feel ready," he confessed. "I can't really even believe it."

His dad reared back his head, dismissing Alex's fear. "In my day, no one was ready for babies. They just happened when they happened and God knows your mom and I weren't ready for you. But we managed not to kill you, eh?"

"That's good to hear."

"You'll do fine. You got a good job and a good head on

your shoulders. And from what June says about your lady, she's a smart woman and she's a good mama to her boy. You're much better off than your mother and I were."

He slapped his knee, chuckling as he bent over and then pushed himself up. "Bring her over soon," he asked as he lumbered into the kitchen.

A good job, huh? What Alex was getting from Daryl now he used to make in bonuses. How was he going to stretch the meager scraps of his savings to take care of his dad, his sister, June, and now Isa, the baby, and Andrew? They were his responsibility when he had the least to give.

29

ROCK HARD IN THE MORNING PART III—
K-Y CAT FIGHT

"You have to see this," June said when Isa checked in at the office. Isa took a deep breath against the unexpected shock of seeing June, who was now technically her baby's aunt. The cold shakes grabbed hold and wouldn't let go.

June took her by the hand and dragged her into the nurse's office. It took a whole minute for Isa to realize they were watching a live Internet feed of Rock Hard in the Morning.

"Oh no—" she started. This she absolutely could not handle.

"Come on, we've got to see," June insisted, gripping her hand harder.

"How could you do this—"

"Honey, look," Lissi, the nurse said. "None of those twits got anything on you."

Isa was curious to see what kind of women would compete for her ex-husband. She liked to think that he was so pathetic that the only way he could get a woman to talk to him was to use his credit card number over the phone.

She peered closer to the screen and the three faces had been set in giant red hearts along the screen. Big hair, lots of makeup, and skin that was so tanned that it would be leather by the time they hit thirty.

"You ever seen women fight in K-Y before?" June asked.

"No."

"I saw it in a movie once," Lissi offered.

"I really could do without this," Isa said, rubbing her temple.

"We think it will do you some good," June said, as Lissi agreed.

"How?"

"Well, you could see the competition."

"I'm not competing for him."

"You know what I mean. Confront this thing and then move on with Alex," June said.

"Who's Alex and since when did you have a thing goin' on?" Lissi demanded.

Isa opened her mouth and then shut it. A thing going on? Honey, did she ever.

"So which one is he?" June asked.

The camera scanned the crowd and zeroed in on Carlos.

Lissi swore under her breath and June blurted, "Good God, Isa! Honey, what were you thinking?"

Carlos wore a green tracksuit, ball cap worn sideways, and three gold chains draped in varying lengths over his bulging stomach.

"He's gained some weight," Lissi commented. "Screwing him must be like doing pudding."

"We were fifteen when we met," Isa explained. "He was thinner and a lot better dressed then."

"I hope so," June threatened. "Or else I'm reassessing my friendship with you."

When Rocco told his wife about this stunt, she'd said, "You'll make our divorce inevitable."

It was his freakin' job! She sure as shit didn't mind taking the damned money from his paycheck.

He pulled in a deep breath, bringing it all back into the moment. The director said through his earpiece, "We're a go in four, three, two . . ."

Rocco looked out at the crowd and then at Carlos, who stood there holding his hands clasped in front of his balls. That fool looked like they'd jumped into his stomach.

On cue Rocco leapt out of the wings, clutching the mic in a fist and drawing screams from the kids crowded into the courtyard at Hollywood and Vine.

"Yo yo yo! This is Rock Hard in the Morning and two contestants remain for that weekend at the Hard Rock Hotel in Vegas. Before we begin the K-Y cat fight in our delightful little rubber pool, I gotta ask our man Carlos, dude?" He stomped on the word and Carlos shuffled out to join him on stage.

"Yo man," Carlos said into the mic.

"Okay brother, do you see any resemblance to your ex-wife in these girls?"

"No man," Carlos answered. "Well, except for the uh, you know . . ." He cupped his hands under his man breasts.

"Really? And her . . ." Rocco waved his hand by his crotch. "That didn't keep you interested either?"

"She never took 'em out."

* * *

"I did too!" Isa shouted and then clamped her hand over her mouth.

"I know you did, baby," June soothed, patting her arm. "I know."

"Never?" the obnoxious DJ asked Carlos on screen.

"Nope," Carlos answered.

Outrage rumbled through Isa. What a pathetic, scum-dwelling, fat-assed mama's boy who—

"What's her number?" the DJ asked.

June and Lissi gasped. Isa felt cold fingers of dread tickling the backs of her legs. She lowered herself onto the cot and wished she could stick a preggie-pop in her mouth.

"Say what?" Carlos asked, surprise evident in his voice.

"I need to see if this is for real, man."

"You can't call her."

"Yes I can. I want to be certain you're for real."

The three women leaned forward, trying to see what Carlos was doing and then he pulled out his cell phone. "Well, here's her number."

June grabbed Isa's shoulders, dragging her back from the laptop. "We need to get out of here."

"I need to find my—"

The dial tone kicked up on the laptop as the DJ reached for a phone from a roadie and then dialed each number from Carlos's cell phone.

"Turn it off, turn it off!" June cried.

Running on absolute irrationality, Isa dug through her backpack as all the crap she forgot to clean out sloshed around.

"Are you ready?" the DJ asked and the crowd roared.

"Honey, where is it?" Lissi pleaded.

"It's in here—" Isa held the backpack against her thigh, reaching down with one hand. "I can't—"

"Oh hell." June yanked it out of her hands, flipped it upside down, and all of Isa's stuff rained down on the floor.

The phone ring burred over the laptop and Isa's phone rang the "1812 Overture." Isa lunged down and made a grab for it, sending it across the floor. June made a grab and it slid under the desk.

They froze when they heard Isa's greeting play over the air.

"Looks like we missed her," the DJ said, ending the call.

The three of them heaved a sigh of relief. Isa pulled out her phone. If Isa threw up on Lissi's shoes, no one would suspect she was pregnant.

When the thing with the ex-wife didn't work out, Rocco got the cat fight started. And it had been a frickin' blood bath.

The two women got in the pool, each wearing bikinis with "Rock Hard" emblazoned on their asses. Becky lunged for the kill, catching Stacy by the knees, flipping her up and into the K-Y. The crowd went nuts and so did Becky.

When Stacy stood up, Becky clothes-lined her WWF-style, then yanked down her bikini top and nearly throttled her with it. The crowd booed as Stacy and her bare boobs fell into the pool. Two roadies ran over and tried to fish her out, but Becky wanted more.

Rocco motioned for the roadies to step in but Becky slammed Stacy face first into the K-Y. A roar rolled up and onto the stage when Becky stood up thrusting her fists in the air. With the assistance of the roadies, Stacy pulled herself up, sputtering K-Y and hair out of her mouth.

"Oh, my God," Carlos whispered fearfully beside Rocco. "She's insane."

Rocco admitted he was impressed but he kinda felt sorry for the dumb ass standing next to him. One wrong move and Becky would send Carlos to the hospital with his dick on ice.

"And she's going to Vegas with ya, man," he reminded Carlos, thumbing the mic back on. "Good luck."

30

Isa's students drew her out into the parking lot of the district headquarters, which resembled more of a tailgate than a meeting of the school board. Pressed well beyond capacity, a fire crew waited outside with the truck, just in case.

"This isn't going very well, Ms. Avellan," Khadija said, winding the ends of her head scarf around her fingers.

"I know, but we can't give up," Isa challenged, not entirely sure that they would win the board.

"But they won't believe us," Phuc insisted.

"They haven't listened to no one so far," Myrna added softly.

Isa had never lied to her students and she wasn't going to start now. The board reduced health education to an elective even after a surgeon, a rape crisis counselor, and an eating disorder patient requested that it not be cut back. And then the board cut the physical education staff to Stan and two part-time instructors, even after one of the board members read a letter of support from an alumnus who had been drafted by the San Francisco 49ers.

Isa knew these kids feared that as new English speakers and immigrants, they didn't stand a chance if the board wasn't swayed by an all-American football player.

"You can only do your best," she said with half an ear trained on the president of the board droning on about the pet construction project, for which he wanted to use money that had been set aside for ESL. "If you do your best, then you will walk away knowing that you stood up for yourself. Understand?"

Still nervous but with a little more courage, they nodded their heads. "We're almost up, so let's go inside."

She gently pushed the heavy door open. Wedged in the back row, June waved her agenda and then raised her eye brows in a question. Isa grinned and nodded that the kids were ready, but June knew her better than to be fooled.

The junior board member leapt at her chance to speak while the president paused to drink from his glass. "We have a lot of people here who need to speak tonight, so may we move on to the next agenda item?"

The other board members shifted away from her as if afraid to be contaminated by her rebellious spirit. Rudolfo Acuna ruled the roost unquestioned and uninterrupted as president for nearly sixteen years.

He struck his gavel and proceeded to read the agenda item to discuss moving ESL students from the eleventh and twelfth grades to mainstream classes. After the board members discussed their way around the issue, Dr. Acuna opened the floor.

Phuc Lee took two steps forward and looked back at Isa for assurance. When she gave it, Phuc took to the podium, laying her paper on the ledge and adjusting the mic.

Isa turned to June, who had her eyes closed in prayer.

"Good evening, board members," she enunciated carefully and Isa caught herself mouthing the girl's speech from memory. In a weak voice, Phuc told of her journey from Vietnam with her two brothers to join their parents after having been raised by her grandmother.

Dr. Acuna's eyebrow lifted at her slight blunders. But when Phuc ended, the board applauded her speech. Isa's students took to the podium, one right after the other, painfully eloquent in their fear. Finally, it was Khadija's turn, but she froze.

Isa put a hand at her back while Phuc and Myrna whispered for her to go. With her pulse pounding in her ears, Isa wondered if Khadija would do it.

"Are there more speakers on this agenda item?" Dr. Acuna called.

Carrie Barcus's father raised his hand and strode to the podium. Unlike the girls before him, his speech was strident and brimming with confidence. He used those tired old arguments that "in the old days" students integrated faster and became Americans.

Isa fought the urge to roll her eyes and furiously fanned her face with an agenda. How many immigrant students left school because they felt stupid and humiliated by a system that refused to transition them into a strange and sometimes aggressive culture?

He ended his speech and then turned a directed glance at Isa before he sat down.

"Will there be anyone else before we close public discussion?"

The audience ruffled and whispered. Isa felt people

watching her, waiting for her to stand up. Dr. Quilley craned his neck, looking pointedly at Khadija.

Khadija took a step forward, whispering "Excuse me" as she pushed her way to the podium.

Isa's hand flew to her neck as she watched her most gentle student unfold her speech with shivering hands.

"I was afraid of America when I came here last year," she said clearly, her accent softening her English. "I was afraid of the students because I know they made fun of me when I read out loud or asked questions, even though I didn't understand them. My parents asked our neighbor to speak for us so that I could be trans—" She struggled for a moment. "Transferred here to this school."

She took a deep breath. "In Ms. Avellan's class, I learned more about my new country and see it as a great place where you can become whatever you want, and where someone will help you achieve your dreams if you work hard, study, and be a good citizen. If you take our money away from us, some of us will be okay. But those of us who still learn English, we will not understand and we will not learn. Thank you."

June leapt out of her chair, the first to applaud. "Sorry," she apologized when every eye turned to her. "Bad back."

Isa held back proud tears when her girls hugged each other and then held hands, emotions quivering as they waited their fate. About to quietly suggest to her students that they listen to the board's discussion, she happened to see Alex crammed against the wall.

He held up his hand in greeting and smiled. Heat crept up her chest, all the way to the top of her head. They'd communicated through voicemails for the last three days. He'd said in the last one that he had something important to tell her. But she'd shoved it away to be dealt with after she got her students through this challenge.

Now he stood there, a head above the crowd, and Isa realized how much she'd missed him. She hadn't asked for him to come, and love for him swelled in her heart until it occurred to her that June probably mentioned it to him.

She turned to June, who winked and gave her thumbs up. It shouldn't have mattered that he hadn't come on his own. Isa was being petty and no matter how much she scolded herself for it, the feeling wouldn't go away.

"You okay? You haven't spoken in nearly thirty minutes," Alex asked, escorting Isa across the parking lot.

She opened her mouth and then shut it. Giving up, she shook her head to tell him she wasn't ready to speak.

He'd give anything to get out of this jacket. Who thought that jackets could shrink across the shoulders? Then again, he'd probably owned this thing since high school. Even worse, he realized his mother bought it for him. As soon as he could, he was getting a new coat.

"Do you need me to drive you home?" he asked when they got to her car.

"No. I don't think so."

"Oh good, you can talk."

She aimed a dirty look at him.

"You're the only person I know who can't talk when there's good news," he said.

"I don't know what to say. My gir—my students, they—" She hiccupped on a sob and pressed the back of her hand to her mouth, tears swelling in her eyes.

"Hey there." He gathered her close and held her under a musky pine tree. "You did good."

"No, they did," she insisted. "Based on what they said, they didn't cut the program. I'm so proud I want to hit something."

"Try not to hit me."

She laughed. "I won't. What are you doing here anyway?"

"I came to see you."

"How did you—"

"I asked June what you meant by that message you left me and she told me about this. So I left Laguna early, showered, changed, and even put on cologne in case you'd let me talk you into a piece of pie at Russell's."

"You did?" she asked as if he were her hero. She sniffed his neck and his hands tightened their hold on her back.

Embarrassed but pleased with himself, he shuffled his feet. "Sure."

She grinned against the damp heat of him. "I'd love to get some pie with you."

"Did you sleep okay?" he asked when the waitress took their orders and menus.

She looked at him dubiously.

"Me neither."

"So what important thing do you have to tell me?"

"I got a job."

"Alex, that's great."

"It's just to tide us over for awhile. Till I can find something better."

"Us?"

"You, me, Andrew and the baby."

Her spoon splashed into her tea cup.

"I can't just sit around and wait for something to fall out

of the sky," he explained. "I've got you guys, June, my dad, and my sister's tuition."

"You pay Christine's tuition?"

"Not all of it. Just what her loans and stuff can't cover."

She blinked and then her eyes dropped to the table, looking as if he'd admitted something embarrassing. "I didn't know."

"She's got another year and then she'll start paying me back," he said, leaning forward and hoping to say this next thing the right way. "But I want to talk about what we're going to do next. I'd like us to get married."

She pulled her hand back and dropped it under the table in her lap. "Because you feel like you have to?"

"I want the baby to have a name. And I'd be a good father to Andrew."

He made it sound like they were planning a trip.

"You knew we were getting married, right?" When Isa didn't answer, he seemed to get angry. "What kind of man do you think I am?"

"It's not that." She pressed her lips together, fighting the urge to curl under the temper simmering in her eyes. "Just a few days ago you and I decided to have a . . . an . . . to be together and now you want to get married and be a father to Andrew."

"But—"

"No, let me finish. I let everyone hustle me into marrying Carlos because it was the right thing to do. And the person who suffered the most wasn't me but my son. I won't do that again."

"Why do you keep comparing me to him?"

"I'm not. But when I get married again I'm marrying because I love that person and he loves me back. Not out of obligation."

The waitress returned with his banana cream and her Boston cream.

"Well I guess that answers that question," she said, picking up her fork.

"What does that mean?"

She sliced into her cake, shaking her head. "Nothing."

31

EMAIL FROM TED TO ALEX

Hey man, just checking in with you about everyone. June said you've got a girlfriend and how come you didn't say anything? Jerk. Watch out for that wife of mine. She's something.

Isa had just finished opening the second bottle of sparkling cider with her students when Lissi frantically waved through the window. Isa forced herself to be cheerful for them. If it wasn't for the festering guilt she felt, she would've been. But all she could think about was that she'd messed up again, just like the last time.

With Carlos, he'd had dreams of going to law school, mostly because his idea of a lawyer was someone with a sleaze-job hairdo and an Armani wardrobe. So when she announced she was pregnant, he left college to work. And now Alex . . . it was like history was repeating itself.

"Ms. Avellan, we need you in the office!"

Isa hadn't seen Lissi walk in. Andrew. The adrenaline rush stung and stole her breath.

"It's Ju—I mean, Mrs. Lujon," she clarified, and Isa breathed again. "She got some bad news."

Thank God it wasn't her son. And then guilt prickled her relief that she thought that.

"I'll stay with your class," Lissi said, hurrying forward. "You go."

Isa raced through the campus, quiet save for the teachers or students speaking from the open windows of the classrooms. They were in the middle of their last period before school ended. Isa prepared herself to face the worst.

"June?" she said when she walked into the nurse's office.

Dr. Quilley shook his head and Isa knew it was bad. Keeping herself strong, she slipped onto the cot next to June who sat there with her hands slack in her lap, her face completely devoid of sorrow or even grief.

Just this morning, June had practically performed a backflip when Isa walked in. Now June had the look of a stranger.

"June, it's me," she said, bringing her arm over June's shoulder. "Honey, what happened?"

"They think Ted died," June said as if she hadn't quite digested the information.

Isa closed her eyes as it sank in. What should she do? She should call Susan—no—Susan had a meeting with the superintendent this afternoon. Isa wasn't a helpless nineteen-year-old girl anymore. But she wasn't Susan.

"I'm taking you home," Isa said in her most soothing mom voice. "Do you want me to call your mother?"

June just blinked. The only movement was her chest moving up and down with her shallow, staccato breaths.

Isa had never seen Ted in person. She couldn't recall his face even though she'd seen the colorful, almost girlish collage of photos at June's desk. She thought how June wanted his baby before he left and grief pierced her with its poisoned dagger. But the more she thought about him, the less she would be able to help her friend.

"Please call us when you learn more," Dr. Quilley spoke softly.

"I will."

A student worker handed over June's purse and jacket, while Isa and Lissi lifted her up from the cot to stand on her own two feet. She walked to June's car because it was the closest. Isa got as far as a block shy of Alex's house when June began to quietly sob.

Tears seared her eyes, but Isa wouldn't break when her friend needed her. She spoke meaningless words of comfort, pulling up to the address that the assistant principal gave her. For a moment it crossed her mind that this was the first time she'd been to Alex's house but then she went back to getting June out of the car and up to the front door.

"Why hello!" Alex's father called through the screen door. "Alex didn't say you were—" He stopped when he saw Isa holding up June. "What's wrong? Did she have an accident?"

He didn't know. How was Isa . . . what could she tell him when she hardly knew?

"No, Señor Lujon," Isa said. "June didn't have an accident." She sat June on the sofa and then laid her down, covering her with her metallic pink jacket. "Could you show me to the kitchen, please?"

He led her to the kitchen and Isa leaned her back on the edge of the counter, taking every scrap of time before she had to tell this man that his son might be dead.

"June found out that Ted might have been injured," she started.

Mr. Lujon's face seemed to tighten against his bones. But with several blinks he pulled himself back together and stood taller.

"I don't know anything else," Isa continued. "She was alone in the office when she got the information and I can't get her to talk."

"Call Alex. He'll know what to do," he said as he moved back to the living room and June.

"Dad?" Alex called through the screen door fifteen minutes later. He stopped short when he saw Isa sitting on a dining room chair beside the sofa, smoothing her hand over June's hair.

"What's wrong?" he asked, feeling the fear rip through his chest.

"*M'ijo,*" his dad sobbed and then clung onto him. Isa shook her head and Alex held his dad, who quivered with the fight not to cry. Seeing the two people he'd sworn to protect fall to pieces, Alex shot into crisis mode.

"It's all right, Dad. We're going to get through this." The words sprung automatically from his mouth while his mind raced with doubt.

"We don't know anything for certain yet," Isa added.

He got his dad seated at the dining room table and then bent over Isa. He was about to kiss her on the forehead but stopped. "Are you okay?"

Isa nodded. "I checked her purse and her desk for a letter or telegram but didn't see anything."

"Thanks," he said. "I don't know how long this will take."

"I called Susan to have her pick up Andrew. And I can order food when your sister comes over."

He deflated when he remembered that he still had to call them. "I just heard from him . . ." Alex's voice trailed off and he shook his head.

"June has a friend she emails whose husband is in Ted's unit," Isa continued. "I could have someone at school check her computer."

Alex never relied on anyone, not in the truest sense, anyway. But having her here beside him made this seem a little less impossible.

"Would you do that?" he asked.

When she grinned, he believed for just a second that everything would be okay.

Two hours later Alex learned that Ted was most likely gone. His helicopter had been shot down over a remote country town that had gained the world's attention as a hiding place for terrorists. Nights of watching news programs report be-headings, explosions, and sneak attacks told Alex that if Ted hadn't died in the crash, he more than likely had been killed on the ground.

Without missing a beat, Isa commandeered food and drinks before the rest of his family showed up. Isa got June to sit up and sip some hot tea. Alex would rather have had June screaming with grief than sitting stone still. Then again, Alex knew when she unraveled, he'd have no idea how to handle it.

Isa turned, feeling him watch her. She whispered something to his sister and then stood up, swaying just a little before she walked over to where he stood in the hallway.

"I spoke with June's mother," she murmured, nudging him deeper into the hallway. "She's flying out first thing to-morrow morning. Did you find out what happened?"

Alex held back from telling her most of the details that tortured his imagination. Isa had been truly amazing in keeping everyone calm and now her eyes looked heavy with exhaustion.

"I don't think he's—" He bit back the rest.

"I'm so sorry," she whispered, placing her hand on his arm. "You don't have to hold it all in, Alex."

He did. If he came undone, then his father and June and the rest of the family wouldn't have anyone to take care of them.

He sucked in his breath. "You'd take some worry off my mind if you got some rest. You look tired."

"I'm fi—"

"There's nothing any of us can do until they tell us more. And I don't want you getting too tired, okay?"

Her hand fell away. "If the tea doesn't knock her out, I want to give June something that will help her sleep. Are you okay with that?"

"What did you put in that tea?"

Isa quirked her lips. "Just some brandy."

"How much brandy?"

"Two shots."

"When are you going to take it easy?"

Isa frowned and then she got his hint. "I'll stay for another hour and then pick up Andrew—"

"Can you stay?" he blurted. "I don't think I can sleep alone tonight."

She stepped back. "Alex, that's not really approp—"

"I don't mean like that. I'll sleep on the couch and you and Andrew can have my room."

She shut her mouth and then opened it to say something but couldn't. "Never mind. Bad idea," he conceded.

"Maybe I should. Just in case June needs anything. But I need to get my things."

"And Andrew?"

"Let me talk to him first." She misunderstood Alex's smile. "You are not touching me unless you want me to throw up all over you."

"That bad, huh?"

"It's good, actually. It means the baby is—" She caught herself.

"Is what?" he asked, genuinely curious as to what she meant.

"Healthy. It's an old wives thing."

By midnight, or sometime around it, everyone settled down to sleep but Alex. He spread out the plans across the dining room table. He'd made schedules and updated Outlook on his Palm and laptop. The work focused him away from the idea that his brother could be dead and that his baby was growing inside Isa.

But at least Andrew spoke to him when Isa brought him over. "Sorry to hear about your brother. Want to play Soul Caliber?"

They went twenty rounds, Alex losing only ten games, until it was time for Andrew to go to bed. Whatever Isa had said to him worked and Alex felt one part of his life click back into place.

"What's that you're working on?"

Alex jerked up. He hadn't heard his dad come into the room. "What are you doing up?"

"Can't sleep. So?" He gestured to the plans as he eased down into the opposite chair.

"House we're working on. The neighbors took the owners to the city and the architect came back with new plans."

"Company got a new project?"

Alex nodded.

His dad made a noise, but his eyes stared at all the fears a parent never wanted to face. And then he focused back on Alex. "Why aren't you with Isa?"

Isa and Andrew were sleeping in his bed. "Dad—"

"Her little boy is very nice. Promised I'd show him the trains before school tomorrow."

"He'll like that."

"Too bad Ted and June didn't have a child."

Alex's head felt like a sponge that was being getting the water squeezed out of it. "Don't say that."

"If June had a little one, this wouldn't be so—"

"Don't!" Alex didn't care if he woke everyone up. "Don't talk about Ted like that. We don't know for sure."

He'd never, ever snapped at his dad like that. Then again, he never faced the horror that his brother's body could be lying on the side of a road somewhere far from them. Ted may never walk through the same door he'd walked out of, or may never have children or coach soccer, or be the center of attention at every party or holiday.

"All I'm saying *m'ijo*, is that if we get the news—" his dad struggled. When Alex moved to go to him, he held up his hand. The whole house seemed to hear his father's sniffling sounds as he fought his despair. But Alex sat there, helpless to do anything about it. "Don't let her go, Alex. Don't ever for a minute regret her, her little boy, or your child."

"I don't, Dad," Alex promised. He got his dad back to bed. He even sat on the couch with the blankets and pillows and stared at the TV as it sent weird shadows over the walls and ceiling of the living room. His mind played his father's words like a needle caught on a scratched record.

As quiet as a thief, he opened his bedroom door and saw Isa and Andrew lying together under the strip of light from the open window over his bed. And this time he made that same promise to himself.

32

Isa thought she felt the bed give behind her and just when she was about to turn, she knew it was Alex as his arm slid over her waist.

"Hi," he whispered against her hair. "Don't pretend to be asleep. I can tell."

She was in bed, wedged between her lover and her son. This was so completely—

"I'll get up before he wakes up," Alex said. "I just need to be with you right now."

She really wasn't comfortable with staying over in the first place, but this? No. And yet she lay there, not saying what she wanted. Damn it, she always kept what she wanted to herself, always too afraid to stand up for herself.

As if he knew by the stiffness of her body, Alex groused, "Okay, I'll go back to the couch."

Her head whipped around, watching his dark shadow get out of bed. Since Andrew slept like the dead, she easily slipped out and followed him into the living room.

"How did you know I didn't want you—" Okay, there must be a better way to ask this.

"You were tense as a wire. Sorry."

Damn it. He'd be much easier to stay mad at if he were more like Carlos.

"It's not that I didn't want you there, I just—" Oh come on, Isa told herself, just say it. "I don't want Andrew to get confused about you and me."

"I'm sorry, Isa, but I don't have it in me to talk about this right now."

Sitting on the couch, Alex pulled his shirt over his head and then adjusted his pillows. "I know you don't," he added.

His stare and those deliciously naked shoulders drew her to him. Primly she covered him up with his blanket and then she sighed. Who was she kidding? She flipped the blanket up and then snuggled down beside him.

"I knew you'd see my way," he said, tucking the blanket over her and then turning off the lamp by the living room.

"Not that way." She propped herself up on an elbow. "I know you're trying to be romantic, but not when my kid's around."

She couldn't see his face in the dark. "What? Say something."

"I'm sorry, Isa. But at some point we need to make a commitment and when we do, I want to be a father to him." He shifted in the dark. "You're not alone this time, okay?"

"I know. I'm just—" In love with you even though you don't love me, she thought. "Tired. And hormonal."

He reached over the back of her thigh and hiked her leg over his. "There," he sighed. "Better?"

Later that night, unable to sleep, Isa sat up from the questions wrestling in her head. Finding her way back to Alex's bedroom so she could check on Andrew, she reached for the lamp on the bureau and the light pushed back some of the shadows, illuminating the picture of Alex's mother.

Isa was pregnant and she was in love. Inside of her another life took root and grew, unaware that Isa had conceived in a moment of lust and selfishness.

Sitting on the edge of the bed, she smoothed her hand over Andrew's hair. At least with him she had been in love, or, at least in the way a nineteen-year-old girl knew of love.

"*I knew you'd come looking for me,*" Joan said from the doorway.

Isa's hand drifted to her belly, not yet hard or stretched. "I have to tell him that I—"

"*No, absolutely not. You make him say it first.*"

"But what if he never does?"

"*What makes you think I'm going to let you stay with a man who doesn't say 'I love you'? Really darling, what kind of woman do you think I am?*"

But Alex cared about her and Andrew. That should've been good enough, but it wasn't. She wasn't going to devote her life to making this up to Alex and doubting his feelings. If he insisted on marrying her, she would insist on the condition that he loved her.

And if he agreed, how would she really know?

"Do you think he does?" Isa asked.

Joan's silk peignoir whispered around her legs. Her cynical smile softened. "*Darling, he's crazy for you and tonight, he learned that he needs you.*"

Isa balled her hand in her lap and she closed her eyes. She loved Alex. But she owed her life to Andrew and her baby, not to validate them to anyone.

"*That's the spirit, my dear. A woman must know her priorities and you should never let a man know that he's at the top of the list."*

"Will you be there tomorrow morning when I—"

Joan lifted a disapproving brow.

"I won't ask him to tell me, I'll just tell him that I won't marry another man who doesn't love me back."

With the wisdom of a woman who'd been married more than once, Joan shook her head. *"Are you prepared to possibly hear the worst? And what will you do if he says no? Could you watch him eventually meet another woman, marry her and start another family with her?"*

Isa took a deep breath, knowing that she had to be honest with Alex. Even if it meant that she would have to face all the possibilities, even the worst ones.

The next morning, the world swam before her eyes and Isa took a deep breath, until everything righted again. There was nothing worse than nausea. Head colds, allergies, sinus infections . . . nothing topped hours of feeling like you were going ralph.

Isa put on a brave face along with her mascara and lipstick. She had to say something to Alex. This wasn't the best time, she knew, but she had to. He was talking about commitment and sneaking into her—no, his bed—while she slept with Andrew.

Holding onto the wall with one hand, she slid into the kitchen, careful not to upset the delicate balance between nausea and vomiting in front of Alex's dad.

"Find everything okay?" Alex asked when she emerged. "You look green."

"Thanks. Is Andrew with your dad?"

"The trains."

She stood there looking at him, curling and uncurling her fists.

"Do you want me to come back after school?" she asked, not ready to say what she had to say.

"If you want. I'll be in Laguna probably till late."

"But what about—" Her sentence hung in the air and she couldn't find the rest. Even though Alex stood in the kitchen with her, she felt like she was talking to a completely different person. "Do you have some Saltines or crackers?"

"Oh," he said, understanding. "How about Ritz and Seven-up?"

"Nothing that smells."

"So Seven-up?"

She gripped the edge of the counter, sinking into the chair by the phone. He got busy getting her the soda.

"You all right?" He offered her the glass and sneaked a glance at the clock. "I can come over later."

"But what about your dad?"

"Then come over and spend the night again."

"No. I can't."

"Why not?"

"Because you—you don't." She smushed her lips together and sipped her soda.

"Do you need to go to the doctor?" he asked, concern softening his voice as he bent down in front of her.

"Do you love me?" Joan was going to get her for that.

He jerked back. "What?"

"Do you love me?" she said, emphasizing each word. "Because if you don't, I can't commit to you, I can't marry you, and I can't share anything with you."

His knees popped when he straightened up, staring down at her.

"So," she started again, twisting her fingers in her lap. "Do you?"

He didn't have to answer. She knew by his silence that she was on her own.

33

ROCK HARD IN THE MORNING:
THE HAPPY COUPLE RETURNS

"You're not going to believe who's out there," Lydia shouted over the hollow burr of the cappuccino maker at Starbucks.

The only person worse than Alex, Isa thought that Friday morning, would be her former mother-in-law. "Surprise me."

Lydia stepped closer, peering at her face. "Are you okay?"

Isa slowly chewed one of the two cinnamon twisty things she'd bought.

No. No, Isa wasn't *okay*. She'd found herself strapped to this emotional roller coaster that she hadn't paid a ticket for, but of course, she kept it all inside.

"I'm just—" Wait. From here on out she was no longer going to hide everything. "Actually, Lydia, everything is all fucked up."

Lydia's brows touched her hairline and she couldn't get any words out.

Outside, they heard someone testing a sound system.

"Okay, okay," Lydia said, holding her by the arms. "When you walk out that door, to the left in front of Casa de Oro, Carlos has his radio show."

Wow, Isa thought. She never imagined her life would ever reach this low.

"Thanks, Lydia. I'll make sure I don't look to the left."

She was hollowed out, numb, and God damn it, knocked up again! It took months, *months*, to lose all that weight with Andrew and now—

"Testing, one two three. Check."

She turned as the voice boomed over the wet parking lot and the empty sidewalks. A giant stage with lights and a "Rock Hard" backdrop had been built in the far corner of the mall in front of the rotting stagecoach.

As if drawn in by a tractor beam, Isa walked in the opposite direction of her car and toward the stage. She had polished off both cinnamon twists, and wore crumbs on her shirt. She peeked around the corner of the stage.

"Stay away from me!"

"Hey baby, I just wanted a good morning hug," Carlos said.

Isa stepped around and saw Carlos and some guy who resembled a weasel circling around what looked like a Britney Spears impersonator with the shoulders of the Hulk.

"Look, you motherfucker, don't you come near me again!" she shouted. On a closer look, she had man hands.

"Hey, I didn't even touch you, bi—" Slap. Carlos jumped back, holding his arm. "Ahh! You see that? Did you see this shit? She hit me!"

"Hey, you're not supposed to be here," a roadie said to Isa.

They all turned and saw Isa standing there.

Carlos stopped nursing his arm and his face screwed into an ugly scowl. "What are you doing here?"

"Nothing, I—"

"Sorry, but you have to go," the roadie insisted.

"No, wait," Isa said. She looked at the blonde. "I'm his ex."

"You were married to this punk?" she asked, smacking her fist into the palm of her other hand.

Both Isa and roadie stepped back. "Unfortunately, yes."

"And you put up with all this?" Smack!

"Not much I could do when I had his son."

The blonde's hands fell at her sides and she turned to Carlos. "You have a little boy?"

"Hey, Isa, get the fuck out of here," Carlos shouted, puffing his chest out and stalking to her. "No wait, everybody! See this! This here's my unfuckable wife!"

Isa heard the roadie suck in his breath beside her. No one jeered or laughed at her. They just stared at him.

"Yeah, the very one," Carlos continued, losing steam. "She's the one tha—"

When the cops asked her later, Isa didn't remember actually walking over and sinking her fist in his flabby middle. But she could remember the sound of the air rushing out of his abdomen and then his body hitting the pavement like a felled tree.

She looked up at his weasel friend, holding up her fist as if she couldn't quite believe what she'd just done. He held shaking hands out to protect himself. "I don't want any trouble."

The blonde walked up, giving her a friendly smile and a handshake. "Hey, I'm Becky and I had to spend four shitty

days in Vegas with this slob and his fat friend. Why did
you . . . how could you marry *that*?"

Isa stepped back. "You wrestled in K-Y for him."

Becky nodded her head thoughtfully. "But I did it for my
career. Did you really love this guy?"

Isa looked down at him and then winced. During the fall
Carlos's pants came loose and his black Calvin Klein
g-string emerged between his pasty butt cheeks.

"Ewww." Isa and Becky both looked away.

Yes. At one point in her life, Isa loved this quivering, pathetic bit of masculinity with every cell in her being. All this
time everyone thought Carlos was the man because he had
women fighting over him on the radio, but really, he was the
kind of man who wore a g-string.

"Come on," Becky urged. "I only had one weekend with
this creep and I can only imagine what you went through.
You deserve a good kick to his nuts."

Then again, if Isa hadn't loved him, she wouldn't have
Andrew. One good punch was enough. It ended this. Because when she thought about it, if she hadn't had Andrew
that meant she wouldn't have met Alex and then—

She drew her right foot back and drove it in the back of
his thigh.

"Ahh!" Carlos screamed. "She kicked me! Help! Help!"

"Oh, shut up," Isa shouted, and kicked him again.

"I'm gonna sue you! My mom has a lawyer, she'll sue you
for—oomph!"

Carlos's friend fell on top of him. Becky stood with
both feet planted wide and arms crossed over her tube
top. "That's for not understanding the word 'no,' you
ass-grabbing jerk."

"Hey, somebody get this on the air!" Isa looked over her

shoulder as the crew scrambled in each and every direction.

Becky grabbed her, marching her to the parking lot. "Just go. Let me handle this."

"Are you sure?"

"Like I said. This is for my career. Maybe they'll give me my own show. You know, like *The Bachelorette Meets WWF* or something." She gave her a little push. "And don't be coming back here to get a show of your own. I'll kick your ass."

"What?" Alex asked, pressing the cell phone against one ear and a finger in the other.

He had the cops here walking an eighty-year-old neighbor down the street who had earlier chained himself to a tree in protest of the new house going up. They'd just got the backhoe going when his phone buzzed.

"Say that again!" he shouted.

"I said that your brother is alive," Dad shouted back.

Alex went cold under the relentless sun. "Is he hurt? Where is he?"

"He's on his way to a base in Germany. We're getting ready to leave now. What's that noise?"

"Work. I'll be right there."

Static garbled Dad's voice, and then the call ended. Snapping it shut, Alex lowered himself on the bumper of Daryl's truck, reaching around to scratch his shoulder.

His brother wasn't dead. He would see him again and joke with him . . . tell him that he was going to be a dad.

Alex didn't know what was worse: getting the call that his mother was dead, leaving him no opportunity to hope, or having lived through the darkness and the mental static of yesterday.

And what if it had been Isa? His shoulders slumped forward on a long sigh. If he lost her, he'd have lost the best thing that ever happened to him. And he loved her. He just screwed up his chance to say it back.

He knew what he had to do. He didn't know how to tell Daryl but he was going to find her and tell her in person.

"And here's the miracle man," Daryl called, coming at him across the site. He ducked under the architect's elevation markers and then swept off his hard hat. "Well, my friend, you just saved our ass. Mrs. Kwan there would've called this whole thing off if you hadn't come along and got us back online."

"The neighbor still chained himself to the tree."

"Eh. Local color. Just trying to get into the papers and if any reporters show up, tell the guys that only you do the talking."

Alex bobbed his head up and down. "Will do."

"I'm thinking with everything moving along now, you might join me for breakfast."

"I can't."

"Sure you can. I'm the boss, I said so."

"No, I have a family situation back home. Just got the call."

"It's not too bad, is it?"

"No, not at all. But I probably won't be able to come back today."

"You sure you want to do that? I'd like to talk about future projects."

Somewhere hidden between duty and doubt, fear and hope, Alex knew he loved Isa. He'd be an idiot to put it off any longer.

Alex stood up and knocked his hard hat on his thigh. "I'm sure."

34

"Hey there!" Isa said when June stood in her doorway after class. She tried to smile even when her stomach felt hollowed out with dread.

"He's alive," June said, her voice unaccustomed to talking. "They found him and he's okay."

Isa flew across the room and hugged her. "June, I'm so happy for you."

June sobbed and tears gushed out of her eyes. Isa walked her to a chair. With her hands covering her face, June cried out all the darkness she'd kept locked inside while Isa held her.

"Look at me," she struggled through her sobs. "I couldn't cry when I thought he was dead and now that h-h-he's alive, I can't stop."

"There's nothing wrong with that. You just deal with it in your own way."

June nodded, pressing her cheek with the heel of her hand. "I'm flying to Germany tonight. I gotta be going in twenty minutes."

"Then you get going. Is your mom going with you?"

"No. I'm going with Ted's father." She settled her shoulders back but she still looked scared. "And I'm really sorry for not being there Tuesday ni—"

"Stop it. When you come back, stop in for a visit with the kids."

June sighed. "I heard what you said to Alex."

Isa dropped her gaze and stood up, not needing to hear this. "June, don't—"

"You're really, really brave. And lucky to be having a baby. I'm gonna remember that when I get on the plane today."

"I'm stupid."

"How dare you say that? Take that back right now."

"Can't." Isa tightened her fingers into fists. "It's true."

"But you love him, don't you?"

It didn't even occur to Isa to lie. "I do."

"And I think he loves you. He's just not smart enough to figure it out."

"There's no such thing as figuring out love. He either does or he doesn't. And people don't learn to love each other over time either. It just doesn't work like that."

June wiped tears from her cheeks and sniffled. "We get to stay friends, right? If I'm still here in California, I get to see the baby, don't I?"

"Now look what you started. I never cry," Isa said.

"It won't be like what you had with Carlos," June said, her voice as calm as Buddha's. "Alex isn't like that. You know my theory about shaving. He's lucky to have any skin left because of you."

Isa laughed and cried harder.

"True as I'm sitting here," June insisted. "You'll see. Now

when I get back, we're going shopping for some sexy maternity clothes. So be ready."

"Come on, let me walk you outside."

They walked arm in arm through the deserted campus. The school seemed a little sad when the kids weren't around, like a host whose party guests were in a rush to leave. Newspaper and discarded tests drifted along the sidewalks and stuck to the chain-link fences.

This was Isa's favorite time of year. The kids were already planning the Halloween dance.

"You missed out on some action this morning," she said to June when they reached the parking lot.

"Yeah?"

"I might have beat up Carlos behind the stage of his radio show."

June's scream could be heard in the next county. "OHMYGOD! Good for you! Did you get a good kick at his nuts?"

"No. He was bent over gasping from the punch I landed on his stomach."

"That's something," June said, clearly not impressed. "But next time, aim lower."

Isa never returned Alex's calls. He drove to her school but found out they had a half day and Isa left.

He went to her apartment to find her and Andrew gone. A desperate call to Susan and he found out she took Andrew up to Tamara's for the night. No note. No phone call. Not even a damn message if Andrew would be playing today.

But her silence told him everything he needed to know.

He'd screwed up. By not being man enough to tell her he loved her.

"She'll come around," Susan said, appearing beside him before the game. "I brought Andrew."

He turned and his eyes caught on the kid, tying his shoe laces. "She didn't want to see me, huh?"

"She told me, Alex," Susan answered, her arms crossed over her chest.

He waited for the knife to slit his throat. "Is she okay?"

"Just very, very sick."

"Yeah, I know."

"When are you going to talk to her?"

Alex shrugged his shoulders. "Isa and I need to talk a few things out, but . . ."

"Well I have a little problem," Susan said, putting her fist on her hip. "I have to take something to somebody but I said I'd take Andrew home—"

"I'll do it," he said.

Susan's lips twitched and she looked strangely very satisfied that he got her Isa pregnant.

"I knew I could count on you," she said. "And don't mess it up."

The car threw up smoke when Susan squealed to a stop in front of La Diosa salon. She'd prearranged for Josie to have her mani/pedi at ten-thirty the second she saw Isa this morning.

Kids these days. Thinking they could pull their excuses over a woman her age! The flu-schmu. She knew a pregnant woman when she saw one and when Alex all but confessed, she almost danced with joy. It was all too easy.

"What's that strut all about?" Patty demanded from behind the cash register.

"You owe me one hundred dollars. Pay up." Susan patted the edge of the counter.

"Don't you order me around. Where's the evidence?"

Susan caught Josie's eye roll and her moaned, *"Hijole.* There they go again."

"They're in love."

"Impossible," Patty declared, not having any of it. "I know my auras and they are not meant for each other."

"But did you look in their eyes? Did you see them together?"

"No," she sniffed. "I didn't have to!"

Susan lifted her eyebrow, giving Patty the look that struck fear in the hearts of her children. "I'm going to be an *abuelita."*

Josie stood up, knocking her soapy water all over Juanito. "Tamara?"

"Memo?" Patty asked.

"No," Susan snapped. They better not be, at least not yet. "Isa."

"With who?" Patty asked.

"What do you mean with *who*?"

"Girls, girls," Josie cautioned, running over with one soapy hand.

"It's Alex," Susan said, relishing his name.

Patty held her hands to her heart, shaking her head with denial. "Impossible. It's can't be—I sense disaster." She folded her arms over her chest. "Mark my words, I told you Tamara would break up with Ruben and sure enough she—"

"Oh Patty, shut up," Josie said. Patty's eyes flipped open. "Now Susan, who else have you told about this?"

* * *

Isa heard a voice and looked around. A second ago she'd been lying on her bathroom floor and now she stood at the helm of the Queen Mary.

"There you are, darling," Joan cooed, sitting atop a mountain of steamer trunks and hatboxes. She wore a white suit with a skirt that did justice to her legs and a large sunhat that covered her dark hair. *"I've been meaning to tell you something."*

"Are you going somewhere?"

"Well darling, you don't need me anymore." Joan cried gorgeously in a lace edged hanky. *"And now it is bon voyage."*

"You're leaving me? *Now?* Look at what you got me into!"

Joan paused in the dabbing of her eyes. *"Into? I gave you a gift."*

"I repeated the same mistake I made at nineteen," Isa informed her.

Joan shook her head as if Isa just didn't get it. *"A child is never a mistake. Men, now that's a different matter. But look at me."* She ran her hand over her long, curvaceous lines. *"I have three children and grandchildren. I loved their fathers, at the time, but I'm still fabulous.*

"That kind of love is not for you, my dear," Joan continued. *"What you could have, and God only knows why, is that delicious man with whom you can spend the rest of your life. That is, if you try."*

Isa tested the hallucination and set her hand on the railing. It felt wet with sea mist. "You make it sound bad."

"Really darling, do I have to be so obvious? No matter how sexy you are, you're still the kind of woman who wants happily ever after. Me? I want happily ever after over and over again."

Was Joan calling her a dud? And what gave her the idea that Isa had the potential for happily ever after with Alex? Was there even such a thing?

Just then the door opened, and of all people, Tamara's little brother, Memo, walked out in a white tuxedo, holding a silver tray bearing a glass of champagne. With his hair slicked back, he held up the tray. *"Ms. Collins, your champagne."*

Joan fluttered her eyes at him and dipped down to pluck it, showing lots of cleavage without toppling over. She sipped and then licked her crimson lips, turning to Isa, *"See what I mean?"*

The ringing phone jerked Isa up from her slumber in the shadow of the porcelain god. She got up to her elbows and her mouth pooled with saliva. No way was she making it to the phone without throwing up again.

But what if it was about Andrew? What if he got hurt at the game?

Cursing Joan, she grabbed the trash can. In degrees she got to her feet with the can poised under her chin. Some of the nausea cleared by the time she made it to the phone.

"Hello?"

"Ms. Avellan, it's Dr. Quilley. How are you?"

"Dr. Quilley?" she managed. "I'm fine. Everything's fine. And you?"

"I was reading the paper today. There's an article on page A3 about you."

Remembering the feel of Carlos's stomach giving to her foot and his black g-string, she swallowed.

"I haven't seen the article." She'd been avoiding the paper ever since the survey had been made public.

"Well, let me read you a quote." He cleared his throat and then said, " 'Ms. Avellan is an example of a local daughter who has returned to her community to teach the next generation of our leaders. We are very proud of the honor she has brought to our ESL program.' "

It had been a long time since anyone had said they were proud of her. But that would be quickly forgotten when word got out about the baby.

Dr. Quilley cleared his throat. "I'll pluck a few copies from the newsstand and have them in your box Monday morning."

"Thank you. I don't know what to say," she said even as her throat swelled. "Who said that about me?"

He was so quiet that she wondered if he'd hung up. "A member of the school board. Alisa Torres."

"Thank you, Dr. Quilley. Thanks for calling."

"No, Ms. Avellan. Thank you."

35

ISA'S HOROSCOPE FOR OCTOBER 30

Your future is not written in the stars,
only the possibilities. The rest is up to you.

"Mom told me that your brother is okay," Andrew said when they got in the 4-Runner.

"Yeah, he is. He got real lucky," Alex said, wishing Isa had come to the game.

Andrew nodded his head, staring out the window.

"So how's your mom?"

"Okay. She's got the flu."

Alex cringed inside. He was responsible for giving Isa "the flu."

He didn't mean to, but he couldn't help but ask, "So what did you do in L.A. last night?"

"We visited with my Auntie Mara and I got to ride the fire truck and stuff."

"Your aunt has a fire truck?"

"Nope. Her boyfriend works in a fire station. We visited him."

Alex gripped the steering wheel. "Yeah, uh, that's pretty cool."

They drove a few more blocks in silence.

"I'm glad my dad wasn't here to see my game. He's not always nice to my mom."

Alex didn't mean to stomp on the brake that hard. "Real men aren't mean to women." He turned to Andrew to drive his point home. "My dad told me that. Look, I need to ask you something. Man to man."

Andrew waited, looking at Alex with his mother's eyes.

"I really like your mom. A lot and uh, I'd like to be her uh—"

"Boyfriend?"

"Actually more than that. Would that make you feel weird?"

Andrew's brow ridged as he considered the idea. "A little. I guess I'd have to get used to it."

"You wouldn't have to call me dad or anything if you didn't want to. We could be friends and if you needed to, I don't know, get something off your chest or something, you could tell me."

"Yeah I could get used to it. When are you going to ask her?"

"I was thinking tonight."

Isa had hoped she'd stop ralphing by the time they came home. This was not how she wanted to see Susan again. She wanted to be confident, serene, and completely in control of her emotional, mental, and digestive faculties.

"Where are you?" Andrew shouted.

She kicked the bathroom door shut, keeping her face over the toilet in case she did an *Exorcist* on the floor.

"I'm in here. Be out in a minute."

Isa thought she was in the clear and that Susan just dropped Andrew off, but she realized she would have no such luck when Alex asked, "Can I come in?"

"He's got something to tell you!" Andrew piped in.

Isa should've known better. Damn that Susan. What if she knew? "Give me a second, okay?" she shouted.

She took a few cleansing breaths and pulled herself up. The ghoul staring back at her from the mirror had lipstick smeared across her cheek and the right side of her hair mashed up from resting her head on the cool side of the tub.

When she switched off the water, she heard masculine voices conspiring in the hallway.

"Give me a few minutes so I can talk to your mom."

"But I want to see."

"Later."

"Aren't you supposed to have a ring or something?"

Yanking open the door, she eyed Andrew and then Alex. "What are you talking about?"

"Nothing," Andrew said. "I'll be in the kitchen."

He skipped away. Her child never skipped.

"Hey there," Alex said. "You look beat."

Isa's smile was about as strong as the feeling in her knees. "Thanks for bringing him home."

"No problem." He walked toward her, backing her into the bathroom.

"What's going—"

He shut the door behind him and flipped the lock. She was hormonal and in no mood for his male stupidity.

"You weren't picking up your cell phone yesterday," he accused.

"I was in class."

He took a deep breath, stretching his fingers wide and then closing his eyes as he exhaled.

"I wanted to answer that question you asked me the other—"

"Don't," her voice rang out like a shot. "I don't want the rehearsed answer."

"But—"

"No. Look, I thought about it and I know you want to be part of the baby's life so we'll figure out how to do this without getting married or living together."

"I let June and my dad take off to Germany and I blew off my boss yesterday to come here and tell you how I feel. Doesn't that count?"

She opened her mouth but he blurted, "I love you."

"Don't." She folded her arms over her chest, which hammered like a drum.

His face fell and he stared at her with his mouth hanging open.

"I appreciate what you're doing, but—"

"Appreciate? Do you think I just said that for my health? You belong with me."

His hand clamped onto hers when she got to the door. "Why are you—What is going on?" he asked.

"You didn't mean it."

"Yes, I did."

"But how could you—" she clamped her other hand over her mouth.

"How could I what?" he asked gently, taking her hand off

the doorknob and holding it between his two hands. "Love you? It's easy to love someone like you."

"Because you feel responsible for me?"

He shook his head and then kissed her knuckles. "I respect you."

"You're just saying this so I'll marry you."

"Wrong again." He pulled her up against him. "Maybe if you'd been someone else, I would marry you because I had to. I know I should've said it but I—I was afraid that it would be, I don't know, associated with my brother dying. So if I have to tell you every single day that I love you, up to the day you give birth or our baby graduates from high school, I will until you say you'll marry me."

She stood there, completely terrified of what he was offering. She'd been used to taking scraps of whatever affection she could find: from her father, her mother, and Carlos. She'd found love from Susan and Tamara but it was the kind that grew out of friendship, not from a one-night stand in the backseat of a Toyota 4-Runner.

What if Alex took it back? Changed his mind, or saw her for what she really was, scared and not always so smart?

"Hey," he said, pulling her away from the horrible places in her mind. "I mean it."

The look in his eyes burned away the ropes that kept her in that dark place where she'd been hiding for so long. Freely, she settled her head on his chest to see how long his love would last.

"Will you keep saying it after you marry me?" she asked.

His arms tightened his hold on her. "Every day."

Epilogue

18 WEEKS AND COUNTING

There was nothing like air-conditioning and ultrasound jelly smeared across her belly to make a woman want to pee.

Isa squirmed on the table, wishing she wasn't thinking of her bladder when she saw her baby for the first time.

"We'll be just a second here," the tech said, wheeling the monitor over. "Boys, are you ready?"

"I guess," Andrew mumbled. "Are we really gonna see what it is?"

"We hope," Alex answered. To Isa, "How're you doing?"

"Fine," Isa gritted between her teeth. The tech twisted on the tap, washing her hands and sending Isa into a new level of hell.

"We just want to make sure everything is developing like it should be," the tech said, wiping her hands. "Do you want a brother or a sister?"

"Brother. Girls are a pain."

"I had brothers and they always stole each other's toys."

Andrew's mouth turned grim.

"Take out your list, honey," Isa suggested.

He searched his pockets. Alex handed it to Andrew across Isa's chest. "Here. You left it on the table." He winked and smiled at her.

"Here we go. Remember the routine?"

Here it came. The pressure.

"If it's a boy I think we should name it Bruce," Andrew said as the monitor came to life.

"Like Bruce Lee?" Alex asked.

"No, Bruce Wayne from *Batman*."

"Nah. How about another one?"

The tech and Isa exchanged a smile.

"Kal-el."

Isa turned to Andrew. "You are not naming this baby Kal-el."

"But it's Superman's Krypton name."

She turned to Alex for help, but he said thoughtfully, "We could tell people it's Irish."

Isa rolled her eyes at the men in her life. "Next."

"What about Peter?" Andrew offered.

"She doesn't like any of our names," Alex said.

"Here we go," the tech announced.

Isa squinted to make out what looked like light green blobs. Trying to make out the head, or maybe that was its butt, the baby's arm jerked.

"Did it just move?" Andrew said.

She felt Alex's hand sneak into hers, his gold band sliding over the back of the engagement ring they'd exchanged as promise rings for Christmas. They'd decided to get married next October, well after the baby was born and the garage apartment he was building for his father was finished.

Alex's hand gripped hers and Isa watched wonder, delight, and fear blossom on his face. "What are we looking at?" he asked. The tech pointed out the head, torso, arms, and legs.

"Can you see what it is?" Andrew asked, straining his neck to see better.

"No, the baby's not turned in the right direction to make a clear determination," the tech said. "We can do an amnio."

"Do I have to?" Isa asked.

"Only if your doctor suggests it." She gave her a woman-to-woman grimace. "Frankly, I wouldn't."

Isa took a deep breath. She didn't exactly come out and say it but she'd been hoping the baby would be a girl. She hadn't told anyone, but she was going to name her Cecelia.

She glanced out of the corner of her eye at Alex and then Andrew, as the tech explained that the baby was oriented in such a way that they couldn't visually make out the gender.

"You've gotta be kidding," Andrew muttered. He glared at Alex. "You should be fired."

As much as she loved the men in her life, Isa needed a female to dress up in cute dresses while teaching her how to be a strong woman who didn't wrestle in K-Y for a man. And frankly, living in a household of males, she needed to even the playing field.

"Tough break, little man." Alex kissed Isa's cheek. "We'll be outside waiting."

"So did you see anything that might give you a clue?" Isa asked while the tech wiped the goo from her belly.

She shook her head. "Sorry." Then she stopped mid-wipe. "Then again, judging from the way you're carrying, you might be having another boy. With my girl—" She rolled her eyes to emphasize her point. "My butt was big enough to have its own time zone."

Isa thanked her and then slid off the table to walk to the bathroom. Another boy. She let her mind test the idea and when the happiness flowed inside, she rested her hand on her belly. Next time.

Want More?

Turn the page to enter
Avon's Little Black Book —

the dish, the scoop and the
cherry on top from
MARY CASTILLO

For starters . . .

Full name: Mary Castillo

How has your life changed since you've become a published author? I hate to disillusion you, but I still do my own laundry, drive the same car, and pick up pug poop. But now I write full time, which in some ways is a blessing and a curse. A blessing in that I don't have to get dressed for work and that "work" is now so much fun that it should be considered a sin. The bad part is that people feel like they can call and chitchat while I'm writing!

What is it like to know that thousands of strangers are reading your sex scenes? I once told a reporter that what this chaotic and too often violent world needs is better sex. Guys like Hugh Hefner and Larry Flynt built empires on sex, but only aimed at men—I don't know about you, but naked, airbrushed girls don't do it for me! Also, when our movie rating system prevents us girls from seeing hotties like Brad in the buff, we need an outlet and that comes in the form of romance novels. So I'm happy to provide!

What does your husband think about all this? As long as I tell the world that all of the love scenes and the male heroes are inspired by him, he's happy.

Okay smarty pants, what does your mother think about all this? Heh. When she read my first book, *Hot Tamara*, she told me that my next book should not only have more sexy scenes, but have them closer to the beginning!

From the book . . .

Where does the story take place? Originally I had parts of *Hot Tamara* and *In Between Men* take place in a real town south of Los Angeles. But the more I wrote about it, I realized I was recreating my hometown of National City, CA. So I made up the name Sweetwater and located it in the vicinity of Montebello. The pizza parlor, Napoleano's, is real and located next to a funeral home on National City Boulevard. The soccer field is located at Kimball Park, down the hill from the old National City Public Library where I hung out as a kid.

If you want to see pictures, check out the *In Between Men* Special Features section on my website, *www.MaryCastillo.com*.

Is Alex real and can I have his phone number? Or, where can I meet a man like him? Sorry, but Alex is a fictional character and if he was real, do you think I'd give you his number after all Isa has gone through to land him? As for where you can meet a man like him, all I can tell you is to wait for the one who treats you no less than a queen. Worked for me!

Where did you get the idea for the Sex Savvy Senior Survey? Okay, it's confession time. When I was in high school, a survey was passed around to the boys about their sexual proclivities. I happened across a copy and was really surprised at how prudish and unadventurous they were. Hopefully for their wives' and girlfriends' sakes, they've loosened up! If not, these women should read my books.

Is there such a thing as the Magic Eye camera? Not that I know of, but the idea came from a conversation I once had with my mother-in-law. One night we met up for sushi and she took out this piece of paper from her purse. She had consulted with a tea leaf reader on the subject of grandchildren and had a list of days that were delicately described as "times of potent sexual energy" for grandchild making. It's a true story . . . I swear! Somehow that got mixed up in my brain and I stumbled upon the idea for Patty and her camera in the third draft of the book.

Did your mom and her *comadres* ever meddle in your love life? Do you want the truth or the answer that won't get me killed? Certainly they have tried to steer me away from the bad ones, and towards the good ones. But when I was seventeen, I was either too stupid or too arrogant to take their advice . . . it's probably a combination of both. While they were right on one too many occasions, they never said I told you so.

Is June's husband serving in Iraq? Yes. I had written a rough draft without June, but when our country went to war, she came to life. The war really hit home with me because our first casualty was a young Mexican man whose funeral took place at the church down the street from my house. The reason why I don't specifically say Iraq is that I want this book to be timeless, and yet, whether one agrees with the war or not, I couldn't help but be moved by the challenges faced by the spouses, family, and friends of those who are serving our country.

Does Rocco Ramie's wife ever leave him? Rocco is really a sweet guy. I pictured him as the kind of man who brings flowers home to his wife, just because. And while he's making hand-over-fist in cash by acting like a drunken frat boy, he's very much aware that his show is offensive to intelligent, strong-willed women like his wife. In other words, at home, he knows where he stands and that he's damn lucky to have a wife like his!

Personally speaking . . .

How was writing *In Between Men* different from *Hot Tamara*? I had thought that Will was my greatest challenge. When I was writing early drafts of HT, I swore the guy just didn't trust me! But when Señora Allende came along, she cracked him open for me. But then with IBM, Alex Lujon came along and he became my greatest challenge.

On the surface Alex seems like a nice guy without much angst. But as I got to know him, I realized he's a pretty angry guy who can't help but be everyone's best buddy, when deep down he really longs to be a selfish jerk. How do you make a guy with that kind of internal conflict a nice guy? Even worse, how wrong was it that I paired him with such a great woman like Isa?

Writing HT taught me a lot about writing novels and if I had tried a story like IBM before, I couldn't have pulled it off. While HT will remain my sentimental favorite, it has its flaws and those flaws helped me to be better at creating conflict (e.g., matching two characters who want nothing to do with each other!), digging down for motivation, and at exploiting my characters' emotional hot buttons.

What is the most unfortunate hair decision you ever made? When I was writing *In Between Men*, I happened to see Lisa Marie Presley's interview with Diane Sawyer. I really liked her hair. In a moment of severely lapsed judgment—I think I might have actually had an out-of-body experience and been temporarily taken over by the spirit of a demented hairdresser—I tried to cut it like hers. It was beyond disastrous but it gave me the idea for Isa's makeover!

Has Joan Collins ever appeared in your shower? There was a time when I came home drunk and—*kidding*! When I wrote the scene in which she appears to Isa for the first time, I was just playing around because I was all out of ideas. But the more I wrote, the more it made sense to have Joan in the character of Alexis (Isa's childhood idol) be the inner voice of Isa's growth as a sexual woman. Joan also serves as a moral tale in what can happen if you're repressed.

What's next? Or, will we ever see a story about Memo? Memo is very much based on my brother. How could I possibly write a love story with sexy scenes using a character like him? Ewww!!! Then again, you never know.

However, to answer the first question, I will tell you that my next book is about two best friends who have grown apart but each think the other has the perfect life. One has the perfect husband, the perfect child, and the perfect house in a perfect neighborhood. The other has the perfect size-four single life with amazing men, an amazing apartment, and even better clothes. But when they switch bodies and have to live each other's so-called perfect and amazing lives, they realize the grass isn't greener! Please visit my website, *www.marycastillo.com*, to know exactly when Mary's new book will be released!

Creating A Male Hero for Fiction

I once overheard a critic of romance and chick lit novels say, "The men in those books are too good to be true." I wanted to ask her, "Did you happen to see the label on the spine of those books that said it was *fiction*?"

Chick lit and romances are what I like to think of as the hopes and dreams of the women who write and read them. The heroine is prized for her intelligence and wit, and no matter what life throws at her, she always wins the race. However, as I met many of you who came to my book signings and asked me about Will from *Hot Tamara*, I realized how important the hero is in these stories.

In our stories, we want a man who is not only gorgeous, but he can make us laugh while listening to our issues without trying to fix them. But most importantly, he's good in bed. I like to create male characters who have touches of realism, who make you, the reader, roll your eyes at his lesser moments and then forgive him when he smartens up and does right by the heroine.

So this is how I create those sexy men you love to read.

Step One: You take a woman and no matter the age, subtract five years of emotional maturity.

Step Two: Program the brain to think the following.

(a) "Pull my finger" jokes are funny . . . remember, that while you are creating a fantasy, there must be some realistic elements.

(b) The heroine is the most beautiful woman he will have ever seen, even when she leaves the house without lipstick or is not dressed like a porn star.

Step Three: Consult with the men in your life on how a male would react to the situations in your story. But you must promise not to get mad at them! They're only men and trust me, they really don't know any better.

Step Four: And this is perhaps the most important element of all, the male hero must have the very best characteristics that men offer: a sense of responsibility, protectiveness and problem-solving. Believe it or not, some actually have emotions and can love as deeply as a woman. With the right heroine who can push his buttons and take him to task when she needs to, your hero will feel secure enough to demonstrate his emotions and love.

The *In Between Men* Sound Track

These are some of the songs that were in heavy rotation on my player while I wrote *In Between Men*. And it just occurred to me that this was a predominantly all-American soundtrack! But you have been warned, these contain spoilers, so if you haven't read the story, continue on at your peril!

1. **"What It Feels Like For a Girl" (Madonna)**
   Isa's main issue in life is her conflict between being a good girl and secretly wanting to be a bad girl like Alexis from *Dynasty*. What I loved about this song is that it communicates all the double standards we girls have to live with: dress sexy and people immediately forget you have a brain, or worse, speak your mind and actually say something smart and suddenly, you're a ball-buster. In this scene, Isa is taking baby steps to start doing what *she* wants, rather than what others think she should do.

2. **"Fell in Love With a Boy" (Joss Stone)**
   Isa has a crush on Alex but she's too shy, too insecure, too burned by love to do anything about it. So a little angel named Joan, assisted by three bumbling "god-mothers" (Susan, Patty, and Josie) may (or may not) have set things in motion to get these two together!

3. **"Paradise City" (Guns 'N' Roses)**
   When my then-boyfriend and I would commute from Glendale to downtown L.A., we'd liven up the drives with Guns 'N' Roses. So when Rocco and his sidekick

Sal popped in my head one day while I was struggling with Chapter Eight, this song and this band typified their frat-boy level of maturity. And you know what? As obnoxious as they were, I actually looked forward to "hanging out" with those guys!

4. "Fighter" (Christina Aguilera)
When Isa hears Carlos on the radio and the girls who compete for a date with him, she loses it. I mean, so bad that in one draft I actually had her crash her car. But then we realized Carlos wasn't worth it and Joan appeared in the backseat.

5. "Dynasty Theme"
When I turned in the first draft of *In Between Men* to my editor, she gave me the go-ahead to unleash my tendency to let things get a bit wild, particularly with the makeover scene and Joan Collins's appearances. You see, when I was a kid and grown out of my Wonder Woman phase, my grandma let me watch *Dynasty* and read Joan Collins's autobiography, *Past Imperfect*. (Did I have a cool grandma or what?) Anyway, Isa's makeover isn't just skin deep, Joan's little pep talks are giving her the courage to let all that fabulousness out of the closet!

6. "Chica Dificil" (Los Aterciopelados)
Isa's feeling and looking good, and girl, she's not about to take any guff from Alex who actually laughed at the prospect of going on a date with her . . . except she still kind of, sort of has a crush on him. So she overcompensates on the attitude and trust me, I've done that a few times. Luckily, Alex is a gentleman—not to mention blown away by the transformation of his team mom—and Isa is woman enough to be honest with him.

7. "I'm on Fire" (Bruce Springsteen)
One day my husband happened to have this in the CD

player and I made him play this song again. Immediately I knew this was Isa and Alex's song in chapter 11, and when I sat down to write their first date scene, I was like, "Whoa there! Keep your clothes on!" I intended the scene not to progress as it did, but as you have probably read, they didn't listen to me. As their writer, I'm now glad they didn't.

8. **"What Am I To You?" (Norah Jones)**
   One of the benefits of marriage is that you get the inside track on how men think and surprisingly, they are just as insecure as we are . . . if only I'd known *that* way back when. Anyway, I knew how Isa felt after her first date with Alex, but I was really interested in what was going on in *his* head. This song spells it all out and when my husband read it, he realized he had inadvertently betrayed his gender.

9. **"I Deserve It" (Madonna)**
   One of the hardest scenes I wrote in this book was the first soccer game and Andrew's incident with his dad. At first I had Isa storming across the field and smashing a water bottle over Carlos's head. But then Alex, like a knight in shining armor, charged in and Isa realized how much she and her son *deserve* a man of character and courage in their lives.

10. **"Something" (The Beatles)**
    Go back to page 178 and read it again with this song in the background. Even though it was written for Yoko Ono, it's a beautiful song written by a man clearly in love with someone who he thought could exist only in his wildest imagination.

11. **"Life For Rent" (Dido)**
    When I wrote the scene where Isa and Alex realize their tryst in the backseat of his SUV has resulted in something more permanent, I was numb. The whole thing

just poured out of me and I couldn't write the next day. Isa realizes that she's not living a fantasy life a la *Dynasty*. This is the real thing and her life lands back on earth with a huge thud.

12. **"Don't Tell Me" (Madonna)**
Part of Isa's journey as a woman is to stand up and say this is what she wants and there's no room for second best. When I was writing this book, I was faced with a professional crisis of this nature and there comes a time when it's all or nothing. Isa decides to go for all that she wants on page 253.

13. **"Piece of My Heart" (Janis Joplin)**
If we caught a glimpse of Isa back when she was nineteen years old and pregnant with Andrew, we would see a very different woman. But after all she's been through, being voted the unsexiest teacher, hearing her ex on the radio, and now this, she's good and angry, plus hormonal!

14. **"It's Now or Never" (Elvis Presley)**
It takes all of Alex's cylinders to fire up for him to realize that what he feels for Isa is more than lust and friendship. After he's hit rock bottom professionally and (nearly) personally, he's got nothing more to lose, and yet if he doesn't move his butt, he'll lose it all.

MARY CASTILLO

The longest **MARY CASTILLO** has ever gone in between men was two years. In her lesser moments, she wishes she could get those years back. But in her moments of clarity, she realizes she's one lucky girl to live with her husband and two pugs in Southern California. Please visit her at *www.marycastillo.com.*